ERIC RITTER

DARK CROSSING

REFLECTIONS OF WORLDS: VOLUME 2

DARK CROSSING

REFLECTIONS OF WORLDS: VOLUME 2

Eric Ritter

Kravitz and Sons LLC
204 E Arlington Blvd. Suite B
Greenville, NC 27858

Published by Kravitz and Sons LLC.

ISBN: 979-8-89639-386-3 (sc)
ISBN: 979-8-89639-385-6 (e)

For everyone who is filled with creativity and ambition, find your art form and share it with the world.

This is mine.

Hope you enjoy the ride!

Table Of Contents

PART 1: Top Side.. 1

  Chapter 1: Acrobats 2

  Chapter 2: The Lodge...9

  Chapter 3: Something 's not right.............................17

  Chapter 4: An Uneasy Alliance.............................25

  Chapter 5: The Roken..30

  Chapter 6: The Warehouse 39

  Chapter 7: Captain Riker 47

  Chapter 8: Surviving the Night 53

  Chapter 9: Roid & Flutter...60

  Chapter 10: Forced Entry..66

  Chapter 11: Pursuit..75

  Chapter 12: Incarcerated 84

  Chapter 13: Reunited...94

  Chapter 14: Discoveries and Preparations...................106

PART 2: Other Side.. 113

  Chapter 15: Long Journey...114

  Chapter 16: Ragu Camp 122

  Chapter 17: Eva 129

  Chapter 18: The Pack 136

  Chapter 19: Late Night Visit 144

  Chapter 20: The Monarch 149

  Chapter 21: Guardians 155

  Chapter 22: The Ancients...164

  Chapter 23: Time of the Brite 171

  Chapter 24: Preparation 176

  Chapter 25: "It Doesn't make sense".................187

  Chapter 26: What's y our plan? 192

  Chapter 27: Clean Up on Aisle 10.....................198

PART 3: Crossing.. 204

  Chapter 28: Dark Season Forever 205

  Chapter 29: Come Out & Play 211

Chapter 30: Sunset or Sunrise 216
Chapter 31: The Battlefield 223
Chapter 32: You Worry about the World....................236
Chapter 33: "Who said any thing about dying?" 241
Chapter 34: Saving the World 246
Chapter 35: The Call....................253
Chapter 36: An Honor and a Privilege 257
Chapter 37: The Fall of Heroes....................262
Chapter 38: Changing of Seasons....................266
Chapter 39: Homeward Bound 274

Epilogue 1 277
Epilogue 2 279

PART 1: Top Side

CHAPTER 1
Acrobats

The less he moved, the sharper the cold stung his skin and burned his lungs with each breath. The longer he stayed still, the more he felt the muscles in his legs slowly begin to cramp up. It didn't matter though, he couldn't move, not now, not when he was so close.

Steph focused on his goal and ignored the cold and discomfort. He had been crouching in the thick branches of the snow-covered pine for what seemed like hours, waiting for his chance to strike.

The pine was one of many covering the valleys between the peaks of the vast, snowy mountain landscape they called home. He had been here only a few months, and had yet to win these near-daily excursions. Sure, he had won two over the course of months of these exercises, but they were close and could maybe even be called lucky. That didn't matter though, the deal was three. Two wins wasn't a victory. No, it took three to be victorious.

"Today is my day. Today, I win and there won't be any talk of luck when I do it," Steph thought with determination, still trying to ignore the freezing temperatures and focus on his mission.

From his position about fifteen feet up in the pine, he could see several miles in every direction. Scattered snow-covered pines littered the valley that stretched two miles in every direction before turning into a snowy, rocky landscape that led up to the peaks of the mountain tops. The top of this vast mountain range in the middle of nowhere had allowed them to be left alone, without any disturbances from the outside world. It allowed them a safe place to rest, to plan, and to disappear after strategic strikes.

"Yeah, strikes that I get left out of most of the time. Not after today though. Not once I win. That was the deal." Steph thought.

He strained his ears and eyes, tuned into all his senses and continued watching and waiting for his prey. They were hunting him, no doubt, and he was ready for them, this time.

Vic crept silently through the deep snow. He tried to stay close to the trees where it was shallower, making it easier to move. These training sessions were getting harder and harder, which meant Steph was getting better and better. The deal was, Steph's participation in missions or 'strikes' as the group called them, was severely limited until he could win three training sessions.

So far, the boy had managed to get two wins.

"The one win on me was lucky. It never should've happened." Vic thought, as he crept through the woods. He wasn't the only one that participated in the exercises with Steph, but he felt the most passionately about it. Vic had already lost his little boy once, and by the time he had found his six-year- old son, he had somehow turned into this twenty something warrior of sorts. Vic was not in a hurry to risk losing him again.

"Still, he's getting damn good." Vic thought. "He's got the strength and speed of those damn Na'gee warriors, but he's learning to mix their fighting style with ours. We won't be able to keep him out of the fights much longer. The kids too tough."

Vic liked to think the progress that Steph was making was all due to him. He liked to embrace the feelings of fatherly pride in that kind of way, but he knew that Halbred's training was doing Steph wonders too.

"Yeah, not to mention facing off against the hairy brute. Still don't know how he beat him once." Vic thought, thinking of Steph's second training win, that had come against G'noch. The large T'kche had not necessarily been bitter, but he had refused to talk about how Steph had beat him and for some reason Steph wouldn't say anything but 'I won and that's all that matters. To Vic, it still seemed fishy.

Vic reeled his wandering thoughts in and focused on the task at hand. "I know he's in the trees this time. He's going to try to come down and pounce. Probably got some sort of damn trap setup too. The sneaky kid's getting desperate for a win. He wants to be in the real fight. He wants a permanent spot on the rotation. I've got to pay attention." Vic's thoughts fueled his alertness.

"Finally!" Steph thought, spotting Vic, and holding his breath. He could see his tall father easing from tree to tree, trying to creep under the cover of the branches and where the thinner snow made it easier to move. Steph had counted on this when he was strategizing. The location of the exercises always changed, and he'd been waiting for the occasion when he would get to use the trees of the valley again. Now was just such an occasion.

Vic was now about ten feet, or two trees away from Steph on the ground. He maneuvered around the right side of the large pine he was passing, which is what Steph had counted on. Steph knew that upon losing, Vic would call that luck, but it was anything but luck.

Hours earlier, Steph had placed the branches on the left side and delicately given them a light layer of snow that made them appear as if they had been resting there for quite some time. Then he covered his tracks and moved on. He knew this would force his pursuer to the right side. He counted on them being so preoccupied with the hunt, that they wouldn't think twice about it, well that and he counted on his father going right... he knew that his father always went to the right.

"Well, it would likely work on any of them except Halbred." Steph thought. "G'noch seems to almost talk to the trees and he's still easier to trick than the old solider." The thoughts brought back many memories of failed exercises at the hands of Halbred. Steph knew his father was no joke, he knew defeating him in hand-to-hand combat was still a very lofty goal, but that wasn't Steph's plan. He'd decided to leverage the woodcraft knowledge that he just kind of had now, to accomplish his goals. He also knew that despite his father's fighting prowess, his tendency to rush into the fray made him the best candidate for some well-placed traps.

"Yeah, today is the day. Today makes three wins." Steph thought, getting more and more excited as the moment he had been waiting for rapidly approached.

Then it happened.

Vic, still two trees away, moved just past the right side of the tree and the trap sprung. The rope instantly tightened around Vic's ankle, and he was yanked ten feet into the air upside down.

As soon as the trap sprung, Steph sprang into action himself. Despite the cold, stiffness in his legs from hours of crouching in the tree branches, he moved fast. The seven-foot tall, pale warrior was no longer the thin man that had come to the mountains. No, now he was thick with muscles. Most of the Na'gee tribal tattoos were now covered up, as he wore a brown and white tightly fitting fur coat, with a short turtleneck type collar, that buttoned up high on his neck. It really left only the tattoos on his hands and face visible. His blonde hair was short and spikey, and his tattoo covered face was shaved clean, showing the strong jaw line of the young warrior. He still wore the black leather warrior's pants of the Na'gee and still wore the belt with the large knife, the .50 caliber pistol, and the numerous clips.

Steph moved through the trees like a jungle cat on the hunt. He leapt from branch to branch, moving from the tree he was in, to the next tree quickly. This placed him one tree away from the one that his father was being yanked up into.

As soon as he hit the branches he reached out and grabbed hold of the rope he had positioned there. He paused for just a moment, knowing that it would happen at any second.

The rope around his ankle had yanked Vic clean off his feet and was instantly pulling him up in the air, upside down.

"Sneaky bastard." Vic thought as he instinctively reached up, grabbed the knife out of his boot and cut the rope. As he fell, he turned himself upright and landed smoothly on his feet. Vic stood every bit of seven feet and was the same lean muscular man he'd always been. He still had the blonde buzz cut and wore all black, only now it was tactical snow pants instead of jeans and a thick black sweater with leather patches on the elbows and shoulders. He had chosen to keep the Na'gee warrior belt with the large blade and .50 caliber pistol as well. He also now carried a knife in each boot and often traveled with a large black carbon fiber spear of sorts on his back. His pale grey eyes had constant dark rings underneath them now days, that he claimed was just 'getting old', but everyone seemed to know it was from constant worry about Mila.

"Gotta do better than that son!" Vic yelled out as soon as his feet hit the snow-covered ground.

Steph saw the swift escape move that he had expected and pulled hard on the rope in his hands, as soon as he saw his father's feet hit the ground. When he did, he saw his father's feet get swept out from under him again, and the upside-down ride started once more for Vic.

This time though, Steph held the rope and as his father was pulled upward, upside down, Steph leapt from the tree and swung towards him. The rope ran over a large branch high in the tree and the trap had Steph swinging at Vic from one side, while Vic was being propelled upwards on the other side.

Steph's feet crashed into Vic's midsection, sending the older man swinging away and gasping in pain. The momentum from the kick swung Steph backwards, like he planned, allowing him to kick off a tree and propel himself back towards his father.

Vic took the kick to his gut and was swinging back in to take what appeared to be another acrobatic kick headed his way before he'd even caught his breath. Instead of going for the knife to cut himself loose again, he leaned into the swing and extended his arms forward, increasing his momentum.

"Ok, you wanna fight like a family of circus acrobats, then that's how we'll fight. Either way you're getting your ass kicked." Vic thought to himself.

As Steph came swinging back with both feet extended to kick Vic again, he noticed that his father had dove forward towards him, and he noticed it too late. As the two collided, Vic used his left forearm to push down Steph's extended feet and then he delivered a mighty downward punch to Steph's groin. The impact sent Steph and his side of the rope, hurtling downward, as Vic's side shot upward. As soon as he started shooting upward, by his ankle, Vic quickly leaned up again, grabbed the boot dagger one more time and this time he reached out and sliced through the rope on Steph's side.

With the rope cut, Steph's speed drastically increased as he crashed downward. He saw Vic coming down fast too and knew his father would hit the ground a couple seconds after him.

Steph readied himself and as soon as his feet hit the ground, he executed a backflip to increase the distance between him and Vic.

"Crap! I had hoped to avoid another fist fight with the old man. This never ends well." Steph thought as he prepared for Vic to rush him as soon as he hit the ground.

Vic, who still had about eight feet of rope tied to his ankle landed nimbly on the ground about five feet from Steph. He saw Steph digging his feet in, preparing for Vic's traditional charge into battle.

"Just when he thinks he's got me figured out, I gotta remind him that they don't call his old man the 'Grim Reaper' for nothing!" Vic thought as he slightly grinned at his opponent and kicked his foot with the rope still tied to the ankle, hard in the air.

The kick propelled the rope through the air, and it wrapped around Steph's neck twice. Vic then yanked his leg back and Steph was hurled forward by his neck. As soon as he started flying forward, Vic leapt up in the air and landed on Steph's back.

The next thing Steph knew he was lying face down with a rope around his neck and feeling the cold metal of Vic's dagger on the back of his neck, just past the rope.

"You're dead son." Vic said.

"Not again." Steph huffed in a defeated sort of way. "I really thought I had you this time."

Vic got off of Steph's back and helped the young man up. The two looked at each other for just a moment and then father and son embraced. Win or lose, they loved this time together. They loved to compete with each other, it truly bonded them in a deep sort of way, and they cherished it.

After they hugged for a moment, they collected the ropes and started to begin the long track back to the 'lodge', but before they got going Steph put his arm on his father's shoulder to stop him. Vic paused and turned to face his son with a questioning look in his eyes.

"Dad, how the hell did you do that crazy rope kick thing? It doesn't even seem possible. You gotta teach me!" Steph said.

Vic just laughed and started walking, "they don't call me the 'Grim Reaper' for nothing kid", he said as he walked away.

"Oh, not that again." Steph said, rolling his eyes as he began to follow.

CHAPTER 2
The Lodge

After a little over an hour of hiking, the lodge came into view. The lodge provided the perfect accommodations for the group. It was a massive cabin or rather, a lodge of sorts -nestled tightly between two mountain peaks. About ten yards away stood the 'hangar' as Halbred insisted on calling it, though to Steph it was clearly just a massive four bay garage with a helipad on the roof. Inside the so-called hanger were two jeeps, two snowmobiles and six dirt bikes. There was also a large four door pickup truck.

The lodge on the other hand welcomed them with a massive front porch that led inside to the main hall. The main hall featured an enormous fireplace and plenty of seating immediately left of the front doors. To the right was a giant dining table that seated twelve and straight ahead stood the kitchen, all of which shared the same grand room. One bathroom was tucked off to the side and steps led up from both the right and the left back corners of the large room. The entire room smelled of cedar, matching the stained wood used for the furniture, floors, walls, and open rafters above. The only décor in the grand room was a large bookcase next to the fireplace and a few lamps scattered about, which barely qualified.

The wide wooden staircases at each back corner connected to a walkway that overlooked the main hall and led to hallways down either direction. The banisters on the stairs and the railing on the walkway were built from thick branches shaved and stained. The entire place definitely had the look of a large ski cabin fit for a group vacation. Down each end of the hallway were three master bedrooms, one at the end and one on each side. The six master bedrooms accommodated the group nicely, but they also served as a constant reminder that the place was designed to house Halbred's previous unit. All members of his six-member unit had been killed fighting the otherworldly threat of the Na'gee-well, all killed except Roid, who had turned into some twisted version of the dark cloaked creatures. The losses weighed heavily on Halbred and despite the old soldier's composure, the pain often showed in his eyes.

The "lodge" was actually much more than a beautiful cabin getaway filled with memories-so much more than that.

On the main floor, the large bookcase directly next to the fireplace didn't just house shelves full of well-written stories, it led to the cabin's true purpose. When you moved a certain hard-backed novel just the right way, the entire bookcase slid outward like a hinged door, revealing a stainless-steel elevator that provided access to the two sublevels.

The first sublevel was an armory of sorts, offering a variety of weapons, tactical gear, two large tables and plenty of tools and equipment for customization. There were racks everywhere and chairs scattered about. The entire room was stainless steel, lit up by large rows of fluorescent lights in the ceiling. On each far side of the room, there were large stainless doors that led to tunnels that connected to the mazes of caves in each of the two mountains flanking the lodge.

The second sublevel was something very different. This one served as HQ for the group and was often referred to as the 'war room'. There were desks, chairs, PCs and monitors all over of various shapes and sizes. This room also had large stainless-steel doors positioned on each side, while the center of the room was taken up by a huge table with a massive, nearly two-sided glass screen a few feet. The screen had a massive map of what appeared to be most of the world with a variety of colored lights positioned sporadically across it. Halbred and Samuel had spent weeks working on this.

"This", was the result of the men trying to mirror the energy signal made by the stone talisman that each of the companions now wore when it opened a doorway to the 'other side'.

The 'other side' was a reflection of the earth they called home-a reflection that was very similar, yet still wildly different. Where the world they knew had advanced technologically, the 'other side' was more primal and well, mystical. It also seemed to be the home to just about every wild creature from far-fetched sighting reports or storybook tales-not to mention ones that the world thought extinct. The more they learned, the more it seemed that almost every legend of an unbelievable 'thing' was somehow rooted in something accidentally crossing over from the 'other side' into the world we call home.

The 'other side' was also home to the vicious tribe of cannibalistic warriors known as the Na'gee. They had developed a way to cross over using the stone talisman each of them wore. Now, they were behind-perhaps even in control of most of the underground drugs and weapons trafficking. Their violent ways, superb fighting prowess, and ability to transport contraband on the 'other side' and then cross back over to our world, or the 'top side' as they called it, when they reached their destination gave them a foolproof way to transport goods without detection. This method also gave them a unique way to infiltrate any oppositions stronghold and wipe them out. The fact that it was impossible to know when or where they would 'cross over' into our world from the 'other side' made them an incredibly dangerous threat.

Well, at least until Halbred and Samuel figured out the energy signature that 'crossing over' made. The system wasn't always accurate. At best, it was only sometimes accurate. After several months and many attempted 'strikes' on the Na'gee operation that ended with them chasing down some wild beast from the 'other side' or finding nothing at all, they realized that ripples that made 'crossing over' possible were far more common than one might think. It seemed that sometimes, they just occurred naturally, like the weather. They also suspected that other beings or creatures besides the Na'gee might have learned to cross over at will, though they had yet to prove it.

After all they had learned, they'd finally come up with a system. They essentially just looked for recurring patterns. If the same location repeatedly showed up, the odds were that it was a highly used trafficking route. Once they thought they had found one, they mobilized and executed a 'strike', which basically meant they killed everyone and destroyed the contraband. The goal was simple: eliminate the otherworldly threat that had already tried to invade once.

They each had different motivations and reasons to want the Na'gee dead, but none of it mattered. The common goal was the common goal. So far, the 'strikes' generally consisted of Samuel, Halbred, Vic and Eva. G'noch, the huge T'kche warrior that had traveled here with them from the 'other side' participated when he was around. He was never too pleased to be left out, but the large T'kche spent more time in the mountain caves than he did in the lodge, which he referred to as a 'little man hut', He refused to carry any form of comms. The T'kche was just over eight feet tall and was entirely covered with thick black hair, except for his hands, feet and face that were more of a black leathery texture. It had a huge head, flat nose, large eyes, and mouth full of huge teeth that G'noch often flashed in his signature vicious grins. Basically, G'noch looked like just about every crazed big foot sighting description, however he was not fond of the term 'big foot' and despite many attempts to explain it to him, he still seemed to think it was a reference to his large feet. Halbred and Vic still used the term often, finding obvious amusement in messing with the large beast and G'noch now often referred to each of them as 'little foot'.

Steph had pleaded to participate in the 'strikes' on many occasions, but his father had insisted that he win three training sessions before he could join. He knew that his father was trying to set an unattainable goal, so that he never had to worry about Steph fighting against the deadly Na'gee warriors, but Steph was determined to get his three wins and join.

"He can't keep me sidelined forever." Steph often thought.

Steph remembered when his father had tried to restrict his mother, Eva, from participating. Vic did not win that argument. From what Steph remembered, his mother had made it very clear that if he wanted to leave them out of it, he failed miserably at that a long time ago and now that she was involved, she would damn sure contribute. Vic hadn't liked it, but he also didn't protest again. Instead, he convinced

Halbred to start training Eva. He knew that his wife wouldn't take kindly to him trying to train her and tell her what to do, but that was the old soldier's specialty and if she was dead set on joining the battle, he wanted her well equipped to handle herself. In no time at all, Halbred had done wonders. Eva's old military experience seemed to come back to her quickly and Halbred leveraged that and built on it, by teaching her numerous new techniques and strategic moves. She now handled herself quite well and even though Vic had admitted it on more than one occasion, he had not told her just how formidable he thought she had become, fearing that it would give her too much confidence and potentially have her take unnecessary risks during the strikes. Despite that, he was often caught grinning at her with pride and adoration in his eyes.

Steph's little sister Mila was an entirely different story. She had grown more and more eerie over the past few months. Her skin now always had a faint glow to it and her eyes no longer showed any form of pupil, they were just, well, lights. Her hair had turned bright white, and she spoke less and less. When she did speak, it was mostly in an ominous voice that didn't seem like hers and it was usually to warn them of a looming threat around a planned strike or inform them about some tidbit from the 'other side'. She never elaborated or explained and never seemed to be wrong. At one point, Halbred had suggested that they include Mila, so that they could attack the 'other side' routes at night, knowing that her light could destroy or at least deter the dark ones that stalked the night there. Vic wasn't hearing it though and exploded at the suggestion. Mila, who had heard it, had said "I will face the dark ones when it is time", and then she had walked away. So far, it had not been brought up again.

Having finally arrived, Steph and Vic climbed the short steps and entered the massive lodge.

Despite it being just past eight am, a fire was blazing in the massive fireplace. The firelight combined with the morning sunshine to wash the room in a warm glow. The lodge smelled of cedar as always, but today scents of cinnamon and oatmeal also filled the air. The delicious smells seemed to be coming from the massive pot on the stove in the kitchen and both men unconsciously began heading straight for it. Halbred and Eva sat at the huge dining table, each with a cup of coffee in their hands and an empty bowl in front of them. They had obviously finished their morning training session and had time for breakfast already.

"How was training? She kicks your ass again Halbred?" Vic asked as he headed for the oatmeal and the coffee pot.

"Just about Vic. She's getting damn good. How about you two? You finally earn your freedom kid?" Halbred said, shifting his attention to Steph.

Steph didn't smile or explain, he simply said "no", as he tossed his fur coat on a chair and headed for the kitchen as well.

"Ahh hell boy!" The old soldier exclaimed.

"Well, what do you think about turning him loose anyway Vic? He's as tough as any of those damn warriors and as tough as just about any of the soldiers I've ever trained." Halbred asked. At the mention of 'soldiers', Halbred's face grew dark. He had managed to hide it well, but the old, seasoned soldier, who still sported his slicked back red hair and big red beard, was tormented at losing his entire unit to the Na'gee warriors. The lodge and the tactical strikes were constant reminders of the people he'd lost.

"Not a chance Halbred! As tough as any Na'gee, ain't the same as tougher than any Na'gee. Steph knows the deal… all he's got to do is win." Vic said, bringing Halbred back from memory lane with his words and signature sarcastic tone.

Halbred knew that Vic was just scared of losing the boy again, so he left it alone. In truth, he didn't blame Vic. He couldn't imagine how tough it would be to have your six-year-old abducted and then get him back as a young man, just days later, not to mention how hard it was to watch how distant his daughter was growing. Whatever change was happening with her, she wasn't a ten-year-old little girl anymore, no matter what she looked like.

"Yeah, it's gotta be tough on old Vic" Halbred thought to himself. "Where the hell is old dark and mysterious at?" Vic asked.

"Samuels in the war room, studying the map again." Halbred said in response.

"Again? He doesn't give it a rest does he. We already know where we think the routes are and we already know that the damn Bermuda triangle stays glowing, which by the way explains a ton, what the hell is hoping to find?" Vic said as he sat down, joining them at the table with his steaming mug of coffee.

"He's verifying the routes we've been watching, one more time and we think we can call it a pattern. He also thinks there's more to it all Vic and he's determined to figure it out. Hell, maybe he's right, but in truth, I don't even know if he knows what he's trying to figure out." Halbred said, half muttering to himself as the words came out.

Suddenly, the communications earpieces that they all wore, erupted with the sound of Samuels voice. The group traded looks, hearing the same message.

It was clearly Samuel and he simply said "It's time. We move in fifteen minutes".

The four of them nonchalantly made their way for the bookcase that would take them to the second sub level or the 'war room'. Not a word was exchanged as they headed to Samuel, this wasn't new to them, no, this was the norm. It was always in the morning too as they chose not to risk the strikes at night, when 'crossing over' could lead them to a showdown with who knew how many dark ones. No, daylight was the time to strike, and leaving in the mornings afforded them plenty of time to take the chopper to most locations.

As the elevator opened and they piled out of it and into the 'war room', they saw Samuel standing in the center of the room, leaning on the large table and staring at the glass screen, which was zoomed in on one specific location.

Samuel was a large athletically built man, who still wore well-fitting black jeans and black t-shirt with his usual black sports coat. When he moved to the left or right too briskly, a sharp eye could see the flash of the holsters he always wore under each arm. He had dark skin and a shaved head and face, and always had a sinister look about him. It was very different than Halbred, who just sounded gruff and mean, like the timeless drill sergeant stereo type, no, Samuel had a much darker presence about him.

Samuel looked up as the group approached the table, he sized them all up, as he usually did, and then began his spill. "It's confirmed. It's definitely a trafficking route. This morning makes the third trip in two weeks. If we leave now, we should have time to fly down, scope the place out for a couple hours and strike before dark. If all goes well, we should be back by tomorrow morning." He stared at each one of them to gauge their expressions as he finished speaking. When his eyes landed on Steph, he paused and asked "You coming with us this time? We could use the extra manpower Steph."

Steph hung his head instead of responding, as Vic spoke up for him. "Not yet he's not Samuel. The boy knows the deal, he's not there yet and someone needs to stay with Mila. Besides, whatcha scared of man, even if you are getting slow, you got the damn grim reaper on your side."

The entire group rolled their eyes at Vic's comments and then Halbred got them going.

"You heard the plan, chopper leaves in fifteen minutes, let's go!" Halbred roared and everyone started moving.

CHAPTER 3

Something 's not right

They'd been in the air heading further north for almost three hours and had covered approximately seven hundred miles, when they saw the city appear on the horizon. They were all used to the abnormally high speeds that Halbred's helicopter achieved, just like they were all used to the anything but steady way that Halbred flew it. None of that, however, stopped Vic from giving the old soldier grief about it every time.

"How the hell are we supposed to fight if we're all nauseous every time we get there, Halbred? Didn't they teach you how to fly this damn thing at military school?" Vic yelled over the roar of the chopper.

"You know a good pilot, bring 'em along and I'll give 'em the reins, Vic. |Until then, I'm what ya got son." Halbred barked back in his usual gruff tone.

"A good pilot? If we could find a half blind one with the shakes, we'd probably be in better hands" Vic retorted, adding, "You gotta smooth this flying out so the Grim Reaper, team Strike Force, and our crappy pilot can handle business when we land!"

This time when Halbred responded, the tone sounded much more angry than gruff: "For the hundredth time, Vic, we're not calling ourselves damn 'Strike Force'!"

Vic mumbled "grumpy, and crappy pilot" under his breath, but didn't yell it back.

The two usually went on like that until Halbred began ignoring Vic or got angry, while the rest of the group paid them no mind-just as they did on this trip.

Eva sat staring out the window, as she'd done the entire flight. She had her thick brown hair pulled back in a ponytail and wore a well-fitting black sweater, with leather patches on the elbows and shoulders. She also wore black tactical pants and still wore the black leather Na'gee belt that held the massive knife and large pistol. She also had a lightweight Kevlar vest as well a large, oversized black duffle bag resting against her leg. She was lost in her thoughts, as she often was before strikes. Eva knew that the men with her thought it was nerves or preparation, and she was content to let them continue thinking it. What Eva really thought about every time--always was her daughter, Mila.

She was tortured by the transformation she saw taking place in her little girl. Every day her daughter was less of the little girl she loved and raised, and more of whatever the thing was that she was becoming. It was something inhuman and otherworldly altogether. Mila assured her mother more than once that it was the way things were supposed to be. She assured her that she had a greater purpose and that she had been the one chosen to serve this generation, but everything she said seemed vague and eerie. Even though deep down, Eva believed her, it didn't make it hurt any less to be slowly losing her daughter to whatever the greater purpose of this transformation was. The fact that she had lost her little boy not long ago only made matters worse. Sure, Steph was still around, and she still loved him, but just months ago he was a six-year-old boy and now somehow, he was a full-grown man. It wasn't the same. She'd lost her baby boy and now she was losing her little girl too. In truth, the only time the loss of her children didn't torment her was during the strikes. It was when she could stop thinking and just act-when she could, for just a moment, unleash the pain she felt onto the people she held responsible.

"Finally, we're here." Eva thought as she saw the city appear.

"Alright team! I'm taking her down onto that large building on the south side of the city. The satellite images showed a helipad there, and it appears to be empty. I'll use my military clearance with the building security to make sure it doesn't raise concerns, while Samuel procures our ground transportation. We meet out front in ten." Halbred shouted as he eased the helicopter towards the building referenced.

Before the chopper had even completely settled on the helipad, Samuel was out, running across the roof. Seconds later he disappeared through the rooftop door, leading into the building.

This was usual for the team. If they landed in the city, Halbred claimed 'military business' and kept property owners quiet, while Samuel 'procured' transportation. No one ever asked how he obtained it- because in truth, they didn't really want to know. Vic and Eva would then casually stroll to the rendezvous location wearing their matching tactical gear and carrying duffle bags full of artillery. They got plenty of looks every time, which Vic consistently claimed were due to his gorgeous wife's figure and well-fitting attire-despite Eva insisting that it was absolutely due to them looking like a couple of terrorists.

Samuel hit the steps and descended the twenty flights of stairs quickly. He exited into the parking deck and slowed to a walk surveying the vehicles that. He looked for the same two things every: a large enough vehicle to fit them all, and one that could handle rough terrain, just in case. He preferred vehicles that looked like they'd been sitting for a long while, which lowered the chances of being noticed missing and drawing the attention of local authorities.

When he saw the large white SUV, he approached it slowly and looked underneath. There were cobwebs around the wheel wells and. It had definitely been sitting there for a while.

"This is the one." Samuel murmured to himself.

As he stood up and eased towards the driver's side door, he sensed movement behind him and turned quickly, only to see a building security guard standing about six feet away, hands on his sidearm.

"What do you think you're doing with Mr. Jenson's automobile sir?" The overweight security guard yelled, drawing an old revolver and pointing it at Samuel.

Samuel checked his watch, "Four minutes. I don't have time for this" he thought. The security guard was clearly in his mid-forties, overweight and had a thick goatee that faded into a long braid that hung to his chest. He wore an unflattering black t-shirt with the word "security" across the front and looked like he had been waiting his entire career for a confrontation like this.

"All he wants is an excuse to shoot someone and then spend the next ten years bragging about it at the bar. I should just shoot him and move on. No, it isn't worth the commotion if someone found his body in the parking deck, while we're gone." Samuel thought, as he raised his hands and slowly moving towards the security guard.

Samuel stared at the man arrogantly and in a condescending tone said "How dare you point a gun at me! They begged me to meet them here and I forget where I parked, and you point a gun at me?! I'll see to it you lose your job over this!" As Samuel berated the man, he kept walking towards him.

The flustered security guard grew nervous and started to panic, still holding his gun, stuttering and mumbling an apology that wouldn't form.

Before he was able to speak, Samuel was in his face and gently touched the man's arm. Instantly the man was frozen in place. The nervous look stuck on his unmoving face. His hands-one by his side and one holding the pistol-were both stuck in position. The "freeze," as Samuel called it, wasn't temperature- related, it was more like pausing someone. He'd always been able to do it. Once he froze someone they were stuck until he willed them -free unless he got a certain distance away, then it just released. It was the effect of "the gene" had on Samuel-just as it had given Halbred impenetrable skin. Its effects varied, and not everyone had it. Samuel had long since grown proficient with his gift.

He quickly surveyed his surroundings and spotted the luxurious sports car directly behind the security guard, so he turned the guard's frozen body to face it and gently squeezed the man's finger that was on the trigger. Gunshots rang through the air, over and over, while Samuel continued to squeeze the guard's frozen finger on the trigger. When the revolver was empty and the back of the once beautiful sports car was full of bullets holes, not to mention a shattered back window, Samuel yanked on the man's shirt and ripped it clean off.

"That should give him and the building management staff a lot more to worry about than a missing SUV. Good luck explaining this." Samuel thought as he walked back over to the white SUV he had been previously inspecting.

Samuel wrapped the security guard's shirt around his right hand and punched it through the driver's side window. The alarm blared, but within thirty seconds Samuel was inside, cutting the right wire to silence it. He then connected the wires needed to start the vehicle and was on his way.

As he approached the exit of the parking deck, he checked his watch again, "right on time" he said to himself.

Samuel made a left turn in front of the building, where he saw Eva and Vic standing out front in their all-black matching tactical gear, each wearing a large knife and pistol at their belts and holding oversized black duffel bags. "They look like a couple of terrorists" Samuel thought as he slowly pulled to a stop in front of them. They both jumped into the back seat and before they closed the doors, Halbred was at the passenger side getting in too. Just like that, the group was off.

"Keep heading straight on this road for ten miles, I'll tell you where to go from there. The old warehouse is just outside of the city. Based on our satellite feeds, it looks like the Na'gee are using this to sell weapons to a large biker gang that operates out of the warehouse." Halbred said, as Samuel drove.

"Perfect. We'll take out the bikers and be there waiting for the Na'gee. You and Eva want to take the 'other side' again to cut off runners?" Samuel asked in response.

"Yeah, might as well. You and Vic will have to handle the bikers on your own. We'll need to cross over as soon as we get there, so we have time to find a hidden position." Halbred replied.

Samuel simply nodded.

Vic and Eva listened intently as they loaded the assault rifles from the oversized duffels. Once they heard that the plan of attack had been agreed upon, Vic nudged his wife with his elbow. "You hear that babe? You get to go play around in dino land again while we bash some biker skulls." he teased, grinning at her. Eva rolled her eyes and kissed him on the cheek in response. The SUV was filled with silence the rest of the way, as they all prepared themselves for the upcoming task. They all knew how savage the Na'gee warriors were. They'd been on several of these so-called "strikes" over the last few months and knew they never went as smoothly as they should. It wouldn't be easy… it never was.

Twenty minutes later, they'd left the city limits and were driving down back roads in what appeared to be a ghost town. Both sides of the street were lined with the old buildings of failed businesses that were falling apart and had long since been abandoned. There were littered streets and walls smeared with graffiti. A few homeless people staggered around, but they were scarce. There wasn't much of anything left here but destroyed remnants of its past. The long road dead ended into a massive grey warehouse. Across the front stretched six large bay doors running across the front of the warehouse and a short stairway that led to a glass front door in the center of them. There also appeared to be a similarly small staircase and doorway down the right side of the large warehouse.

"That's where we're heading. Let's stash the ride behind one of these old, abandoned buildings", Halbred said.

Instead of replying, Samuel simply pulled sharply down a small side street about two blocks away from their destination. He took a right into a lot behind what used to be a strip mall and parked the vehicle so that the old dumpster in the lot somewhat hid it from the street. They piled out. Vic handed Eva and Halbred assault rifles, tossed Samuel his preferred shotgun, and within seconds they were jogging down side streets toward their target.

A few short minutes later they slowed to a stop and peered around the corner of the last building before the warehouse. Halbred turned to Eva and asked, "Are you ready?"

"Let's go." she said coldly. While running, Eva's thoughts shifted-from worrying about her daughter Mila to anticipating vengeance. She was ready and eager, as she often was just before the attacks began.

Halbred nodded at her reply and then began rubbing the stone talisman that he wore around his neck, in varying circular motions that made it look like he was working a combination lock of some sort. Instantly, the 'blur' appeared.

The 'blur' was like a ripple in the air that stretched five feet high and three feet wide. It seemed to rip right through the fabric of the world itself. Halbred and Eva stepped directly into the 'blur', and it disappeared behind them. Just like that, they were gone.

"We splitting up out here, or easing in the side door and then splitting up?" Vic asked.

"Let's get inside, then we'll find our positions… and Vic, be ready, something is off." Samuel said as he stared at the building.

"Oh, you mean, because we're supposed to be bashing biker heads and there's no bikes? Yeah, I see it, Samuel. Maybe the pansies valeted their hogs. You never know." Vic said as he took off for the side door of the warehouse. Samuel quickly followed, shaking his head. He could always count on Vic rushing into the fray and making smart remarks along the way. In truth, Samuel appreciated Vic's confidence- it lightened the atmosphere and showed he was never worried or nervous, both of which could prove disastrous.

Upon discovering that the side door was locked, Vic reached into one of the many pouches on his black leather belt and removed two long metal pins and made short work of picking the lock. He replaced the pins, eased the door open quietly and the two men slipped into the warehouse.

The warehouse had a large main room that seemed to run across all six of the bay doors that they had seen from the front. It was mostly empty, except for a handful of doors that lead to other areas of the warehouse scattered about on the walls and the hundreds of huge crates stacked on pallets in various locations across the warehouse floor. The main floor was overlooked by a second level walkway that circled the entire warehouse floor and appeared to also have stacks of crates and a few doors. There were a couple tables with chairs around them off to the side, that were littered with empty beer and whiskey bottles, but there were no signs of bikes or any bikers. The inside of the warehouse was no warmer than the freezing temps outside, allowing both men to see their breaths in the air as they crept through the large building.

"Maybe we're just early." Vic whispered, although he didn't really think that was what it was. "Something's not right Vic, this place should be crawling with bikers. Doesn't matter though, as long as the Na'gee show up, we still do what we came to do, just stay on your toes. You want high ground or low ground?" Samuel said.

"I got the terrace level baby. My assault rifle will be much better at shooting Na'gee fish in a barrel, then that shotgun you love so much." Vic said with a sly grin, and then he took off for the metal stairs that led up to the walkway overlooking the warehouse floor. Samuel watched him go, and then headed for a stack of crates in the corner, where he took up his position.

Neither man noticed the eyes that were watching them from all over or heard the faint whispers of "Not yet, hold your position until our primary target arrives".

CHAPTER 4
An Uneasy Alliance

Dante casually lounged across the room from the desk that Primo sat behind and listened to the older man's phone conversation.

"Clear the damn warehouse, like I said. You can take back your clubhouse next week. The guns will be left there for you. We'll come collect our money in a couple days." Primo stated in his raspy voice.

Dante didn't like the wiry Native American man with the ponytail, who always wore suits. He didn't trust the man. So far, Primo had kept his word, Dante was paid well, and they had taken over several Na'gee trading routes. As long as the Na'gee were being wiped out, Dante was good with it all. Still, he hoped to one day cross paths with Samuel and finally avenge his family, but at this point he didn't think it was likely Samuel had survived the 'other side' in pursuit of Camacho. So, Dante had settled for the next best thing, working with Primo and his mercenaries to kill off the Na'gee tribe and take over their trading routes.

Although Primo had saved his life-or rather, had his mercenaries save him and had shown him the video evidence that Samuel was behind the death of his family, Dante still didn't trust him. He'd seen Primo appear with Camacho outside of the club explosion and overheard their casual remarks.. To Dante, it seemed that Primo was as responsible as Samuel, Camacho, and the Na'gee tribe. He had decided months ago he'd kill Primo once the Na'gee were dealt with, and deep down, he thought Primo likely felt the same about him. Dante kept a close eye on the man, never letting himself forget who he was working with, or overlooking the fact that Primo had seemingly betrayed the tribe he was loyal to, out of ambition.

"Still, his resources and his 'gift' of knowing what's coming are handy to have… for now." Dante thought.

Dante let his thoughts wander as he sat back in the chair of Primo's large penthouse office. He had his black boots comfortably propped up on the coffee table before him, relaxing while he listened to the phone call.

Dante had indeed taken advantage of Primo and the mercenary group's resources and was now much better equipped than the jeans and t-shirts he used to wear when competing in the knife fight arenas. Now he always wore black tactical pants, a black T-shirt and was never seen without the leather holsters that crisscrossed over his chest packed with daggers. He also wore a belt similarly loaded with blades. Dante still wore his jet-black hair slicked back, although it had now grown nearly to his shoulders. He still sported his well-trimmed goatee. Another change to his look was the Na'gee stone talisman hanging from a black leather strap around his neck.

Primo had taught him to use the talisman to travel to what was called the 'other side'. Dante had never spent much time there and had caught glimpses of enough strange things while chasing fleeing Na'gee warriors to know he didn't want to linger there. Still, it was a useful tool. The young man had grown much harder over the past few months, and it seemed to have significantly darkened his demeanor and aged him.

"So? Are we all set, Primo?" Dante asked.

"Yes. We're all set young Dante. The bikers are clearing out now and the Na'gee will be there to deliver to them tomorrow. We'll be waiting." Primo said.

Dante's skin crawled every time he heard the older man's raspy voice. "It's like listening to a hissing snake make words." He thought.

Dante stood up, staring at Primo the entire time. "When do we leave?" he asked.

Just then Riker, or Captain Riker, as he insisted his men call him-walked into the office. Riker was the lean, muscular man that commanded the mercenary group, after killing the previous Captain. He had renamed the worldwide gun-for-hire organization,

'The Renegades' and had increased their already large numbers significantly. Even before he had taken over, they had several outposts in key locations around the world and made a wealthy living running military-style missions for the highest bidder. Riker himself and a large number of his troops stayed posted here with Primo and were focused on taking over the trading routes that the Na'gee used on the 'other side' to traffic weapons, drugs and all sorts of other illegal contraband. Riker always wore the black and grey camouflage tactical uniform, as did all of his troops, and often wore a black ball cap pulled low over his eyes. The man was vicious and often lashed out violently at his men for failures, disrespect, or sheer whim.

Dante knew it was Riker who had saved his life-not only rescuing him from the previous captain who would have killed him, but also from the exploding building. Despite that, he didn't like the man and definitely didn't trust him. He often thought Riker planned to kill him and Primo once the trading routes had all been procured, especially now that he and several of his officers had the talisman that the Na'gee warriors used to cross over-and had learned how to use them.

Yes, it all made for an uneasy alliance, but they all had their reasons for making it work and so far, it had.

Upon entering, Riker stood rigidly and stared from one man to the other, waiting with a degree of impatience.

Primo spoke first. "We're all set for tomorrow. It should be late afternoon when they arrive, so we'll have to move fast," he said, his voice hissing.

"Perfect. We leave in the morning at zero five hundred, Dante. The birds will airdrop us right on top of the warehouse in that frozen ghost town, and we'll hit them hard as soon as they show up." Riker said, then he turned and left the room.

Dante looked at Primo and asked, "You going with us this time? Your gift for knowing what's about to happen could come in handy." Primo only stared back without answering.

"Yeah, I figured," Dante muttered, and then he vanished.

A split second later, he was in his loft apartment, shedding his gear. He liked showing off his teleporting skills to Primo-reminding him who he was dealing with. Dante figured it was safer if Primo believed he could appear anywhere at any time. The truth was more limited: Dante had to have seen the place first and picture it clearly in his mind, unless he was looking at it directly. He doubted Primo knew that. Stripped down, he sank onto his couch and thought of the family he'd lost.

He thought of Samuel, a man he had respected, who'd taught him to expand his gifts in such a short time-yet had also been the one who killed his family. He thought of Vic, a man without "the gene," without any special gifts, yet who still fought with bravery, courage, and humor no matter the odds. Dante's mind was haunted by all of those he thought were dead and gone, ones he had loved and ones he now hated. These thoughts kept him awake staring into nothing deep into the night, until the tormented young man finally fell asleep on the couch.

Early the next morning, Dante stood on the airstrip just out of town with sixteen mercenaries or 'Renegades'. Three large helicopters sat nearby, waiting to transport the men. At five am on the dot, a black SUV came speeding onto the air strip and stopped next to the gathering of men by the helicopters. Riker got out of the back seat and walked up to the group, who all immediately lined up in formation. All, except Dante of course. He just stood to the side and watched them, like he always did.

Riker walked up and down the line, supposedly inspecting his troops, but Dante thought it was really just to remind them he was in charge. He didn't like Riker, but he didn't judge, for all he knew, it was things like this that kept them functioning at such a high level.

After Riker had walked up and down the line, he yelled "Load up!" The men scrambled to the three helicopters. Riker then turned to Dante and said, "You sure you don't want a firearm or two this time slick? It'd make things a lot easier for you." Dante knew the question was coming in some shape or form; it always did. At this point, he knew Riker already knew his answer but insisted on asking every time anyway.

"I don't do guns" Dante said, as he walked past Riker and headed to the nearest helicopter. Riker followed him and moments later they were all airborne, heading to the warehouse.

It had been hours since the sixteen mercenaries, Dante, and Riker had taken up strategic positions all over the cold warehouse, inside large crates equipped with "peep holes," when he saw them. Dante couldn't believe what he was seeing.

It was Vic and Samuel, both of whom he thought were dead. He had not seen either man since he had fought the Na'gee warriors with them at the hotel, in what seemed to be a lifetime ago. He'd thought both men were dead and yet now he watched them warily move through the warehouse. Dante was flooded with mixed feelings. In truth, he liked and trusted both of those men more than Primo or any of the ruthless mercenaries he now found himself aligned with, but he also blamed Samuel for the death of his family and hated him at the same time. He felt relief and excitement to see them alive and safe, while also feeling hatred and spite for the man that had taken everything from him. For a moment Dante didn't know what to do, but then he pushed all the thoughts and feelings out of his mind and steeled himself.

"It doesn't matter how I feel or what I think, Samuel must pay. He has to die. I owe it to my family. I don't want to hurt Vic, but if he gets in my way…well." Dante thought to himself. He didn't finish the thought though. He couldn't think about killing Vic, but he knew he would if he had to.

Riker sensed Dante's reaction and whispered to him, "Not yet, hold your position until our primary target arrives".

CHAPTER 5
The Roken

Halbred and Eva stepped out onto thick, frozen grass, with their weapons ready. They knew that every trip to the 'other side' could mean death. While the world seemed somewhat like a mirror image of their world, it was very different and full of dangers. The landscape was rough, wild, and unkempt. Lush forests, overgrown fields, hills, and rocky mountains were everywhere they looked.

Frost covered the ground; the air was crisp and cold. None of them had ever been this far north on the 'other side' and did not know what to expect. The frigid temperatures and the differences in the landscape made them speculate that the inhabitants of this part of the 'other side' were bound to be different too.

They all had terrible memories from their first visit, to this strange land, having witnessed unimaginable otherworldly creatures that lived here. They understood now that it was some sort of parallel earth – a reflection of their world- primal, magical, and the root of ~~ so many unbelievable legends and stories once dismissed as mere imagination. None of that made them feel more relaxed or comfortable in this strange land.

They also knew they had only scratched the surface, and what little they had learned could terrify even the most hardened soldier. The key to these trips was to hide quickly, stay alert, and wait for the Na'gee to appear to cross into the world they knew. If all went well, they'd give it the allotted amount of time and cross back over. If not, their mission was to eliminate any Na'gee warriors who tried to flee back. There was usually at least a couple who tried to escape. The group had agreed that the secret to their success was to make sure that none escaped alive. Right now, they were the hunters. They had no desire to alert the remaining Na'gee to their 'strikes' and then become the hunted.

After quickly surveying their surroundings and seeing no immediate dangers, Halbred signaled for Eva to follow him as he headed across the frost-bitten landscape toward a nearby hill. It wasn't a very large hill, more of a mound rising about ten feet out of the ground, covered in thick grass and a few large boulders around the base. The path leading to an oddly large boulder was clearly visible at the base, as were the strange etchings on the boulder itself. Halbred pointed at it, quickly looked around and then pointed at the tree line about twelve feet away. He pointed directly at a huge tree that seemed to loom above the well-worn path and offer a good view of the hill and its distant continuation.

"That's where we'll post up. Keep your head on a swivel; it's too quiet. Something is watching us," Halbred said as he scrambled toward the tree, assault rifle with sound suppressor up and ready to fire. Eva followed closely, sharing his feelings of being watched. She knew the landscape here was usually filled with strange sounds of wildlife. When it went quiet, a predator was always near-and humans were far from the top of the food chain.

The two cautiously made their way across the path and had almost reached the tree line when shapes emerge from the shadows of the cold forest.

Three enormous jungle cats stepped out onto the path before them. They each looked to weigh at least five hundred pounds, far larger than any lion from their world. The cats were orangish-brown, their thick fur bristling, and each bore two massive eight-to-ten-inch fangs protruding from rows of bloodstained teeth. The beasts' massive muscles rippled as they moved with slow menace, eyes fixed on Halbred and Eva, stalking their prey.

Halbred motioned with his left hand for Eva to back up, while he kept the assault rifle aimed at the enormous predators. He stared, unable to believe he was facing what could only be a saber-toothed tiger- or something eerily close. The beasts stared back at Halbred like a rabbit standing before wolves.

While Halbred watched them, waiting for the inevitable attack, Eva slowly eased backwards toward the way they had come. As she moved, the beasts on the right and left started to spread out, slowly beginning to circle their prey. They moved with a slow, powerful grace, tense muscles flexing, appearing ready to pounce at any moment. Time seemed to stand still, and the world was silent outside of the heavy breathing of the large cats.

"You got left Eva!" Halbred suddenly shouted, deciding the longer he waited the more of a tactical advantage he'd be giving away and he squeezed the trigger, opening up his assault rifle on the large cat directly in front of him. As he did, he heard Eva simultaneously begin firing at the beast on the left.

The high-powered rifles did their job, quickly dropping two of the enormous predators but before he could turn his rifle towards the one on the right, Halbred was hit. The massive jungle cat leaped on him tackling him with crushing force, its jaws clamping down on Halbred's head. His impenetrable skin kept him from getting eaten alive, but it did not help him get out from under the weight of the creature or get his head out of its mouth. The tiger savagely chomped down again and again on Halbred's head, while keeping his body pinned with its back legs and tearing at his chest with its front legs. It took mere seconds for the giant creature to tear through his bulletproof vest, while it kept chomping down on his head with relentless fury. Halbred's gift of impenetrable skin kept him in one piece, but he was still trapped, helpless under the weight of the massive beast.

Then the familiar sound of gunshots muffled by a sound suppressor rang out and Halbred felt several bullets hitting him and the beast on top of him. In moments the dead weight of the beast fell on Halbred and the vicious attack stopped. The bullets had no more luck piercing his skin than the teeth did, but he was still stuck under the weight of the massive jungle cat.

"Thanks Eva," he grunted. "Now see if you can help get this thing off of me," Halbred said, sounding like he could barely breathe.

Eva rushed to his aid, set down her rifle and shoved the dead cat's body as hard as she could, while Halbred pushed from under it.

It did not go smoothly, nor did it go quickly, but eventually they managed to roll the creature off to the side. Halbred did not get up immediately, instead he rolled onto his hands and knees and huffed and puffed, trying to catch his breathe.

Eva watched him with concern. She had never thought about Halbred not being able to breathe. In all her time working with the old soldier, he had seemed pretty much invincible, due to his skin as tough as steel. Now she realized that had nothing to do with crushing weight or breathing at all.

As Halbred, worked to catch his breath, Eva began growing concerned that the Na'gee they were supposed to be ambushing would walk up on them at any moment. The old soldier noticed her looking down the path and seemed to read her mind.

"You're right, we don't have time and we won't be able to move these things. Pick up all the bullet shells you can find, especially around the path. I'll make this look as natural as I can." he said, huffing and puffing the entire time, as he rose to his feet unsteadily.

Eva didn't question it, she immediately began gathering bullet shells and tried not to look as Halbred pulled out the large hatchet he wore on his belt and began hacking and slashing the beasts open where they'd been shot, obviously trying to make it appear like they'd been attacked and shredded open by another predator. After a few minutes of both of them working hard on their tasks, Halbred called out, "We'll have to hope that's good enough. If we stay out in the open it won't matter, they'll either see us or we'll be facing off against the next thing that comes along with an appetite. Let's get in the tree quick!"

Ten minutes later they were about fourteen feet in the air, perched on large branches, well hidden by thick leaves, breathing in the icy air as they watched six Na'gee warriors approach the sabertooth carcasses. The six warriors were followed by four, slightly smaller people who pulled a massive wooden cart on wheels that was filled with long wooden crates.

As they neared the bodies of the large cats, four of the warriors spread out on the path and peered into the forest, while two slowly examined the bodies. The people with the cart stopped where they were. They did not look anything like the Na'gee warriors, who all wore brown leather pants, sleeveless matching leather vests and the leather belts which held the huge knives and large .50 caliber pistols that all Na'gee warriors seemed to carry. No, the people with the cart wore tan cloth cloaks of rough burlap-like material, and they did not have the tribal tattoos covering their entire body, face and head like the warriors.

Halbred and Eva had never seen any others like them with the Na'gee before. They had seen the Na'gee with slaves and prisoners when they had raided one of their settlements very far to the south, but they'd never seen them with any 'workers' on trafficking routes. Halbred didn't like it. He knew if he left anyone alive it would put them all at risk, but he didn't like the thought of killing people that may be as much victims of the Na'gee's brutality as anyone.

After several moments, they saw the two warriors that were examining the bodies signal for the others. When the four warriors that had spread out approached them, still looking this way and that cautiously, one of the two who had inspected the carcasses said "This is strange. It does not appear normal. Keep a close watch on everything. Once we deliver the packages, we'll take the bodies back with us. We will feast on their flesh and learn more about what has happened here, brothers." Once the words were spoken, by what appeared to be the leader of the bunch, the other five all bowed their shaved tattoo covered heads in unison and headed towards the hill. The lead warrior that had spoken, waved for the four others with the large cart to follow.

One warrior, who was slightly larger than the rest, stepped away from the group, removed the talisman from around his neck, and placed it against the strange design etched into the face of the large boulder. After holding it there for a moment, the design on the boulder began glowing blue and a doorway opened on the boulder. The warrior then stepped back and waved for the people pulling the cart to come to him. No words were said, but they apparently knew what this meant, because when the signal was given, the four people pulling the cart, set it down, walked past the Na'gee warriors and into the doorway. As soon as they entered, the doorway closed behind them.

"Locking up their workers for safe keeping?" Eva whispered to Halbred, as they watched it all take place before them.

"Yeah-or just making sure that they don't become cat food while they're gone." the old soldier said quietly in response.

As soon as the doorway on the boulder closed, the large warrior did the same circular movements on his talisman that Halbred had done earlier, and a 'blur' appeared in the air. As it appeared, two warriors the apparent leader of the group that had given the instructions and the larger one who opened the boulder doorway - stepped through the 'blur', while the four other warriors grabbed hold of the cart and pulled it through with them. The 'blur' disappeared as the last one went through.

"I'll take out the stowaways. Keep an eye out and let me know if anything's coming my way." Halbred said as he started to make his way down the tree.

"Halbred, how can we be sure they aren't just victims of the Na'gee like the rest of us?" Eva said, considering the differences between the warriors and the apparent workers.

"They're all Na'gee. They're all a threat, Eva. These aren't innocent villagers just following them around, they're part of it… besides, if we leave them alive, we're all at risk" Halbred said.

"Do you really believe that, soldier, or is that what you're telling yourself to feel better about killing them?" Eva said. She usually didn't argue or challenge the group's tactics, but she felt compelled to speak now. She hated the Na'gee for what they had done to her and her family, but she also didn't want to end up just as bad as them.

Halbred didn't respond; he just kept climbing down the tree. Once his feet hit the ground, he looked up at Eva, who was still looking down at him, as if waiting for his answer.

"Okay, Eva. I'm here to kill the damn monsters, not become one of them, but if we're wrong this could be bad for all of us," he said solemnly. With the decision made, Halbred turned and headed towards the large boulder at the base of the hill. He leaned his head close and held his talisman to the design the way he'd seen the large warrior do.

The same doorway appeared and Halbred found himself staring at the four cloaked workers.

They stared back with a mix of surprise and.

"I'm Halbred. I'm here to free you. You no longer need to serve the Na'gee. You are free to go." He said this while wondering if he and Eva had been wrong, bracing for the men to attack.

One of the four cloaked workers stepped forward and, standing face to face with Halbred, removed his hood. The man had red eyes, a strong jaw, and short thick brown hair on his head and most of his face. The veins stood out on his thick neck, and Halbred instantly realized that while these men were not large, they were much stronger than they appeared beneath the rough cloaks.

The man stared at Halbred for a long moment, as if weighing his words and deciding whether to trust him. Then finally he spoke in a rough voice that sounded more like growling than speech.

"I am Grifter. We cannot leave, Halbred as we are bound to the Na'gee. If we move too far from them, we will grow weak, and they will track and kill us. We cannot leave with the chains around our necks, nor can we remove them ourselves without risking death. We are trapped in servitude," Grifter said in his harsh, growling voice, pulling down his cloak to reveal a large stone chain of some sort that was wrapped tight around his thick neck.

"Lean forward and let me help you, Grifter," Halbred said.

The man eyed Halbred warily, but eventually bowed his head forward. Halbred wrapped one hand around the stone chain and pulled out his hatchet with his other hand. He felt the tension rise from the others as they watched. In one sharp movement, he tried to snap the chain against the blade of the hatchet, but the chain didn't snap. The man gasped, his body shaking in pain, before jerking back quickly.

"It cannot… be broken stranger. I have… told you. The more attempts to break the chains… the more pain we endure… until finally we meet death", Grifter said, the broken words filled with pain and anger as if forced out by sheer will.

Halbred thought for a long moment and then asked, "What happens if they're dead?" Grifter eyed him warily and said, "We do not know."

Halbred nodded resolutely and said, "We'll see then. Maybe that will free you." He then turned and headed toward the hill's exit.

Grifter watched him curiously and, despite the pain he still felt, he half grinned at the man's apparent nonchalant attitude towards killing their captors. Right as Halbred was exiting the doorway in the boulder, he stopped and turned around. He had one hand on the stone Na'gee talisman that he wore around his neck and had a speculative look in his eyes.

"What do you say we try one more thing Grifter? The worst thing that can happen is it hurts, a fair price for the chance of freedom, don't you think?" Halbred said.

Grifter looked at the strange human for a moment and then bowed his head forward without responding. Halbred approached him and placed the stone talisman against the chain. Instantly, the chain glowed a faint blue color and then fell to the floor.

As soon as it broke free, the man let out a deep, low growl and slowly raised his head. He stepped back, staring at Halbred the whole time and said, "Please Halbred, help free my brothers as well."

Halbred performed the same act on all three of the other captives. None of the others spoke, instead they let out low, deep rumbling growls and stared with the same eerie red eyes as Grifter. After the last one was freed, they looked at each other and then the three stared at Grifter, apparently waiting to follow his lead.

"You have freed four of the Roken, Halbred. We owe you a blood debt," Grifter said in the same growling voice. Then he walked past Halbred and out through the doorway in the boulder into the cold night air. The three others followed Grifter, and Halbred did too.

As soon as they were outside, all four of the so-called Roken leaned their heads back and howled into the air loudly. As they howled their bodies grew larger, changing in shape and slowly ripping through the rough cloaks they wore. In seconds, Halbred found himself staring at what appeared to be four huge, monstrous creatures. They all had heads like that of a massive wolf and stood tall like an oversized man. Their bodies appeared to be just under seven feet tall, covered with hair that did little to hide their massive muscles with huge sharp claws on their hands and feet. Each of them still had bright red eyes.

They noticeably eyed the corpses of the massive jungle cats on the ground and then Grifter made a loud growling type noise. Each of the other three beasts grabbed one of the dead cats and threw it over their shoulders with ease. None of them looked back at Halbred. They all simply took off with incredible speed, three of them carrying the massive cats over their shoulders while they followed Grifter into the woods, leaving the old soldier standing alone in the path. He stood wondering what he had just witnessed and questioning his own sanity.

Once they were gone, Eva let out the breath that she hadn't realized she'd been holding and wondered the same thing from the branch of the frozen tree. Finally, Eva snapped herself out of her thoughts and surprise and yelled out to Halbred, "Enough daydreaming! Take cover before any of them return!"

The old soldier slowly turned his bewildered eyes up towards the tree, then visibly shook his head and started to head towards Eva.

While he walked, he thought, "What the hell are we going to run into next, in this cursed world?"

CHAPTER 6
The Warehouse

Samuel hid behind the large crate in the corner, waiting. He knew Vic had taken a similar position on the second level above him. He also knew that if he was impatient with all the hiding, Vic must be going insane. The thought was somewhat amusing to Samuel and helped distract him from the cold that seemed to cut through his clothing.

As he waited, he continued to survey the warehouse. He knew that at any moment, the Na'gee could appear and he had to be ready. Then Samuel's eye caught what looked like warmer air, coming from a small hole in a nearby crate. It looked like what you see when you breathe out in the cold, except it came from the hole in the crate. He looked around and saw other crates on the warehouse floor, many with similar holes. Here and there, he'd see the mist or discolored air briefly before it vanished.

After a moment the realization washed over him. "This is an ambush", Samuel thought.

Immediately, Samuel whispered into his earpiece.

"Vic, the bikers aren't gone, they're hiding in the crates. They must be waiting to ambush the Na'gee and they must see us too. Be ready." Samuel whispered.

The only reply he got from his tall companion was "Shit! Sneaky damn bikers."

Just then a large blur appeared in the center of the warehouse floor, tearing through the air. The rift was like a rip in the fabric of the air. Six Na'gee warriors poured through it. Despite the cold, they still wore their sleeveless leather vests, and despite this supposedly being a meeting to sell weapons, the two in the lead emerged with cautious looks and hands resting on their pistols. The four that followed pulled a massive cart loaded with long crates, undoubtedly weapons.

As soon as the last of the Na'gee emerged it vanished.

Then… it all started.

The warriors looked around, scowling at the empty room, when suddenly crates burst open and the warehouse exploded with gunfire.

In a split second the large Na'gee warrior in the lead took several bullets, although he still kept moving, as he and the fighter beside him ran for the cover of nearby crates. They moved with incredible speed, shifting side to side as they ran, making it hard for the camouflaged men emerging from from the crates to land a clean shot.

The four Na'ge that pulled the large cart through the 'blur', quickly flipped the cart on its side, creating a large barrier and began firing back with their .50 caliber pistols.

Samuel stepped back from the crate he had been using as cover and fired his shotgun three times, directly into the side of the crate closest to him. The entire side shattered under the powerful shotgun blasts, revealing the bodies of two men, wearing black and grey camouflage.

They definitely weren't members of the biker gang, but he didn't waste time figuring out who they were.

"There'll be time for that later", Samuel thought as he rolled past the side of the destroyed crate and unleashed his shotgun on another pair of camouflaged soldiers who were trading gunshots with the Na'gee. Both men were torn apart by the close-range shotgun blast.

As soon as he fired, he instinctively ducked and barely avoided the bullet that exploded into the crate behind him. Samuel looked toward the shot's origin and saw the lead Na'gee aiming a large pistol at him.

Samuel started to roll away, knowing he wouldn't have time to get a shot off before the warrior fired at him again, but before he could, the man in black appeared behind the Na'gee warrior, seemingly out of nowhere, and slit the warrior's throat. The man held a dagger in each hand and stood staring at Samuel as the dead warrior's body fell in front of him.

"Dante!?" Samuel thought in shock. He had thought the young knife fighter was dead. He had grieved for the young man carrying the guilt that he was somehow responsible for his death. Yet now, the man stood before him.

As soon as the shooting started, Vic grinned and leaned over the metal railing in front of him. He took aim and shot one of the Na'gee warriors in the head, just as he stood up from behind the overturned cart to shoot at one of his attackers.

A second later, Vic shot another one in the head in the same manner.

"Two down, two to go. Not sure what's got the bikers hell bent on robbing the Na'gee, but the distraction is certainly making my job easy." Vic said aloud as he took aim and waited for the next Na'gee to poke his head up.

Before he could take the next shot, however, he caught movement in his peripheral vision and heard the boom as the side of the closest crate crashed to the ground, and two soldiers emerged from the crate with rifles aimed at him.

Vic knew he didn't have time to turn from the railing he was leaning over before they filled him with holes, so he dropped his gun and leaped over the railing itself instead. Hearing the clangs of bullets ringing off the metal banister behind him as he dove over the edge.

As soon as Vic dived over the edge, he turned his body around, reached out and caught the flooring of the walkway he had previously stood on. In one fluid motion, the tall man went from leaping off the walkway, to catching the flooring and swinging his body, legs first, back up under the railing.

The timing was perfect. His extended legs and body shot under the railing and collided into the legs of the approaching soldiers, sending both men crashing down on either side of Vic.

With his momentum still carrying his outstretched body forward, and the two soldiers crashing on either side of him, he reached out with both hands, driving his elbows down on the backs of their heads.

The crunching noises Vic heard as he delivered the elbows, told him he had likely broken both of their noses. He jumped to his feet and turned to face the two men, who were lying face down and trying to roll over to face their attacker who had somehow gone from leaping over the railing of the walkway, to taking out their legs and smashing their faces.

Neither man had the chance to roll over before Vic pulled his large pistol and delivered one shot to each of their heads. He saw movement to his left and quickly shot the other two soldiers who were rounding the corner with their rifles ready.

"These sure as hell ain't bikers", Vic mumbled as he quickly looked this way and that, waiting for the next attack.

Samuel yelled out "Dante! You're alive!" Just then, he saw the soldiers coming around the crate directly behind him with their weapons drawn. Despite his shock and surprise at seeing his young friend alive, Samuel's timing was still as sharp as ever. He turned and slammed the butt of the shotgun into the face of the closest man, while simultaneously kicking out his right leg to knock the rifle from the other soldier's grip. Before either man could recover from Samuel's initial moves, he reached out and touched the man he'd hit with the shotgun, freezing him in place, while he turned and cut the other man down with the shotgun. Before the body hit the ground, Samuel turned back and shot the soldier he'd frozen with the shotgun as well.

A split second after shooting the second soldier, Samuel felt the impact of a boot slam into him in the center of the back and sending him flying into the shattered crate in front of him. As he stumbled into the debris, he was kicked again, this time in the back of the head.

Samuel saw stars as he crashed to the ground but didn't let it slow him down. As soon as he hit the ground, he rolled onto his back and kicked out with both legs, catching his attacker- who was coming down on him with a large knife drawn-directly in the chest, sending him flying backwards.

Samuel immediately saw that it was the large Na'gee who had been shot multiple times while taking cover at the beginning of the chaos. He also saw that his kick hadn't done much more than the bullets had to slow the large warrior down.

Samuel rolled backwards, jumping to his feet as the warrior rushed back in at him. Before the gap closed, Dante appeared out of nowhere, crouching behind the large warrior with a knife in each hand. He swung both hands slashed open the tendons on the back of the warrior's knees, sending him crashing to the ground.

By the time the warrior hit the floor, Dante had thrown both of the daggers into the back of the man's neck, killing him instantly.

With the warrior dead, Dante directed his attention to Samuel, pulled two more daggers out from the crisscrossed sheath he wore across his chest and disappeared.

Samuel was shocked that Dante had disappeared without a word, just as much as he was shocked at the look of hatred in the young man's eyes when he looked at him. Then he felt the air move behind him right before the knives slashed open his back.

Samuel spun around and saw the flash of Dante disappearing. His back screamed in pain, and he felt the warm flow of blood streaming down from the burning wound. Then he saw Dante appearing to his right and instantly felt his right arm being torn open by a knife slash as Dante vanished again.

"Don't know what's got into him. Maybe he thinks we left him to die. Doesn't matter. This stops now." Samuel thought as he steeled himself for the attack he assumed would come from his left side.

Sure enough, he saw Dante appear on his left, slashing a dagger towards him. This time Samuel was ready.

He leaned back, evading the swing and smashed a hard left hook into the side of Dante's head, sending the younger man staggering several feet across the floor. Samuel had no intention of killing the young man he cared about, but he also had no intention of continuing to be sliced up like a piece of sushi.

He charged after the staggering Dante and delivered another powerful left hook into the side of Dante's head. This time the young man went down, crashing to the floor.

Vic leaned on the railing of the warehouse second story walkway once again, looking at the gunfight between what appeared to be two soldiers and the two remaining Na'gee still using the large crate for cover. Then he noticed Samuel fighting what appeared to be his old friend Dante and he froze.

"There's no way he made it out of the hotel explosion!" Vic thought in shock. As he watched the teleportation and slashing of knives, he knew without a doubt it was Dante. Instantly, the shock of seeing the man alive again was replaced with frustrated bewilderment that Dante was attacking Samuel.

He thought of shooting the man as he saw him slash Samuel's back before vanishing again, but couldn't bring himself to pull the trigger. Instead, he quickly holstered his pistol and pulled the carbon fiber spear out of the sheath on his back. He flipped it upside down and prepared to send it flying, the dull butt end of the spear first into Dante's chest.

"Don't want to kill the kid, just stop him from cutting old Samuel into pieces" Vic thought as Dante appeared to the right of Samuel and slashed the man's arm wide open before disappearing again.

Vic expected him to appear to the left of Samuel next and readied himself to throw the spear. "The kid's good, but he's still predictable" Vic thought.

Then before he could throw the spear, he saw Samuel turn and deliver a powerful punch as soon as Dante appeared. Vic wasn't surprised at all. He'd fought with Samuel on many occasions, and knew that Samuel was as calculating and dangerous as anyone anywhere.

Vic watched as Samuel hit Dante a second time, sending him flying to the ground. Vic knew if Samuel wanted him dead, he would've frozen the young man when his fist connected and then quickly dispatched him. He found it heartening to see that Samuel obviously didn't want to kill Dante either.

Then an explosion lit up the entire warehouse and heat flared up from the center of the building.

Vic looked up in time to see, the 'blur' disappearing from beside the overturned, exploded cart and was shocked to see the lean soldier with a black hat, who was holding a rocket launcher, create a 'blur' of his own and step through in what could've only been, pursuit of the fleeing Na'gee.

"Oh no!" Vic said out loud, realizing that Halbred and Eva would be expecting fleeing Na'gee on the 'other side', but they definitely wouldn't be expecting someone firing rockets at them.

He instinctively grabbed hold of the Na'gee talisman that he wore, attempting to cross over to the 'other side' to help, when he saw Dante on his feet below him.

Samuel's attention was on the explosion and his back was turned to Dante, who approached with a dagger in each hand. Vic watched the young man raise both daggers and knew that Samuel would be dead before he ever saw it coming.

Vic released the talisman, raised his carbon fiber spear and hurled it, butt end first.

Just as Dante's daggers were swinging down towards the back of Samuel's neck, the butt end of the spear struck him in the chest. The young knife fighter dropped both daggers and flew backwards, crashing into a crate.

Samuel whirled around to see and saw Dante crash into the crate from the impact of the spear. He looked up and saw Vic standing on the walkway overhead.

Dante looked up too, albeit very disoriented, scowled, then his eyes widened and he disappeared. Samuel instantly saw what Dante had seen and yelled, "Vic, look out!"

Vic whirled around to see another soldier with a rocket launcher aimed directly at him. He watched the man pull the trigger, sending the rocket flying in his direction. He leaped over the side of the walkway with no thoughts of hanging on this time.

The walkway exploded, along with a portion of the warehouse itself, sending chunks of crates and pieces of the ceiling crashing down.

Vic hit the floor of the warehouse hard. Large chunks of crates and debris crashed around him, as he slowly pulled himself to his feet and glanced back at the soldier who fired the rocket. He saw the man quickly reload the massive weapon and then aim the rocket launcher at him once again. As the soldier fired, he felt Samuel grab his arm and jerk him to the side, then everything went black as the air filled with the thunderous sounds of explosions and immense heat washed over them both.

CHAPTER 7
Captain Riker

As the warehouse went up in explosions and flames, Riker and two of his men engaged the stone talisman they had previously procured from the Na'gee warriors, and the 'blurs' appeared. All three stepped through to the 'other-side'.

In an instant, they went from the chaos of a burning warehouse caving in on itself, to the unnerving silence of the frozen wilderness. Two of the Na'gee warriors had used this same route to escape and now stood on a clear path catching their breath. They both shared shocked looks when three mercenaries appeared in various positions around them, and they took off for the nearby woods.

Riker didn't bother chasing them. Instead, he fired the rocket launcher that he still held, and the tree line-along with one of the warriors exploded. The second warrior leapt behind a massive tree overhanging the path for cover, successfully dodging the explosion.

Another of the three mercenaries was about fifty feet from Riker He took aim at the tree, but before he could fire, muffled gunshots pummeled his chest. The mercenaries bullet proof vest took most of the impact, but it still knocked him off his feet and sent him flying backwards, causing his rocket to fire straight up into the air.

The stunned Na'gee warrior, looked up from the base of the tree, searching for the source of the shots that had saved him. He spotted a strangely beautiful, dark-haired woman pointing a rifle down at him from the branches above. He instinctively rolled his body back towards the path, hoping to dodge the deadly hail of bullets to come. The roll saved his life, but it did not save the agile warrior from taking several bullets to the back of his legs.

Eva repositioned herself on the high branch to aim more cleanly at the fleeing warrior, while Halbred fired several rounds at Riker's position.

Riker saw his man get shot and the rocket fly straight up into the air. He knew there was no self-destruct on the munition they were using – meaning it would soon come crashing back down on them.

"No time for that now. Have to deal with the shooter first." Riker thought as he ducked behind the hill next to him. Bullets peppered the side of the hill directly beside him.

Riker looked over to see his soldier who had been shot back on his feet, taking cover as well. He was grateful he had insisted they all wear vests during these ambushes.

"It's supposed to be us ambushing the damn Na'gee! Who the hell is waiting to ambush us?!" Riker thought furiously. "Whoever it is, Dante knows them, that much was obvious. The kid has some explaining to do once we get back."

As Riker's thoughts tried to make sense of the unexpected turn of events, he did not fail to notice that the third soldier with them had yet to be seen. He quickly moved to the other side of the hill he was using for cover and peered down the path, roughly twenty yards ahead. In the distance he saw his third soldier, just as the man unleashed another rocket towards the injured Na'gee warrior on the path.

"Not the path, you idiot! The tree! The damn gunfire is coming from the tree!" Riker yelled furiously.

The injured warrior and the entire area of the path where he stood erupted in a massive explosion. Eva saw the explosion and quicklyadjusted her aim from the warrior she had been about to finish off, to the mercenary with the rocket launcher several yards down from him and let the rifle loose.

The mercenary never knew what had hit him, as a shower of bullets riddled his body. The vest provided some protection against the center-mass shots but did nothing against the bullets tearing into his arms and head. In an instant the soldier fell to the ground lifeless.

Halbred was still firing at the soldier she had wounded, who had crawled into a ditch on the other side of the path, almost directly opposite to the large tree.

Still using the large branch as a tree stand of sorts, Eva turned back towards the hill where the other mercenary was using for cover. She took aim, just in time to see the rocket fire towards them.

As soon as Riker yelled, he rolled around the side of the hill to shoot back, thinking "Last rocket, this better do the trick"

Riker fired the rocket directly at the tree.

Eva took aim and saw the rocket fire, instead of shooting she just dove into Halbred without thinking, sending them both flying off of the fourteen-foot-high branch of the tree.

They hit the ground hard, just as the tree and everything around it exploded directly behind them. In less than a second the massive tree was on fire and falling towards them fast. Eva was facing the ground from the reckless dive, but Halbred saw it coming.

"No time! Have to save her!" Halbred thought as he shoved Eva to the side as hard as he could. Eva went flying off to the side just as the massive tree came crashing down where Halbred lay.

Riker watched the destruction caused by the rocket he had fired with satisfaction and pride. He loved the violence, he loved to win, and in this moment, he felt the joy of both. Confident that he had dealt with whoever had been foolish enough to interrupt his slaughtering of the Na'gee, he dropped the rocket launcher and casually approached the soldier hiding in the ditch.

"You look like shit, man! How many shots did you take?" Riker asked as he came upon the bleeding mercenary in the ditch.

The man had several bullet wounds to his legs, arms, and one near his neck. He was losing a tremendous amount of blood. He looked up at Riker with pain in his eyes but didn't manage to deliver an answer before Riker pulled out his pistol and shot the soldier in the head.

"I don't have time to play nursemaid," Riker thought as he holstered his weapon and removed the dead mercenary's talisman. He put it in his pocket and then looked up, just in time to see the rocket that had been sent flying straight up into the air come crashing down towards them.

"Oh shit!" He yelled as he quickly used the talisman to create the 'blur' and dove through just before the area he had been standing in erupted.

As soon as Riker stepped back through the 'blur' into the world he knew so well, he felt the sting of flames all around him. The entire warehouse was on fire and chunks of walls and ceiling were falling around him, crashing to the ground. He spotted an exit, ducked his head and took off running through the flames. Although he held his breath, to keep the smoke from burning his lungs, there was nothing he could do to keep the hot flames from singing his body as he ran.

Seconds later Riker came crashing out the side door of the burning building, falling down the short steps and collapsing onto the cold concrete outside. He lay there coughing and hacking, as the white SUV pulled up to him.

The last remaining mercenary in his unit jumped out of the vehicle, ran up to him, and began helping Riker to his feet.

"I used our satellite feed to find this vehicle parked a couple buildings away when you sent me to find transportation sir. The driver's side window is smashed and it's been hotwired, so I'm guessing that whoever our attackers were, they used it to get here." The older mercenary said.

He was a veteran of the 'Renegades', who had been loyal to Riker since before he had taken the position of Captain. The man was slightly older than Riker, had silver/grey hair that hung almost to his shoulders and always sported a scruffy five o clock shadow on his face. The soldier's name was Earl, but everyone just called him 'Brick'.

Riker didn't respond, as Brick filled him in and helped load him into the white SUV.

"Captain, the helicopter can't get us from here anymore with the building up in flames. They said the next closest spot is a helipad on top of the tower in the city, but there's already an unscheduled chopper sitting there. Something vague about classified government business. Sounds like what we would say." Brick stopped talking and looked at Riker questioningly while they both sat in the unmoving vehicle.

After a few brief moments without a response, Brick decided he would be more direct with his thoughts.

"Captain, the way I see it, we got two options… we can head further away from the city towards a clearing the satellite feed shows about twenty miles south of here and have the bird pick us up, or we can go take that chopper parked on the tower and fly out of here ourselves. What is your orders sir?" Brick finished.

"The choppers got to be theirs. We're taking it Brick. Then we'll find that damn knife fighter and get some answers." Riker said, still somewhat gasping.

Without another word being said, the white SUV skidded out of the burning warehouse's parking lot and headed towards the city.

Before long, the two men were approaching the large tower. They noticed several police cars in front of the tower, so they pulled into the tower's parking deck and discreetly parked the white SUV. They exited the vehicle and made their way towards the stair well and had almost made it there, when two police officers stepped out of the doorway. Before either officer was able to say a word, Riker pulled his pistol and shot them both in the head.

Neither Riker or Brick said a word, they just stepped over the dead officers, into the stair well and began running up the stairs towards the roof. In no time they emerged onto the roof top, where two more officers stood, and were immediately dispatched the same way. Both men jumped into the chopper and Brick took the controls and had them airborne in seconds.

As they flew, Riker radioed Primo.

"I need the last ten minutes of camera footage at the tower scrambled quick; there were a few casualties. Then I need a copy of the footage from the rest of the day sent to my phone asap. We were ambushed and your little knife fighter knows who it was! Take care of the video stuff Primo, I'm headed your way." Riker barked it all out quickly and then turned off the radio and looked at Brick.

"Whoever the hell they were, they'll be remembered for killing a bunch of cops at the tower and flying off in a chopper. Assuming their bodies at the warehouse aren't too burnt up to connect to the footage." Riker said viciously and then leaned back in his seat and closed his eyes, while Brick flew them away.

CHAPTER 8
Surviving the Night

It was almost dark when Eva woke up freezing. She had no idea how long she had been unconscious but knew it had been long enough for the flames to die down around her and for the freezing temperatures to sink into her bones. She shivered violently as she forced herself to sit up, despite the stiffness and pain that she felt everywhere.

"How in the world can I literally hurt everywhere?" she thought to herself. As she sat up, she looked around trying to get her bearings and recall the last moments before she blacked out. The frost covered forest around her still had small fires here and there amidst the destroyed trees and foliage. It looked like what was left of the land after huge man-made wars took place. The needless destruction disgusted her. She turned away – only to see Halbred's head sticking out from beneath a massive fallen tree.

Eva gasped and scrambled towards him the memories of the recent events flooded her mind. She remembered that they had both been in that tree when some soldier in black and grey camouflage fired a rocket at them. She remembered diving into Halbred and knocking them both out of the tree. Then she remembered him kicking her away as everything exploded. That was it. The next memory in her head was waking up just now.

"Who were those guys, and how did they cross over to this place?" Eva thought to herself as she neared Halbred, fearing the worst.

The old, seasoned soldier was still breathing, but didn't appear to be conscious. She didn't know how he could possibly be alive under the weight of the tree and figured that his impenetrable skin must have something to do with it. Eva figured it didn't matter how tough

53

the old soldiers hide was. If he lay trapped under this tree, he'd be slowly crushed to death. She frantically thought through her options and decided she needed help to try to free him-though she figured it would take dozens of men to move the tree far more than they had.

"Still, maybe Samuel and Vic can help." Eva thought as she stood and engaged the stone talisman that she wore. When the 'blur' appeared in the air, flames leapt out of it, making Eva jump back several feet. She tried to peer through, it, however nothing but flames and heat poured through, making visibility and entry impossible, so she quickly let the 'blur' close.

"I hope Vic and Samuel are all right," She thought to herself as she redirected her attention to Halbred. She could see his head, right arm and part of his right hip sticking out from under the tree, but the rest of him was trapped securely.

Eva grabbed his arm and pulled with every bit of strength she could muster, but the man didn't budge. She tried again and again, but made no progress. She finally stopped pulling on him, realizing she was accomplishing nothing more than wearing herself out needlessly, and began looking around for something that could help her free him.

As her eyes scanned the woods around her, she couldn't help but notice that the sun was starting to set. She tried not to think about the implications but knew deep down that 'they' would be coming soon.

"If I don't get him out of here quick, we're both done for," Eva mumbled to herself. She looked back at Halbred worried and noticed the handle of the hatchet he wore on his belt peeking out from under the tree. Without a second thought, Eva grabbed it with one hand and started digging away at the dirt underneath with the other, slowly working it free.

After a few minutes that seemed like forever, she got the hatchet loose and held it in her hands. Eva began savagely chopping away at the tree just above Halbred's head, desperately trying to save the man before the quickly approaching darkness brought the dark ones upon them.

As the sun set and she found it difficult to see Halbred beneath the tree, she realized how little progress she had made. Eva knew her options were fading and understood that she wouldn't have a chance at saving Halbred if she got herself killed in the night. So, she stopped trying to free her friend and looked around for cover-someplace to hide through the night. She first looked for a tree that she could climb and hide in, but there was so much destruction from the earlier battle that none were climbable. What she did see, as she scanned her surroundings was the hill with the boulder in front of it.

Her memories of Halbred using the talisman to open a doorway in the boulder just hours before came back to her in an instant. Eva jumped to her feet and ran for the boulder, realizing just how dark it was as she ran. She reached the boulder and pressed the talisman against it, watching impatiently as the blue light started to glow and the doorway in the stone appeared.

Eva stepped through and turned around to close the doorway behind her, and as she did, she saw two black-cloaked shapes appear on the path before her. Under their tattered black cloaks, pale translucent looking skin could be seen covering the lean muscular bodies, as well as the long claw like fingers that extended out of the sleeves of the cloaks. Their dead black eyes locked with hers and they both hissed loudly, showing off rows of sharp teeth and long deadly fangs. Suddenly they both began racing towards her at inhuman speeds. Eva jumped back, pulling her pistol and nervously watched the doorway close, just seconds before they reached her.

The creatures banged and beat on the boulder for what seemed like forever, while Eva sat curled up in the corner of the small enclosure, trying to keep warm. She was freezing and terrified that at any moment the evil creatures she had only ever heard referred to as 'dark ones' would break into her shelter, but at the same time, she thought that the longer they focused on her, the less likely they'd find Halbred trapped helplessly under the tree.

Eva didn't think the creatures would have any more luck biting through the old soldier's tough skin than the jungle cats did, but she had no idea what they were capable of and didn't want Halbred to be the one to find out.

After what seemed like most of the long night, the noises stopped, and silence filled the small cold shelter. Eva had found a stack of firewood and started a small fire, hours before, deciding that they already knew where she was and freezing throughout the night, wouldn't be much better than getting devoured by the creatures trying to break in.

The silence that finally came, seemed more concerning than the savage attempts to break in hand, leaving Eva to wonder just what the creatures were up to now as she crouched by the small fire.

Outside on the small hill where Eva had hidden just moments before, Halbred awoke with a groan.

"What the hell?" the old soldier exclaimed as he unsuccessfully tried to move. He groggily looked around as best he could. His view, however, was severely limited by his precarious position. With most of his body trapped under the tree, Halbred was stuck. His right arm was free, so he used it to try to push the tree off him, but it didn't even begin to budge.

"We're gonna need a damn bulldozer to get this thing off me." He thought to himself, yet he still tried to push it away again, this time letting out a loud roar as he pushed with all strength. Still nothing, not even an inch. Then he saw the hairless pale long face with black eyes peer over the tree. It was directly above him, leaning over the tree that had him trapped and staring at him with a predatory look. Then its mouth opened wide to reveal sharp teeth, long fangs and a long black flickering tongue, just before it dove in biting at Halbred's face. It didn't manage to penetrate his skin any more than the jungle cat had earlier, but it was just as diligent about trying.

Seconds later, a second creature had joined it and began chomping down on Halbreds exposed arm. He tried to swat it away, but the creature was too powerful and had too much leverage, so Halbred lay helpless as the two beasts tried to eat him alive.

After what seemed like forever of being an oversized chew toy, the creatures stopped. They eyed him with a sense of curiosity and then looked at each other. The one by his arm reared its head back and let out a loud screeching, hissing kind of sound into the silent night, while the other one leapt over the fallen tree and began digging away at the ground around Halbred. After a moment of screeching, the second creature joined in on the digging efforts. Before Halbred knew it, two more creatures had arrived and began tugging at his arm while the first two kept digging around and underneath him.

The soldier felt his body start to slowly move, inch by inch. He tried to prepare himself but knew that his body wouldn't likely move right after being crushed for who knew how long under the massive tree. He also knew how formidable these violent creatures were and knew his odds against the four of them wouldn't be great in the best of circumstances.

All of the sudden, a powerful jerk on his arm, released Halbred from under the weight of the tree and sent him flying across the forest floor.

Two of the creatures darted off, while the other two circled him. Halbred tried to get to his feet but couldn't manage to move his body that way. He didn't feel like anything was broken, it was just that the muscles were locked up and not moving right.

His arm worked though, so he quickly pulled the pistol on his hip and took aim. He managed to get two shots off, before the gun was violently kicked out of his hand. He felt for his hatchet but found it missing. With his weapons gone and his body not wanting to listen to him, the old soldier felt a feeling of helplessness wash over him, that he'd never felt before.

He didn't think the creatures could actually kill him; in truth he wasn't even sure if he could even die, but the realization that he was at their mercy seemed to weigh heavier on him then the idea of death. He was shaken from his thoughts of doom and gloom when he caught the movement out of the corner of his eye. It was one of the creatures who had darted off, back with a long vine of some sort in its hands. Halbred watched it closely, so closely in fact that he never noticed the second creature with a similar vine until it had it wrapped it around his feet.

Halbred looked down, just in time to get slung by the vine wrapped around his feet into a nearby tree. His head took most of the impact and stars instantly started swirling around him. The first creature swooped in and wrapped up his arms with the long vine that it held and minutes later, Halbred was being drug across the ground at incredible speeds, wrapped up tightly like a mummy in the thick vines.

Halbred didn't know where they were taking him, all he knew was that they were getting him there fast, as he was helplessly pulled behind them, dragging and bouncing off the rough terrain.

Hours later, Eva checked her watch. "The suns got to be up by now" she thought.

She had given it an extra thirty minutes, not wanting to make it through the night just for her impatience to get her eaten alive minutes before sunrise. Cautiously, she approached the stone wall, and pressed the talisman against it, seeing the blue glow once again just before the doorway in the boulder appeared.

Sure enough, the sun shined brightly on the frosty terrain that surrounded her. With Halbred's hatchet in hand, Eva made her way over the frost covered ground to the fallen tree, ready to begin her efforts to free the veteran soldier. Instead of seeing Halbred though, she saw the ground dug up and claw marks everywhere. There were unmistakable tracks of long clawed feet and a wide trail heading away from the scene that looked like a sled had been drug across the ground.

She stood for long moments taking in the scene around her, piecing together the events from the previous night the best she could and weighing out her options. Finally, Eva switched the apps on the watch she wore and zeroed in on Halbred. She knew the tracker wouldn't work from one world to the other world, but it would work just fine in one world.

She saw his location many miles away and continued to think through her options. She figured that the creatures wouldn't be able to kill Halbred, so he was likely still alive. She also figured that as long as Vic and Samuel were alive, that they'd come in search of them sooner or later and that once they crossed over into this world, the trackers would lead them to her. To Eva, those facts made her decision clear. She would track down Halbred and try to free him while the sun was still shining. The way she saw it, if she didn't get to him by nightfall, she would just cross back over to her world until the sun came up. She hoped Vic and Samuel were ok, she worried about the flames that she had encountered when she tried to cross over to them the day before, but Halbred was with her in this world, so she felt it was her responsibility to do what she could to save him.

With her mind made up, Eva searched around the area and found the assault rifle she had dropped in her wild dive from the tree the night before. She threw the weapon over her shoulder, tucked Halbred's hatchet into her belt and began to follow the apparent sled trail towards the tracker. As she moved along the trail, her mind shifted from the dangerous creatures of the night to all of the potential dangers that came in the daylight in this strange world, and she focused on the woods around her, straining ears and eyes as best she could, hoping she wouldn't be caught off guard.

CHAPTER 9
Roid & Flutter

The darkness of nightfall covered the snowy mountain terrain like a warm blanket. They didn't have to see it to know that the night had come; they just felt it, knew it deep down. The night awakened themit brought them life, and with life came the hunger. The hunger a thirst for blood, and revenge.

They had crossed over to this world, the 'top side' several months ago and had beenhunting ever since. Despite the fact that they were from here, they knew that they didn't belonganymore. They knew that 'their kind' or the species that they had somehow become, roamed freely on the 'other side'. That they hunted together and congregated together at night, in those pyramids that kept them safe from the deadly rays of sunlight that cursed the daylight hours. They also knew that there was some form of hierarchy within their species, some form of order and ranks-but neither of them had stayed long enough to learn what it meant.

"Maybe when we're done. Maybe when he's dead, when they're all dead. Maybe then we'll go learn what we've become," Roid thought to himself as he slowly crept out of the shelter of the mountain cave and surveyed the snowy landscape around him.

"Then again, maybe we'll just take this entire world by the throat and make it ours," the large man, or what used to be a man, thought.

Roid was an abnormally huge and muscular specimen. He'd already been long before the change. He had served on Halbred's special military unit and was often describe as looking more like a giant ape or bear than a man. He had huge muscular arms, legs, and a massive chest that seemed straight out of a comic book. The muscles weren't just for show either. The 'gene', as the world called it, affected each human that had it differently, for Roid it gave him this enormous physique and an otherworldly strength to match it. When he had transformed into the creature that he was now, none of that went away, -instead it enhanced his speed and strength even more, heightened his senses, and 'blessed' him with the strange long claw like fingers.

The creature that was Roid now, still sported the enormous muscles under pale almost translucent skin. His hair had all fallen out, leaving the pale, almost glowing creature hairless but even more monstrous. He wore no shirt, and still sported his black camouflage tactical pants and combat boots. He didn't need a shirt, as he felt no temperature, hot or cold, something that he'd gotten used to over the past few months.

His eyes were solid black, -no pupils, no color-just endless dark. His mouth had grown larger and was filled with rows of pointed teeth that seemed to surround his two massive fangs like background singers.

He stood in the snow outside of the cave thinking that this night would finally be the night.

Roid and Flutter had been hunting Halbred, their old commander for months in this world, which their species called the 'top side'. No one had told them the rules when they had been transformed into the creatures that they now were, but still they somehow knew deep down that they were forbidden to be in this world. Neither of them cared. They blamed Halbred for what they had become and now obsessed over finding him and killing him.

In truth, Roid blamed Halbred. Flutter accompanied him and desired to kill her old commander, but no more than she desired to kill every living thing since her transformation. Deep down, she didn't blame Halbred for their fate, she blamed that Agent 17, or Samuel or whatever he wanted to call himself. Their unit was fine, they were happy, and they were unstoppable until they had run into that man. He had led them to this cursed fate. He had been the reason the rest of their unit had died. Yes, Flutter was along for the hunt, she hungered for the blood of these humans, but her lust for revenge would only be satisfied when Agent 17 – and everyone he cared about-was torn limb from limb-and she intended to see it done.

Flutter stepped out into the snow next to Roid. She still wore her black-on-black camouflage pants and combat boots, like Roid. She, however, still wore her matching tactical shirt, although she'd torn the sleeves off at the shoulders, freeing her muscular pale arms that extended into unnaturally long fingers ending in pointed claws. She had torn her shirt off just above the waist as well, making it almost a crop top -claiming she couldn't move properly in constricting human clothes.

When she'd torn open her shirt Roid had suggested that she just go shirtless like him, which earned a vicious look and no response from her. Despite their changes, her oversized companion was still the same old Roid in some ways.

Unlike Roid, Flutter had not lost her hair; it remained the short, blonde messy hair that she had before the change. Her black eyes, large mouth, and razor-sharp teeth, surrounded by the menacing fangs were very much like Roid's features though. Like Roid and the rest of Halbred's old unit, Flutter also had the 'gene', but it had not given her strength and size like Roid or impenetrable skin like Halbred, instead, the 'gene' had 'gifted' Flutter with the ability to fly. Several humans with the 'gene' had been affected that way. What made Flutter even more unique was that she could touch others and objects and make them weightless and floating, almost like a helium-filled balloon. She did not have to be touching them to make it stop;she could release them at will. The skill had come in handy on many tactical missions and in the past several months, it had been just as handy for her and Roid.

The two of them had covered a lot of ground in the last few months, hunting Halbred at all of the safe houses that they remembered. They had left trails of bodies behind them along the way and had done nothing to hide or conceal the scenes.

"Let them fear us! Let them be scared of what's out here hunting them." Roid said.

They had been careful to remove the heads of their victims -most of them, at least. They had learned that when they fell into the feeding frenzy their bodies instinctively implanted some sort of eggs or parasites into their victims, turning them into creatures like themselves.

Roid and Flutter had agreed that this world was theirs and they didn't intend to share it, so they had begun removing the heads of their victims early on in their hunting endeavors. Well, most of them. When they crossed paths with their old comrade-in-arms, Unoko, at one of the safe houses, Roid had insisted that the world deserved to have the small martial artist running around devouring people, so they left him to turn. Outside of that incident there were no others.

Now Roid and Flutter stood at the base of a large mountain, just outside the cave they had used to hide from the sunlight the night before. They had both been here long ago, before they had been changed. The mountain cabin was the next of Halbred's safe houses on their list. They had searched several so far, hunting the old soldier, and both felt this one would be the one. Of course, they always thought the next one would be the one.

In the distance they could see the cabin lights glowing in the night and knew that someone had to be there. They didn't bother discussing their plan of attack, as they knew each other too well. They already knew how they would attack the cabin.

Flutter leapt into the air and began flying towards the cabin lights, while Roid took off on foot at inhuman speeds towards the same lights.

Before long, they were both outside the large cabin nestled between two mountains. Lights poured out of the windows, but they did not see movement inside, not yet.

Roid stood just off the porch, in the snow, staring at the house. Despite the lights seeming to indicate signs of life, the chopper missing from the helipad on the roof of the garage concerned him. He had been on several missions with Halbred from this safe house and knew the chopper was always their primary means of travel from the snowy mountain safe house.

"If they ain't home, then I guess we just wait on them" Roid thought as he stared into the windows. Suddenly, Flutter landed next to him in the snow.

"Upstairs window, far right," she said coldly.

Roid shifted his gaze to the window she indicated and noticed the light was different there.

"How did I not see that before?" he thought, only to be answered by the dark voice in his head saying, "You miss much when the bloodlust clouds your vision."

He had grown used to the voice that came with the change, as had Flutter. Sometimes he listened to the voice and sometimes he ignored it, but it was always with him. It was like another entity altogether that lived within him and told him what to do, warned him, provoked him and so many other things.

Roid pushed away the thoughts of the voice as he often did and focused on the window with the different shade of light coming from it.

He backed up several feet to try to get a better view inside and saw the glowing little girl.

"You have found the Brite. Leave this place and hunt elsewhere, lest her sunlight bring death to you," the voice in his head said.

Roid ignored it and stared at the little girl who seemed to glow a bright white light. She sat cross-legged a few feet back from the window, staring out at the night sky, unmoving.

"You cannot kill a Brite, fool! They can only be harmed by one of their own blood! Hunt elsewhere!" The voice in his head screamed.

"The voice in my head is telling me to run from this glowing little girl, Roid. It keeps calling her a Brite and saying we can't hurt her," Flutter said to Roid in her raspy, dark voice.

"Yeah, the damn voice in my head's saying the same thing. We didn't come this far to run away from a little prepubescent human night light, though Flutter," Roid said viciously as he turned and began walking towards the woods.

"Where the hell are you going?" Flutter asked as she watched him walk away.

"I may not intend to listen to the damn voice, but I also saw that little flashlight girl burn up several of our kind on the 'other side'. I'm not going out the same way. I say we test this 'no one but her own blood can hurt her' theory from right out here." As Roid finished speaking, he stopped at a small pine tree. The small tree stood only about ten feet high, and its trunk was only about a foot and a half around in diameter. Roid quickly ripped the tree from the ground and used his sharp claws to strip the branches and roots. He then swiftly shaved a point onto the bottom of the tree, leaving the large beast with a crude oversized spear.

Flutter watched him fashioning the spear with curiosity and then watched as Roid marched back through the snow to the same spot where he'd stood while peering through the window. The large, muscled beast that was now Roid, looked over at Flutter and winked as he said, "Time to break a lightbulb."

Then Roid hurled the oversized spear through the air with incredible force, sending it crashing through the window and straight for the small body of Mila.

CHAPTER 10
Forced Entry

"I can't believe they left me again! At this rate, I'll never be able to prove myself!" Steph thought as he paced the kitchen area of the cabin. "They know I'm ready! They just want me to stay here and play babysitter!" he fumed.

At the thought of his sister, Mila, Steph's eyes shifted to the staircase at the far end of the room. After staring for a moment, he let out a long exhale, set down his cup of hot tea, and headed for the stairs.

This was how it usually was when everyone else left for their so-called 'strikes'. Steph would spend the time shifting from being angry and upset he was left out, to worrying about and caring for (or trying to care for) his sister. He didn't know how to care for Mila, no one really did nowadays, but it didn't stop him from trying. Sure, she was strange and eerie and seemed to be just a shadow of her old self, but she was still his big sister.

In truth, her transformation seemed to bother Steph less than anyone else in the group. He had loved and admired his older sibling for as long as he could remember, and he knew she had always been a little more eerie and strange than his parents seemed to notice. She had always just known things and would randomly say things in strange voices. Yes, Steph knew there was always something special about his sister, he just didn't know what it was.

As memories of him and his sister flooded back, he realized that he still didn't know what it was, none of them did. What he did know was that no matter what, he would still be here for his big sister; he would watch over her and protect her. In a strange way,

Steph felt deep down that was the true purpose of him 'being aged' on the other side and turned from a six-year-old child to a twenty-something year- old man.

"No matter what the Na'gee's intentions were for doing this to me, they were really just so I could protect my sister," Steph thought as he hit the top of the staircase and headed down the hall.

In moments he was standing in the open doorway of Mila's room. He saw her sitting cross- legged on the bed, staring out the window across the room. She didn't seem to move at all, as she sat there glowing brightly and filling the dark room with a strange white light.

Steph watched her as feelings of love and concern flowed through him.

After a few long moments he was about to ask her if she was okay and if she needed anything. He did this quite often and was usually ignored or politely dismissed by her, but it never stopped him from asking. This time, however, she spoke first, before he could even get the question out.

"It is almost my time, Steph. I will cleanse the other world to maintain the balance of life. You will be needed. Be vigilant. Be strong. You cannot fail, young warrior," Mila said in an ominous, otherworldly voice. She turned her head to face him for a brief moment when she spoke and then turned back towards the window and went silent.

"What do you mean 'cleanse the other world, Mila?" Steph asked in shock at what was just said. Mila did not respond.

"Mila! What do you mean 'maintain the balance of life'? What do you need me to do? What does 'your time' mean? You've got to tell me more!" Steph blurted, with slight panic creeping into his voice.

Mila did not respond. She simply stared out the window across the room, with glowing eyes and white light radiating from her small body.

Worry and frustration overtook Steph as he marched further into the room, standing at the side of the bed so he could see her face better.

"Mila! Please!" Steph pleaded. "You've got to tell me more! At least tell me what you need me to do!" Steph's voice started to trail off in despair and sadness.

"I'll do anything for you Mila. Just tell me what you need. Please…" he said, knowing that an answer was unlikely. He started to hang his head, when a blur of motion from the window caught his attention.

Suddenly a small tree with a sharp point on the end came crashing through the window, heading straight for the small glowing form of Mila. Steph didn't have time to think, he could only react. By the time he saw what was happening the flying tree was passing him and was about to hit her, so he did the only thing he could do. He dove for the tree.

Steph dove over the bed in a wild leap, catching the front of the tree with both hands and taking it with him. The result was that the tree spun and while the front went with him and avoided hitting Mila, the back of the tree spun around and struck her in the side of the head with incredible force, sending the small girl flying across the room into a wall.

Her body went limp, and the glowing light disappeared, leaving the room dark.

Steph jumped to his feet and was immediately horrified. He rushed over to Mila and checked for a pulse. He let out a small sigh of relief when he found the faint pulse and heard the short breaths but was still mortified at what had just happened.

"Nothing is supposed to be able to hurt her! They said nothing can hurt her but her own blood! How could this happen?!" he mumbled to himself. He jumped up and rushed over to the window, looking for the source of the flying tree. Steph barely caught glimpse of two shapes, one of them extremely large, creeping on the porch and then they were out of view.

He looked at the branch on the floor and realization struck him.

"I moved the branch. I made it hit her. I'm her own blood," he gasped. "I tried to save her, and I may have killed her myself. No, no, no. I couldn't just let it hit her. I had to do something. Oh no, oh no." Steph's panic-stricken mumbling was harshly interrupted by the loud, booming sound of the front door crashing in.

His head perked up and the worry washed away. The Na'gee had trained him for this. Halbred and his father had trained him for this. He would not let these intruders hurt his sister further. This was what she needed him for. Somehow, Steph knew that Mila knew this would happen and that protecting her was what he was forbidden to fail at.

He touched his belt and felt the reassuring cold handle of the pistol in one hand and the large knife handle in the other.

"And they always tell me to take off my weapons in the house," he thought.

Steph rushed across the room, picked up Mila gently, slung her over his left shoulder and rushed out into the hallway. He silently made his way to the top of the stairs and saw the smaller intruder about halfway up the steps.

It was a woman wearing dark-colored camouflage pants and a matching shirt that had the sleeves ripped off, showing her muscled arms. The woman was built like an Olympic gymnast and moved up the steps with the predatory grace of a lion, stalking its prey. She had short blonde hair and skin so pale it seemed translucent and contrasting with her black eyes in a disturbing sort of way.

Steph's eyes immediately shifted to the sharp teeth and fangs flashing from her mouth and weirdly long fingers that ended in sharp, pointed tips. Memories flooded back to him of his trip through the trees at night on the 'other side'. Memories of the Na'gee settlement getting raided by these creatures that seemed to feed on humans. He knew in that moment that he was facing a dark one.

He immediately pushed away the thoughts he had of setting down Mila and dispatching the intruders. He had seen what these dark ones did to trained Na'gee warriors. No, Steph decided, this was not the time to test his prowess in battle; this was a time to get Mila out of here safely.

He looked past the quickly approaching dark one and his eyes locked on the bookcase just past the bottom of the stairs, the one by the large fireplace, which hid the elevator to the sub levels.

"If I can just get to the sub levels, I can lose them in the caves." Steph thought.

He knew his time to decide was quickly running out. He saw her approaching and saw her long black tongue flickering in and out of her mouth, as she bared her fangs. He felt like a mouse being approached by an alley cat intent on toying with it before the kill.

Steph decided he wouldn't play the role of the mouse any longer.

"You haven't found the prey you thought you found, vile creature," he said softly, and then he leaped over the handrail of the steps, keeping a hold with his free right hand.

In a flash, he leaped, and Flutter lunged towards him, but Steph had expected it. He held the banister tightly with his right hand and swung himself back up with both feet extended, just as quickly as he had jumped. The result was both of his booted feet crashing into Flutter's face and smashing it into the wall.

Steph, still holding Mila tightly over his left shoulder with his left hand, jumped back and rushed down the steps while his pursuer tried to pull herself together. As soon as he hit the bottom of the steps, his peripheral caught the massive shadow swinging at his head and without slowing, he dropped to his knees and slid forward.

The ducking slide caused the swinging claw of Roid to miss him, going right over his head.

Steph then leaped to his feet and whirled around to face his attacker. Right when he turned, he took a boot to the chest and went crashing into the wall across the room. Mila fell from his grip and slammed to the floor next to him.

Shocked at how quickly he was kicked, and still pulling himself out of the wall, he instinctively went for the pistol at his side. He was too slow, in a flash Roid was on him. The large, shirtless creature kicked Steph's right arm that was reaching for the pistol with incredible force, and then used its left hand to grab Steph by the throat.

Roid yanked Steph out of the wall with ease and held him in the air by his neck. Steph's brain turned off. His body just moved in the ways that it had somehow been trained to move during the aging process and with incredible he speed he pulled both legs up, planting them on Roids bare chest, while he pulled his large knife with his left hand. He kicked with his feet while twisting and swinging the blade.

The result of the quick complex movement sent Roid flying backwards with a slice diagonally across his face and Steph flipping backwards to land on his feet.

As soon as Steph's feet hit the ground, he saw Flutter rushing him from the side and, so he grabbed the end table to his left and swung it at her hard. The table crashed across Flutter's face and sent her stumbling backwards a couple feet.

Roid roared loudly and rushed at Steph, just as Flutter regained her balance and did the same.

Steph leaped straight up, flipping over Roid, but as he did, the large creature caught hold of his ankle and slammed him into the wooden floor of the cabin. Steph saw stars and heard Roid roar again, even louder and more animalistic than before -followed by crashing sounds.

As Steph jumped to his feet, trying to regain his balance, and stay alive, he realized quickly that the second roar had not been Roid at all, it had been G'noch.

The large T'kche had emerged through the elevator that was hidden behind the bookcase, like he usually did. Only this time, G'noch had burst into the room with a roar and struck Roid in the side of the head, with such intense power that it sent the enormous dark creature flying through the air across the entire cabin and crashing into the far wall.

Flutter darted in from behind and slashed open G'noch's side with her claws. The black hairedT'kche, over eight feet tall, roared again and swung his arm at Flutter, but she ducked leaning in to slash open G'noch's midsection the room was filled with the sounds of gunshots.

Steph fired three times into Flutter's chest, sending her flying backwards and crashing into the floor of the cabin. Then he turned and fired three times into the body of Roid, who was getting up and beginning to head their way. The gunshots did not send Roid crashing to the ground like Flutter though. They pelted his body and left large wounds, which seemed to slowly close up right before their eyes.

"Get Mila, young Steph," G'noch growled. "We must save Brite."

Steph shook himself away from staring at the healing bullet wounds on his opponent and rushed to Mila, throwing the unconscious child over his shoulder once again.

Roid looked at G'noch, grinning, showing his fangs, and said "I've killed a much bigger one than you, hairy, and he even had a spiked club. Playtime's over." Then he rushed G'noch.

G'noch held his ground for a split second, before turning, grabbing the entire bookcase behind him with both hands and spinning with it, just in time to meet Roid's charge. The bookcase smashed into Roid's face, and a large, hairy black fist came crashing through the debris behind it, connecting with Roid's face and sending the large dark one crashing backwards yet again.

Steph ran into the exposed elevator with Mila over his shoulder and yelled out, "G'noch! Come on!"

The large T'kche took three steps backwards without turning around and was in the elevator. They both saw Flutter rushing them and Roid jumping up as the doors closed shut and the elevator began going down to the sublevels.

As soon as the doors of the elevator shut, G'noch grabbed his side. Although the large T'kche was mostly covered with thick black hair, the wound on his side was still visible. Blood poured out his side from the slash that Flutter had delivered.

"Are you going to be okay?" Steph asked G'noch.

"We go. Fix wound later. No time, young Steph," G'noch said with clenched teeth.

It was obvious that the large T'kche was hurt. Steph had never seen G'noch hurt before and the sight tested his nerves. He had come to think of the T'kche and Halbred both as invincible seeing G'noch hurt was a devastating blow to his own confidence.

"If we don't get out of here and find a place to hide, they'll kill us all," Steph thought.

G'noch spoke up, seeming to respond to Steph's thoughts. "We go caves. G'noch know way out.

Know secret path to home world," he said.

"G'noch, why don't we just cross over now?" Steph asked, grabbing hold of the stone talisman that he wore around his neck. Before he could work the combination on the talisman that would open the 'blur' to 'other side', he felt G'noch wrap his large, leathery hand around his.

"Did you not see, Steph? Dark ones wore talisman. They cross too. Need to take T'kche path, not Na'gee path." He said it in the broken growling words that he often used, only now there was the distinct sound of pain behind the words. Regardless of how the words sounded though, they still sunk in. Steph replayed the fight upstairs and realized that both the dark ones were in fact wearing talismans.

"How can they do that, G'noch? I thought dark ones couldn't cross over?" Steph exclaimed.

"Not normal dark ones. Different. Special humans from your world. Made dark ones in my world.

Not good, Steph. Not good," G'noch said.

Their conversation was interrupted by the large crashing boom that came from the roof of the elevator above them, just as the doors opened. As they rushed out, they saw a large clawed fist punch through the roof of the elevator.

Steph reached back in and selected the top floor button, then stepped out as the elevator doors closed and Roid's ride back upstairs began.

"That won't buy us much time. Let's go!" Steph yelled as he rushed to the door on the right, leading into the cave system in the mountain.

"G'noch yelled, "No, Steph! Right means death. Left leads outside. Outside leads to T'kche path out of this world." As soon as he finished growling the words, the large T'kche was on the move, headed for the door in the far left wall. Steph turned quickly and followed the large beast.

As they entered the door, G'noch reached down and picked up his massive club leaning against the wall just on the inside. The large carbon fiber weapon was a gift from Halbred and designed for mass destruction in the hands of the mighty T'kche warrior. As G'noch picked up the club, he paused and looked back into the sublevel room with a contemplative look.

Steph knew what his friend was thinking. He knew how lethal G'noch was with his weapon of choice, just as he knew how proud the T'kche was. Running away from a fight was not in G'noch's nature.

"Not now, G'noch. We need you! I need you. The, uh, Brite, needs you," Steph pleaded, knowing that he did not know the paths of the cave system well enough to find his way out as quickly as G'noch.

Strangely enough, it seemed that was the last statement that snapped G'noch out of it and turned him around-the part about 'the Brite'. Steph made a mental note to ask G'noch more about this if and when they made it out of here.

G'noch quickly pulled the door shut and then stepped back and swung his mighty club at the ceiling of the cave, a foot or so back from the door, sending a small avalanche of rock and dirt down to partially block the doorway. Then he turned and took off jogging with a limp, one hand holding his massive club over his shoulder and the other clutching the wound on his hip.

CHAPTER 11
Pursuit

Roid was furious! Anger and rage burned within him. This was the same beast that he had fought at the Na'gee settlement and the same glowing little girl who had been there too. They were right there within his grasp and somehow managed to slip away.

The thoughts rolled around in his head, fueling the rage within him. He channeled frustration and pulled as hard as he could on the steel elevator doors before him. Despite his incredible strength, the doors barely moved. They were clearly reinforced steel doors. Roid knew this from his time here with Halbred and the special unit he had served with, before the change.

He strained and pulled with all of his might. He refused to think there was anything he wasn't strong enough to do. Slowly, the doors started to ease open. Once they started to give and open just a few inches, he was able to squeeze his massive hands inside the opening, giving him more leverage. Suddenly he ripped the doors open wide.

Flutter stood back and watched. She did not fear her partner, but she did know better than to get in the way when he was overtaken with the rage, that he obviously felt. She was angry too, but not like Roid. She did not like being bested, but Flutter didn't see it like that. To her, the scared little humans and the large T'kche were running for their lives. She did not know who the man or the little girl were, but she knew G'noch.

She had been with Halbred and Samuel and the T'kche tribe before she woke up as this 'thing' that she now was.

Once the doors were open, Roid leaped through.

"All he had to do was wait and I would have flown us down," she thought as she glided through the doorway and down the elevator shaft behind Roid.

Roid landed on top of the elevator with a boom. He could smell them inside the elevator below him. He could feel their fear. He grinned, envisioning the taste of their blood and slammed his fist through the roof with a roar.

Roid then pulled his hand out, grabbed the hole his fist had made, and began to rip open the roof. As he did, the elevator suddenly started rising upwards.

Flutter saw it coming and quickly changed her direction, flying back the way she had come. She looked up as she flew and saw that when the elevator came to a stop at the cabin level, its roof would butt up against the steel ceiling of the elevator shaft. She looked down as she flew out into the cabin level and saw Roid riding on the roof. She saw him look up and knew she would not be able to pull him out quick enough to save him from being crushed.

The open shaft she looked at was suddenly filled with the sight of the elevator as it came to a stop before her.

Flutter wondered if Roid's new form could survive being smashed by two steel plates the way it had seemed unfazed by bullets. Then the doors opened and she saw Roid standing inside. She walked into the elevator, joining the large dark one, and looked up. The roof had been completely torn open, as if an animal had torn into a can of tuna.

Roid saw her looking up and knew she must've thought he'd be smashed between the elevator and the shaft.

The large dark one, grinned his evil, fang-filled grin and said, "I don't go down that easy, Flutter." Then he selected the second sub level button. The doors shut and they were on their way back down.

Within a few short minutes, the doors opened again and they exited into the 'war room' they both knew so well.

It seemed like a lifetime ago they had been in this room with Halbred and the rest of the unit, preparing for whatever mission good old Uncle Sam had decided to send them on. Now here they were again, only this time they had chosen their own mission and it was to hunt down and kill the same commander they used to follow.

Roid took off quickly searching the room and sniffing the air, while Flutter walked slowly over to the large screen in the center of the room.

She looked at the screen and the corresponding monitors closely, while Roid ripped open the door on the right and sniffed the air.

She heard the large man growl and mutter, "I can't pick up their scent," She saw him rush across the room to the doorway on the left. As he ripped that one open, rock and debris came pouring into the room. She didn't have to see Roid, to know he was grinning. The hunt was on.

"The fools tried to create obstacles and really just let him know which way to go," Flutter thought. "We have them now! Let's go, Flutter!" Roid roared, with obvious excitement.

He was stunned at Flutter's response, though. "You go" she said. "What?!" Roid asked.

"I care not for the fools you hunt. Hunt them and kill the Roid. Then come back here. I've grown tired of hunting and guessing. I'm going to use this to track down Halbred and that damn Agent 17 or Samuel or whatever the hell he's being called now, and then we're going to finally kill them. Enough letting the animalistic voices in our heads rule us, we know how to find people. We were the best at finding and taking out targets. These new forms, should advance us, not reduce us to Cro-Magnons." She said it all with the usual hissing sound in her voice, but the words made sense.

Roid let the words sink in, even as he did, the ancient voice in his head-the one had been there since he changed into the creature he now was, urged him to hunt. It emphasized the thirst and spoke to him of how sweet their blood would be.

Flutter was right though, there were better ways to hunt. Roid decided the voice was also right this time.

"You find them then. I'll kill these fools and bring you back one to feast on Flutter!" Roid roared, and then he dove through the debris in the tunnel and took off.

Steph grew more and more worried, as he followed G'noch. The T'kche was slowing down and leaving a large trail of blood. He didn't know how much farther his friend could go, and he also worried about how easy it would be to follow their trail.

Once again, G'noch broke the silence, seeming to respond to Steph's thoughts, "G'noch good Steph. Dark ones can follow. No matter. We will be gone."

The cave system was elaborate. They had entered many openings that accessed several different caves, and G'noch had taken them twisting and turning without hesitation. The T'kche definitely knew his way through these caverns well.

"Still, I don't think he realizes how slow we're going," Steph thought, with another worried look backwards. Just then a gust of icy air seemed to hit him in the face and take his breath away. As he looked up, he saw the blackness of night out of the opening in the cave ahead. It seemed to abruptly end with an opening to the outside.

G'noch stood in the opening, looking out, and Steph approached him to take in the scene as well.

The cave seemed to open into the side of a sheer face of the snowy mountain. Steph leaned forward and looked down. It was steep and snow-covered, making it impossible to tell what type of terrain was hiding under the thick snow.

"Where's the T'kche path, G'noch?" Steph asked.

G'noch simply pointed about a hundred yards out, towards a thick patch of massive old trees at the bottom of the mountain face.

"How in the world are we supposed to get to them, G'noch?" Steph blurted out.

'We go, Steph," G'noch said and then he walked right off the ledge, into the darkness of night and in a crouched manner headed straight down the snowy side of the mountain.

"Well, we sure can't just walk down like a T'kche can we Mila" Steph muttered to his unconscious sibling that he still held over his shoulder. Then he heard commotion from down the tunnels behind him and knew they didn't have much time.

Thinking quickly, he pulled Mila off his shoulders and held her with both arms in front of him, then he backed up and took off running towards the opening and jumped.

He jumped further than he intended, but he gained the momentum he was hoping for and then some, landing on his back and his butt, with one leg out and one leg bent. He began flying down the snow-covered side of the mountain, like a human sled.

As Steph went, he gained speed, flying past G'noch, going faster and faster.

The smell of fresh blood seemed to float on a breeze that shifted through the tunnels, leading Roid to his prey. He didn't even need to look at the clear blood trail on the ground to track them. The smell was so strong, it did the trick. He ran through the twists and turns in the cave system, his nose guiding him closer and closer to the fresh blood that would be his.

As he rounded a corner, he saw the night sky and knew that the journey through the caves had finally ended. He slowed to a walk and came to the opening at the end of the cave. It opened on the side of the snowy mountain.

As he surveyed the mountain side below him, he saw the blood streak, like a twisting red line on the white snow background, leading him to the large black shape of the T'kche a little more than halfway down the mountainside. He also saw the speeding man, who appeared to be sledding on nothing, still carrying the little girl, fly past the hairy beast and keep going.

Roid did not hesitate. He leapt off the side and began hurtling himself down the steep snowcovered side of the mountain towards the dark, bleeding T'kche.

G'noch more sensed it than heard it and he looked up. He saw the oversized dark one, half- running, half-leaping down the steep side of the mountain, heading straight for him. He knew that he was weak from blood loss, just like he knew that the smell of fresh blood would undoubtedly enrage the dark one and increase its speed and strength.

G'noch's first instinct was to hold his ground and battle the vile creature until only one of them remained, but he fought to push those thoughts from his head. He knew this was no ordinary dark one, he knew he was injured, and he knew he must get this Brite to safety. He hoped it wasn't too late to save the 'Brite', but he was worried. She had not moved, and the blow to the head had seemed to eliminate her glow. He decided in that moment that he had to get Steph to the path and help him get her the help she needed, for the fate of his home world rested on it.

With his mind made up, he sped up his pace down the mountain side, grimacing in pain as he held his side and glancing over his shoulder every few feet to see how close the rapidly approaching dark one was.

In what felt like seconds, Steph was down the mountainside and sliding very fast at a large patch of massive old trees. His back and butt were numb, and his planted foot didn't seem to be doing much to slow him down. He knew he couldn't roll with Mila in his arms, but also knew if he didn't come up with something quick, then they'd both inevitably crash into a tree. He figured a crash would kill them for sure, so he decided to risk it, and in one quick motion, he planted both feet, kicking himself up and throwing Mila into the air.

The momentum sent him flying forward but he manaed to flip through the air and roll on the ground when he hit, breaking the impact of his fall. As soon as the roll ended, he stretched out his arms and looked up, just as Mila came flying back down and landed in them.

"Holy crap! I can't believe it worked!" he exclaimed, experiencing a combination of sheer shock and excitement.

Then he heard the loud roar echo across the night and looked up towards G'noch.

Roid saw the T'kche speed up. He saw the way the hairy beast limped and held its bleeding side. He knew that the injured prey would be his and the thought itself made the bloodlust kick in. The voice in his head craved the blood and seemed to take over. The entire world around him, seemed to fade away. It was just the voice in his head urging him forward, urging him to kill and the prey before him; nothing else existed.

The T'kche was almost at the bottom of the mountainside. Almost to the cover of the trees, when Roid closed the distance between them and leaped at his prey.

"First I will feed on this monster, and then I'll feed on the humans!" he thought as he flew through the air at his prey.

G'noch was almost at the trees, but he knew the dark one was on him. He knew that it would hit him any moment. He felt the ground move beneath him and knew that the creature had leapt; that was his moment. The large T'kche warrior roared a furious roar and spun with his club. He timed it perfectly, batting the dark one out of the air with a powerful swing.

Steph heard the roar and looked up to see G'noch's club catch the oversized, muscular dark one in the ribs and send it flying twenty or more feet through the air.

His excitement dissipated instantly, though, when he saw G'noch fall to the ground after the powerful swing. Steph laid Mila on the ground gently and ran to his friend.

"You've got to get up, G'noch! We're at the trees! We're almost there! We need you!" Steph pleaded as he tried to help the large T'kche up.

Slowly the two worked together and managed to get G'noch to his feet, but he was anything but steady. Steph served as a human crutch of sorts and G'noch made it over to the trees, he passed the first couple and kept going, staggering from side to side as he stumbled through the trees. Steph let himself be guided and kept glancing back at where the dark one had landed.

So far, the large creature had not moved, but Steph didn't think anything that big would have been killed from a blow to the ribs, not after he saw the way it healed from the bullets anyway.

Finally, G'noch stopped at a huge old pine tree in the middle of the patch of trees. It appeared to be the oldest tree there and was at least ten feet around in diameter.

The T'kche stared at the massive tree for a painfully long moment, and then placed his hand on the center of it. After a moment, a faint blue glow lit up the area, and a doorway appeared in the center of the large tree trunk.

Steph eased G'noch through the opening and then rushed over to Mila. As he picked her up, he glanced over and saw the dark one rising to his feet and staring at him.

He took off for the opening in the tree and didn't look back.

Roid rose out of the snow to his feet. The T'kche had played the victim and he had been overconfident. He knew that his recklessness had cost him his prey. Or had it…

As he rose, he looked up and about thirty feet from him, he saw the young man, picking up the unconscious girl from the snow. He stared at them as the man darted off into the mess of trees that filled the level ground at the base of the mountain.

Roid took off in pursuit. He darted through the trees, this way and that way, but could not find them anywhere. Then it hit him…

"They think they can cross over and hide from me, huh?" Roid thought to himself, as he rubbed the talisman around his neck in the distinct pattern that opened the 'blur' before him. He stepped through and searched the area just as thoroughly but found nothing.

Frustrated at the fact that his prey seemed to have disappeared, he stepped back through from the 'other side' and searched for another hour before roaring into the night sky and turning to head back to the cabin, swearing to himself that now it wasn't just Halbred he was after. Now it was Halbred and that damn T'kche!

An hour later, Roid walked back into the sublevel of the cabin from the cave access door he had left through earlier. Flutter was still standing at the screen in the center of the room and turned to look at him when he entered.

"Did you kill them?" she asked in her sinister hissing voice.

Roid just looked at her with hate in his eyes. No other response was needed. "Well, it appears I've had more success than you," Flutter said.

"You found Halbred?" Roid asked.

"No. Not yet. His tracker isn't registering, which I'm guessing means he's on the other side. We should go hunt him there, but first..." She paused for seeming effect, which just managed to annoy the shit out of Roid, and then she continued. "Let's go kill the Samuel character that got us into all of this in the first place. I found him and the tall one, Vic, who was with him when we first ran into them. You'll never guess where they're hiding." Flutter said it all with a cocky sense of accomplishment.

"Well, you gonna make me guess Flutter? Where the hell are they?" Roid asked impatiently.

"They're in a large city about three hours north of here... in jail" she said with a sinister grin. "What do you say we go pay them a visit Roid?"

CHAPTER 12

Incarcerated

Samuel still heard the ringing in his ears and felt the pain in his body from the warehouse explosion. He had no idea how long he'd been unconscious; he just knew that he hurt all over.

He instinctively went to wipe the debris from his eyes before opening them, but found that he was unable to move his arm. He started blinking his eyes, trying to open them, and tugged with both arms to no avail.

"Ahhh, looks like our friendly neighborhood terrorist finally decided to wake up, Bob." He heard a rough voice say loudly.

As Samuel was finally able to open his eyes, he saw bright fluorescent lights above him. He was lying on his back, and both his arms were restrained. As he turned his head to the left, he saw two overweight men in jailer's uniforms approaching him. He saw the metal fencing-type wire in the glass of the door behind them and the cold grey block walls, and it immediately sunk in.

"I'm in jail. Don't know if it's county or city, but this is definitely not the police station." Samuel thought with frustration. "Shit! How long was I out? How the hell did this happen?" He thought. Then Samuel forced the frustration out of his mind and thought, "Doesn't matter. It will be a bit more complicated getting out; that's the only difference it makes. First, I'll need to figure out what happened to Vic, though."

"Where am I?" Samuel asked out loud, turning his head left so he could see the two jailors.

"Oh, he wants to know where he is, Bob… should we tell him?" The man who had spoken before said in a sarcastic tone. To Samuel, he looked to be in his late twenties, heavily overweight, with pale skin, a short brown buzzcut, and a thick moustache. The second guard, that was obviously named Bob, was also overweight, but looked like he was packing a lot more muscle under his weight, kind of like a defensive end on a pro football team. This guard was dark-skinned, had a shaved head and thick goatee.

The second guard, Bob, approached, and Samuel noticed him pulling his baton out of his belt. "That is not a good sign," Samuel thought.

"Yeah, let's tell him, Ricky," The dark-skinned guard, Bob, said as he slammed his baton down onto Samuel's midsection.

Samuel let out a grunt. In truth, his body hurt so bad that a little extra pain didn't make much of a difference.

"So, this is how you treat prisoners here?" Samuel asked softly and coldly.

"No, this is how we treat terrorists and cop killers! Those officers at the building were my friends, you bastard!" Bob yelled as he slammed the baton down again.

This time Samuel definitely noticed the pain, but he still didn't understand what was going on. He did figure that the way this was going, he couldn't just ask about Vic and hope to get a straight answer, though.

"What are you talking about? I didn't hurt any officers," Samuel said through clenched teeth. "Yeah, well your buddies that took off in the chopper sure as hell did, while you were killing people and blowing up a damn warehouse!" Bob yelled, as he came down with the baton for a third time.

Samuel's body screamed, but he refused to. He held in the pain.

"Doesn't matter though. We got you and your buddy. We know that renegade soldier and the girl took the chopper off. You idiots just messed up some of the video, we salvaged the rest. We know who you were with." Ricky said as he pulled his own baton and sent it crashing down on Samuels right shin. The baton made a loud cracking noise as it connected with Samuel's shin, and he let out a loud groan.

"You think we don't know who the hell you are, man? You're the damn terrorist that blew up that hotel months ago. Your pictures plastered everywhere, and now we got ya," Bob said loudly as he leaned in close and spit in Samuel's face. Then Ricky hit his other shin with the baton, and both men laughed and walked away.

As they left, Samuel heard Ricky talking… "I don't care how long we're supposed to keep him in the infirmary. He's conscious now; that's good enough. Let's throw him out there and let him figure it out himself."

"Yeah, I'm with you, Ricky." Bob said.

"Well, it sounds like Vic is alive and here somewhere. It also sounds like Eva and Halbred might've killed a few cops on their way to the chopper… strange, though, that doesn't sound like them, and I wouldn't think that they'd leave us." Samuel thought, trying to piece it all together.

In moments, the two guards were unstrapping his arms and hauling him roughly to his feet. Samuel thought about taking them both out right then and there, but figured it was better to wait, find Vic, and figure out what the hell was going on first. So, he let them throw him around and drag him down to what appeared to be general population.

The main area of the jail was wide open and full of rough-looking prisoners. It had three stories of cells that surrounded the open area that was filled with tables, where groups of prisoners were hanging about. The guards dragged him to a cell in the back of the main level and hurled him roughly into the wall on the inside.

Samuel crashed into the wall and then hit the floor. He looked up, expecting them to take their batons to him again, but they didn't. Instead, Samuel saw a large muscular man that looked like an oversized wrestler. He had South American features, long black hair, and a smooth shaved face. The man yelled at the guards like they were the prisoners.

"Just what the hell do you think you're doing?! That's my cell! You know the deal; I don't share a cell with anyone!" The large man yelled at the jailers.

Bob looked at the man and said, "You deal with it then." With that two jailers walked off.

The large man stared venomously at Samuel as he slowly got up from the floor. Samuel could see over the man's shoulder and noticed that a small crowd had gathered outside the cell and all of the jailors on the floor had seemed to vanish.

Samuel decided that despite the pain and stiffness from the explosion, he would need to send a message immediately or finding Vic and getting out of here would be a much more difficult task. He also decided that none of them needed to know he had abilities from the "gene" yet. That would get him locked up elsewhere as soon as the guards heard people talking about it.

Samuel stared back at the large man.

"You got two seconds to get out of my cell. You come back, you die, little man." The large man roared the last part, obviously making a statement for everyone.

Samuel stood straighter and stared into the man's eyes.

"Tell me what I need to know, and I'll be on my way soon," Samuel said coldly. He paused for effect and then went on, "There was a tall man that came in with me. Where did they take him?"

The large man roared and jumped forward into the air, swinging a hard right hook downwards towards Samuel's head. Samuel saw it coming, caught the man's fist with his left hand and simultaneously came up hard with an open right hand into the bottom of the forearm that connected to the fist he had caught.

"Snap!!!"

The sound of the large man's forearm snapping filled the cell and echoed out. A large bone protruded from the man's right forearm as Samuel finished the motion with a yank that used the large man's forward momentum to slam him to the hard concrete floor of the cell.

Then Samuel stomped down hard on the man's left knee and shattered his kneecap.

He saw the blur of motion behind him and spun around, catching the prisoner who was rushing him in the throat with a hard left jab, crushing the man's windpipe. Then Samuel dropped to his knees, just barely ducking below the swing of a third prisoner rushing in.

As soon as his knees hit the ground, he delivered a powerful right uppercut to the man's groin and jumped back up to his feet. Then he kicked the man in the face, shattering his nose and sending him flying across the cell.

Samuel turned to stare at the gathered prisoners outside the cell and calmly repeated his question. "A tall, pale man came in with me. Where did they take him?"

No one said a word, so Samuel slowly walked out of the cell and grabbed the closest man. He was shorter and well built, but he never saw it coming. Samuel grabbed his head and twisted, swinging his body to yank the man off his feet, smashing his head into the wall outside the cell door. The man's body hit the ground in a clump, and he did not move.

Samuel turned as another man rushed him. He ducked and used his back to flip the man over him. Without turning, he kicked backward, shattering the man's jaw as he fell.

"A tall, pale man came in with me. Tell me where they took him, and I'll be on my way," Samuel said again to everyone gathered around, in a calm sinister-sounding voice.

No one answered, but no one else rushed him either. They slowly backed away, leaving a wide space around him. Samuel surveyed the gathered group and then heard a loud whistle from the second floor and looked up.

Leaning on the railing, looking down at him was Vic, smiling. "Damn Samuel! I didn't know you cared so much… that's real sweet, buddy. You want to catch up or keep smacking around these poor assholes?"

The tall man's face was bandaged up and he had a splint on one leg, but other than that he looked relatively well considering what they had been through. Samuel let out a frustrated sigh, walked through the crowd, which quickly separated for him, and headed for the stairs to go meet up with Vic.

As he went, he thought to himself, "Doesn't matter where we are or what's happening, Vic is always Vic."

As soon as Samuel made it up the stairs to the second level and turned the corner towards Vic, the lights started flashing and the sound of sirens began blaring.

"You had to make a mess of them, didn't you Samuel…" Vic said, as he watched the main doorway to the open hall, waiting for the squadron of baton-swinging jailers to burst in.

"How long have I been out?" Samuel asked.

"Two days man. You saved me and took the brunt of the damn explosion, but in truth, I think the cops gave you a real good once over while you were out. They're calling us terrorists, Samuel, saying we blew up the damn Hotel that the Na'gee took out months ago. They're saying we killed some officers at the business building where we landed the chopper." Vic paused then looked at Samuel's eyes and asked, "Did you kill some cops when you took the SUV?"

"No." Was all Samuel said in response, as he too watched the door, waiting for the inevitable violence that would come with the arrival of the jailers.

"Well, I haven't quite figured out how to get out of here yet and I'm not sure where they're holding our stuff, but I'm also not sure you can let them give you another beating, man. They're likely to kill you this time." Vic said, with a rare tone of serious concern in his voice.

Samuel knew that by "stuff", Vic really meant the Na'gee talisman that allowed them to cross over to the "other side", just like he knew that Vic was probably right about the cops.

"Okay. Then we leave now. When they arrive, we leave. How bad is your leg?" Samuel asked, as he looked down at the splint Vic wore.

"I'm good." Vic. The tall man leaned down and took off the splint.

A moment later, they still had not seen any of the guards pour in, but they heard dozens of gunshots and yells coming from outside the main hall of the jail.

"Something's not right," Samuel said.

"Maybe old Halbred is busting us out?" Vic said with a grin.

Suddenly the door burst open, and dozens of jailers burst in. They were not focused on the prisoners as expected though, they aimed their firearms at the doorway they had just come through and walked backwards with fear in their eyes. Then Samuel and Vic saw the large shape fill the doorway. They knew the oversized, muscular monster at first glance.

"Oh shit. That's Halbred's muscled soldier turned monster freak! How the hell did he get into this world?" Vic exclaimed.

Samuel didn't respond. He just watched the guards open fire on the monstrous being as it lunged forward and began shredding them to pieces. Left standing in the doorway was a muscular woman, or what used to be a woman. It was something much different now. She had short, blonde hair and a sleeveless shirt that showed her pale, muscular arms that extended into overly long finger-like claws.

Samuel knew it was Flutter at once, just like he knew that whatever those things had done to change Roid, they'd done to her as well. As if she sensed his thoughts or presence, she looked up and their eyes locked, then she leapt in the air and took off flying straight for them both.

"Let's go!" Vic yelled at Samuel, as he vaulted himself over the railing and down to the main floor. Flutter didn't even bother glancing at him, her eyes were locked onto Samuel.

"She blamed me before this happened to her, I'm sure she's no less angry now." Samuel thought to himself, as he waited for the distance to close between them.

Flutter stopped just out of Samuel's reach and floated in the air before him.

"You think I'll let you freeze me, Samuel?" Flutter hissed. Then she continued, "You see what you have done to us? All of this is your fault! Tell me where Halbred is and I'll just kill you, but don't and I'll turn you into one of us." She flicked her oddly long black tongue out between her fangs as she spoke, staring at Samuel with sinister black eyes.

Vic saw her floating in front of Samuel, just like he saw the huge muscled monster tearing through jailers. He saw two dead guards on the ground not far from him and ran to them, grabbing both pistols from their hands. Then he threw one directly at Samuel and yelled.

"Samuel!" Vic roared.

Samuel shifted his eyes, just in time to raise his hands and catch the pistol that was flying at him.

In one quick motion, he caught the gun, aimed, and unloaded into Flutter's face.

She roared and crashed to the ground, just feet from Vic.

Samuel vaulted over the railing and landed next to her. He gently touched her arm and froze the injured monster of a woman in place.

He looked up and saw Vic running for the door, with a pistol in one hand and a baton in the other. He saw several prisoners running for the door as well. Samuel looked back and saw the large muscular beast facing off against the last three guards. He took off running out the door of the jailhouse's main floor, right behind Vic.

The two companions darted down the large hallway, as did several prisoners who were fleeing for their lives and their freedom. As they turned the corner the hallway opened up into three directions. The prisoners didn't slow; they all ran straight ahead, which Vic knew to be the direction of the front doors from when he was brought in days ago. Vic and Samuel halted and looked the other two ways.

Samuel looked at Vic and asked, "I assume you think it's to the right?" Samuel knew that Vic had a thing with 'always going right'. He had challenged the man's 'we always go right' philosophy on many occasions, but in truth he thought teaching your family something like that early had a ton of benefits. The thoughts brought a wave of painful memories back to Samuel of the family he had lost, so long ago. He pushed them out of his head and said to himself, "Not now. I need to focus now."

Vic just took off to the right and yelled back, "Finally you're learning Samuel!"

This time Vic proved to be right. After what seemed like a one-hundred-yard dash, they stopped before a doorway labeled 'Property Room'. Vic immediately produced a set of keys that he'd obviously taken from one of the deceased guards. After several tries, he located the correct key and the door opened. Both men slipped inside the property room and pulled the door shut behind them.

After several minutes, they had changed back into their tattered outfits that smelled of smoke and fire. Despite it being torn in several places, Samuel donned his black sports coat over his black T-shirt and black pants once again. Vic also proudly sported his black tactical pants and long sleeve black sweatshirt with leather patches on the elbows and shoulders, despite the tears and burns in it. The only things that surprisingly seemed unscathed were the black boots that each of them wore, their sturdy leather belts, and the stone circular Na'gee talisman that they wore around their necks with black leather straps. To their relief they also found their watches which everyone in the group wore, well everyone except G'noch and Halbred, that served as a way for them to track each other. The only other items were a lighter, a utility knife and a few other random belongings that Vic had either sported in the pouches of the black Na'gee belt that he wore or Samuel had stashed away in one of his many inside jacket pockets, but their weapons were not there.

Vic dropped the 9mm pistol he'd confiscated from the guard into the empty holster on his belt and it sat in place loosely, being much smaller than the .50 caliber gun, he usually carried. Samuel's empty shoulder holster fit the 9mm pistol he had perfectly, as that's was, he usually carried. It still left him with an uncomfortable, unbalanced feeling having only one of the shoulder holsters with a gun in it and the other empty, but he decided he would fix that soon enough.

Both men looked at each other. "Well, we sure as hell look like we were just in a damn exploding warehouse, that's for sure." Vic said with a grin, then he continued. "What do ya think Samuel, should we cross over even though its after dark and take our chances with those dark one thing on the 'other side' or try to get out of here past the cops and the crazy steroid solider dark one, that if I'm being honest, seems to really just be after you. You sure have a way of pissing people off man; you know that don't you?"

"Let's stick to the rules Vic. We stay on our side after dark. We need to get out of here, get back to the cabin and figure out what happened." Samuel said.

Vic nodded in agreement and they both headed out of the 'Property Room' and begun quickly backtracking to the hallway that would take them out of the building. They heard a gunshot and yelling in the distance, but there was no one left in the hallways at all, no one alive anyway. Neither of them bothered to check the watches for the location of their companions, both assuming that everyone was safely gathered at the cabin.

CHAPTER 13

Reunited

Dante appeared on the open field in front of the county jail. He used to be very limited to only being able to teleport to places he had been before, but he had since learned that if he could see the place, see it in detail in his mind, he could teleport there. He knew the risk was that if an obstruction was there, it could hurt him or possibly kill him, but Primo's satellite views mitigated these risks significantly.

"This is worth the risk," Dante thought viciously.

Just a day ago, he had confronted Primo about the appearance of Samuel and Vic, accusing the older man of keeping things from him. He soon realized, or rather saw it in Primo's eyes that this was as much a surprise to him as it was to Dante. The older man had immediately begun searching satellite footage, news feeds and government communications that he intercepted and tracked, searching for Samuel, while Dante hovered impatiently.

After a day of scouring data sources, the older, thin man in the suit had identified the news feed that described Samuel perfectly, claiming that he was the terrorist responsible for blowing up the hotel that Camacho had blown up, the same hotel that Primo had saved Dante from.

Dante heard the report and saw Primo quickly match it with satellite footage of Samuel being wheeled off in an ambulance from the warehouse explosion.

The fact that the government communications blamed Samuel for the hotel explosion so many months ago, that Dante knew he wasn't responsible for, bothered him.

"Could I be wrong? Could he not be responsible for the death of my family?" Dante thought. His eyes shifted to Primo, "I wouldn't put it past this man to lie to me in order to get me to help further his greedy ambitions... but no, I saw the videotape. It had to be Samuel... unless it wasn't real footage..." His disturbing thoughts trailed off and he forced them out of his head, deciding to himself that first he would find Samuel, then he'd confront him and decide by the look in the man's eyes if he was guilty or not.

"If I've been misled all this time and it wasn't Samuel, then Primo and all of the twisted 'Renegades' will die by my hands." Dante thought.

"That's him alright." Primo said in his raspy voice. "Looks like the feds are coming to 'collect' him and Vic from the local jail. If we're going to hit them, now is our best chance." Primo looked up at Dante, who had refused to leave the office for the past day of searching.

"Not 'we' Primo. I'm handling this on my own. I'll go now, show me satellite views of the jail and the surrounding landscape, I need an open space." Dante had said it coldly and softly, but in a way that left no room for debate.

That was all before, now he was here. The moment he had longed for, for so long, was finally here. The moment where he would avenge the death of his family. Still, in the back of his mind he was haunted with doubt. He knew that Primo had worked closely with Camacho and he knew that both Primo and Camacho were pure evil. He also knew that when he'd met Samuel, the man had been doing the same thing as him right now, hunting these evil men who had killed his family. Samuel had taken him in instantly, had helped him use abilities to fight these evil men, that Dante now worked with.

"I will confront him and then I'll know. I have to know," Dante thought to himself as he stared at the jailhouse ahead of him.

As he thought to himself, he walked closer to the large jailhouse and quickly realized things were not right. There were over a dozen police cars in the parking lot in front of the doors. The officers themselves were gathered around what appeared to be twenty or thirty prisoners on the ground in cuffs.

Sirens were going off and lights were flashing on the building itself, and he heard random gunshots coming from inside the building.

"It must be Samuel." Dante thought as he continued to creep closer.

No sooner did he think than, as if on cue, Samuel and Vic came bursting out the front doors of the large jail.

Immediately, all of the officers pointed their guns at the two men, who raised their hands quickly into the air. Dante watched the officers scream at them both to throw their guns on the ground. He watched Samuel and Vic comply. He was close now, crouching just behind a police car watching, and then he heard the comments from the gathered cops.

"Their cop killers, they probably caused all this. Let's just gun them down now and be done with it." He heard one of the officers say. Dante watched as more and more of the other officers nodded and then started to redirect their attention to Samuel and Vic.

"No." Dante thought. "Samuel's mine to kill if he's guilty and if not, then he doesn't die." The officer's dialogue brought back memories of the dirty police officers from his home country that caused so much persecution and suffering. Things his family had to endure before he brought them away to what he hoped would be a new life.

Anger flooded through Dante's veins, and he decided these officers who were planning to murder unarmed men were no better. Once the decision was made in his mind, Dante disappeared.

"The dark ones on the 'other side' don't seem that bad right about now Samuel. Think we can manage to trigger these talismans to take us away without these cops filling us with bullets?" Vic mumbled as he and Samuel stood side by side with their hands in the air.

"Don't move a muscle Vic. They think we're cop killers. They may fill us full of bullets anyway, but they definitely will if we move an inch." Samuel muttered through clenched teeth, as he racked his brain for a way out.

"It can't end like this." Samuel thought.

He counted fifteen officers spread out in a half circle, directly in front of them. All of them pointing assault rifles at him and Vic and most looking scared and shaky.

Then Samuel saw the flash of movement as a smaller, Hispanic looking man in all black appeared in front of the officer in the center, knocking the rifle down with one hand and quickly slashing the officer's throat with the other hand. Then as fast as he had appeared, he was gone. The man appeared again as fast as he had disappeared, this time behind the next man down the line. Again, he used one hand to reach around and knock the rifle down towards the concrete, while he used his other hand to slit the man's throat. Before the body hit the concrete, the man in black had disappeared again.

He appeared in front of the next man down the line and performed the same move.

By now the guards had turned their attention from Vic and Samuel to each other, watching in horror as this new assailant appeared and disappeared, seemingly at will, killing them one by one. A terrified officer towards the end of the line, opened fire with his rifle when he saw Dante appear in front of one of his fellow officers, several people down the line from him.

Dante saw the movement and knew it was coming when the trigger was being squeezed. He disappeared and left two officers to receive the hail of bullets from the scared young copDante used both hands to turn the man sideways, while he still had the trigger pulled. The remaining officers fell to gunfire from their own and then Dante slashed the young man's throat and turned to face Samuel and Vic.

In what seemed like seconds, Dante had murdered all fifteen officers, while Vic and Samuel watched. The two men were both prone to violence, but the needless slaughter of these men who were just doing their jobs disturbed them greatly. They knew it was done to save them, they knew if it hadn't been done, then they'd both probably have been gunned down, but it still bothered them.

Dante stared at them both, with rage and bloodlust in his eyes.

They stared back, knowing this was not the same young man whom they had first met months ago.

Dante shifted his stare to Samuel and shouted, "Did you kill them, Samuel? Did you blow up the club and murder my entire family in some reckless attempt to kill Camacho?"

Samuel looked at Dante and thought how easy it would be to lie to this young man. He could tell that Dante wanted to believe that Samuel didn't do it. He knew that the best thing to do would be to lie to him. He knew that Dante was somehow being manipulated by evil people, and that he could get him away from them and maybe save this young man if he just lied to him in this moment and denied everything. Samuel knew it was what he should do-he knew it's what he would have done without hesitation after losing his family, but somehow these past few months had changed him, taught him to care about more than just vengeance, taught him to care about others again.

All of these thoughts and feelings ran through his mind and finally Samuel spoke, and when he did, he told the truth. "Yes, Dante. I am to blame. In my attempt to end Camacho's evil reign, I failed to consider the innocent lives that would be lost in the process. I failed you, and your family is dead because of it. I am sorry Dante." Samuel said with a softness that neither Vic nor Dante had ever heard from him before.

Dante was moved by the words, but even more so by the honesty. He never expected any admittance of wrongdoing. He expected denial and then to have to decide if he believed Samuel or not. He didn't know how to process it.

"Why would you tell me that? Why wouldn't you lie?!" Dante screamed in frustration. "That's a good damn question" Vic mumbled quietly.

Samuel ignored Vic and stared at Dante as he responded, "Because it's the truth Dante. I was wrong. I am sorry. I blame these evil Na'gee and all of Camacho's associates, but it is my fault your family is dead. I will kill every one of these evil men to avenge my family and for what I did to your family trying to kill them. That is all I can do now. Forgive me Dante. Come with us and let us end them all." Samuel said earnestly.

Dante let out a savage roar of confusion and frustration. Then screamed, "You don't get to feel sorry for them! You killed them! Why are you telling me all this?! It's your fault!!!" As he screamed it all, his eyes changed.

"Oh shit." Vic said aloud as he watched Dante disappear.

Dante reappeared in front of Samuel and slashed his chest open, before disappearing again and appearing behind him to slash his back open. He disappeared again and when he reappeared in a crouch before Samuel to slash the man's legs, he instead appeared to the bottom of a boot kicking him, hard in the face and he fell backwards.

Samuel stared at him on the ground and said "I am guilty, and I am sorry Dante, but I will not die yet, there are too many I must save from these evil men. I cannot let you stop me."

Dante screamed "Cannot let me?!" and disappeared. Samuel didn't bother turning around-he knew what was coming and just swung backwards with a hard right elbow that caught Dante right in the face, sending the young man stumbling backwards.

Samuel did not use his ability to freeze Dante; instead, hejust quickly turned and said, "Dante, we're fighting the same evil, we're on the same side. It doesn't have to go like this."

Dante stumbled backwards from the impact of the elbow into the arms of Vic and heard Samuel's words. Vic caught the younger man and added his own comments, "We're all on the same side kid. Let it go." Vic said with compassion.

Dante was in a rage, he didn't process the words, he just knew he was losing, so he tried harder. He delivered a backwards kick to Vic's groin, disappeared and this time reappeared low in front of Samuel and slashed open the top of one of his thighs.

Dante instantly disappeared again and reappeared behind Vic and slashed the tall man's back open. Then he disappeared again and reappeared at Samuel's left swinging the dagger towards Samuel's face. Samuel saw the swing coming just in time to duck, and when he did, he touched Dante's right leg and froze the young man in place.

Both Vic and Samuel stood bleeding and breathing heavily, staring at the frozen young knife fighter whom they both had considered a friend. Before they could process what had happened though, a loud crashing noise caught their attention and they saw the body of a guard hurled out through the front doors of the jail. The thrown body took both double doors completely out and bounced roughly off the concrete parking lot.

The handcuffed prisoners were scrambling away in fear, and then Roid burst out of the smashed doorway with a wild roar and began immediately pouncing on fleeing prisoners, slashing and tearing them to pieces with his claws and fangs.

Samuel and Vic did not say a word to each other. They just took off in the other direction, towards the closest police car that was parked behind the firing squad that Dante murdered.

In seconds they had made it to the car, jumped inside and took off out of the lot. Vic drove, as Samuel looked back to see Roid finish off the last of the prisoners and turn his attention to Dante, who was still frozen.

"I can't leave him like that. It doesn't matter that he's trying to kill me, I deserve it." Samuel said out loud. He 'willed' Dante free from the frozen state, like he did to any of his victims whom he wanted to free.

Vic muttered, "Yeah, poor kid" and just kept on driving.

Roid finished off the last of the prisoners and noticed the only other person standing was a strange looking man in all black. He noticed that the man did not move, didn't even seem to be breathing and instantly knew that it was Samuel's handiwork, the same handiwork that still had Flutter frozen on the jailhouse floor.

Roid scanned the area and saw a car fleeing in the distance. He knew that was Samuel fleeing. "I'll have to kill him another time, but now…" Roid hissed to himself, as the voice in his head urged him to taste the blood of this frozen man before him. Roid often ignored the voice, but he slowly approached the frozen man intent on adhering to the voice's urging this time. As he got closer, he realized he recognized the man.

"This is that teleporting knife fighter from the hotel rooftop." Roid growled to himself. He remembered that day, he remembered this knife fighter had been with Samuel and the tall man. He became angrier at the man as he got nearer. Roid stopped inches from the frozen man and leaned in close, sniffing the man. He noticed the stone talisman around the young man's neck and ripped it off, crushing it in his hand before dropping the broken pieces to the ground.

"You won't be needing that anymore," Roid hissed.

Then suddenly Roid noticed the man turn his head and look into his eyes, before disappearing.

Dante instantly knew he had been frozen and then released. He'd seen Samuel do this to others before. Everything was different. He went from swinging a dagger at Samuel's head to staring at the oversized muscular soldier from Halbred's unit, only now the massive man was more monstrous creature than he was soldier, still Dante knew it was him. He also knew that he had seconds to save himself, so he acted.

Dante teleported behind the monstrous creature, the one he remembered as 'Roid', and stabbed it in the back of the neck. The beast roared and flipped around, as Dante teleported behind him again and stabbed a dagger in each side of the beast's lower back. All killing blows to any normal human.

"Well, Roid wasn't a normal human before he turned into whatever he is now. So, I guess I'll have to work harder." Dante thought coldly to himself, as Roid spun around swinging his massive, clawed hand with incredible speed. As fast as it was, it wasn't fast enough to catch Dante before he disappeared and appeared behind Roid in a crouch, a fresh dagger in each hand slicing the large man's tendons right above the back of each foot.

Roid roared and staggered forward, both of his massive legs wobbling.

Dante took his chance and teleported in front of the beast, still in a crouch and slashed sideways across Roid's gut, with both hands. Roid's insides opened up, and he started to fall forward. Dante teleported behind the large man who had fallen face first on the concrete and was about to turn away, when he saw the wounds on the back of Roid's legs closing up on their own.

To his astonishment, he saw the large beast pushing himself up to his feet again, although still leaning over holding his midsection. Dante didn't know how the large monster could still be alive, but he didn't let it slow him down. With trained precision and speed, he slashed at the back of Roid, cutting the large creature open from neck to ankles, with what must have been a hundred slashes. Roid didn't turn around, Dante didn't think he could, he just gurgled as his body was slashed to pieces faster than it could heal itself.

Then Dante heard the approaching vehicles and looked up to see dozens of black SUVs pouring into the parking lot.

"Time to go." Dante said to himself, and he teleported back to Primo's office.

Roid fell to the ground face first, his body not responding when he tried to move it. He could feel it healing itself, but there was so much to heal. He turned his head and saw the vehicles approaching and knew that he could not defend himself in this state.

"Go home. It is time," the sinister voice in his head whispered to him.

He didn't think, he just did what the voice said and rubbed the stone talisman he wore in the correct sequence, opening a 'blur' to the 'other side'. Roid kind of crawled, kind of rolled himself through it, the blur disappeared, just as several federal agents approached him with guns drawn.

Dante appeared back in Primo's office. Although it happened often, it still always startled the older man. This always amused Dante, since the 'genes' effect on Primo was to alert him of approaching danger, a kind of warning sense. He figured that if it wasn't danger, then maybe it didn't warn the man the same, but it still usually amused him. Today, however, he was not amused. Today, he was disturbed.

Dante didn't say a word, he just stared at the wall and wondered why Samuel had freed him from the frozen state. He wondered why

Samuel had not killed him while he was frozen, as he'd seen Samuel do to so many others.

"Why didn't he just kill me?" Dante wondered in frustration.

Primo saw the young man and said, "We have used the flight patterns in the stolen helicopter's database to find their base of operations. We were waiting for you, now we'll send a unit and wipe out all of them, and every one of their damn friends and family. You've been waiting for this moment, Dante, now it has finally come. We'll slaughter every one of them." Primo said it all in his usual slimy, raspy voice.

The words caught Dante's attention. He realized in that moment while he could never forgive Samuel, Samuel was not the true villain. He had made a mistake in his efforts to avenge his family and murder these monsters and he could not ever make up for those mistakes, but it was the Na'gee and men like Primo who were the real monsters. Dante realized that every minute he worked for this evil man, he was making the same mistake that he hated Samuel for making.

"And now, I'm becoming the same as the evil villains that I fought to get my family away from." Dante thought to himself. He raised his head and turned around to face Primo.

"Is Riker here?" Dante asked coldly.

"Of course, Dante. He has a unit ready and has been waiting on your return to make the trip to their base and bathe the mountainside in their blood.

"Call him in here." Dante said.

Primo eyed Dante warily and then hit the button on the communication panel on his desk and said, "He's here. Meet us in my office."

Moments later, Riker walked into the office. The slim mercenary in the black hat looked from Primo to Dante and asked, "We ready?"

As soon as he said it, Primo jumped to his feet and screamed "Kill him, Riker! Kill him now!"

By the time the last word came out of his mouth, his throat had been slit. Dante teleported behind him, let the thin man's body fall forward onto the desk.

"I always wondered if his power of 'knowing what was coming' would be enough to save him. I guess not." Dante said coldly as he stared at Riker. Then he went on to ask: "Do we have a problem now Riker?"

Riker didn't go for his gun, or even look surprised, he just responded, "Hell, if it wasn't for you backing him up, I would've killed the slimy bastard a long time ago Dante. No problem here. What now though?" Riker said as casually as if he was talking about the weather.

"Give me the coordinates to their base. I don't want anyone touching any of them… ever.

Understood?" Dante said.

"Whatever you say Dante. This was your revenge mission. You know I'm only interested in the high paying jobs." Riker said with a half-smile. "I'm guessing you want them all for yourself huh?"

"No. I'll never forgive them, but they don't deserve to die. Leave them alone." Dante said.

"Fair enough man. What're you gonna do now? I could use someone with your skills, and I'd damn sure pay you more than that guy did." Riker said, pointing at the body of Primo.

Dante hesitated before answering, somewhat surprised at the question, then after a moment he said, "Well, I'm not going back to knife fighting. I'll only work alone. No innocent people, and the price is high. I have to do something first, but you know how to reach me Riker. Send the jobs my way and I'll get them done." Dante said, staring at him.

Riker smiled broadly. "I got plenty of jobs right up your alley. I'll be in touch kid. Oh, and here's the satellite coordinates of their base, you know… just in case."

With the final words said, both men nodded, and Riker left the office.

Dante shoved Primo's body onto the floor and typed the coordinates he'd been given into the keyboard, pulling up the satellite view of a cabin nestled between two snow covered mountains.

As the 'blur' disappeared, Roid rolled over onto his back and lay there in pain as his body worked to heal itself. He was hurt, but more than that he was infuriated that the little knife fighter was able to injure him so badly. He was infuriated that Flutter had been immobilized by Samuel, and he was infuriated that they had gotten away again.

As he lay there caught up in his thoughts, he became more and more angry, so angry that he didn't notice the pairs of black eyes hovering over him. When he did finally look up, he saw several of the dark creatures, like him, crowded around. They were busy moving here and there as he realized they were binding his arms and legs with some sort of tough vines. Roid started to struggle, but it was too little too late. Several of the creatures pulled tightly on the vines pulling, his legs and arms out straight.

One of the black hooded creatures leaned over his face and hissed at him before saying, "Your resistance is pointless. We have been sent to take you to the monarchs. You have crossed over. You have failed to return to the temple since your conversion. Your actions are forbidden. You will be judged." When the creature finished hissing out the words, it leaned in closer and flicked its long, black tongue in the air directly above Roid's face. Then it looked up and hissed at the others as they took off, dragging Roid behind them across the ground.

CHAPTER 14
Discoveries and Preparations

Samuel and Vic stood in the far shadows of the snow-covered truck stop parking lot, watching and waiting. They had ditched the stolen police car about two miles down the road and walked back to the truck stop in the snow, intent on getting new transportation. Both men knew they had to move fast, just like both men knew that if they were wanted before, they were surely being looked for now after the bloodbath at the jail.

"Well, maybe they'll just think old big and toothy killed us and give up the manhunt." Vic said softly as they surveyed the dark lot.

"It doesn't matter what they think Vic, there are tons of bodies and a missing cop car. They'll follow the car and they'll be looking for anyone who didn't end up in a body bag." Samuel replied coldly.

The two men had been on the road for a couple hours, headed towards the cabin. As Samuel drove, Vic used his watch to confirm that Steph was still at the cabin, just like he confirmed that Eva and Halbred were still not showing up. Both of them knew that meant they were still on the 'other side' and both of them knew the implications were terrifying. Regardless, it was still night and crossing over was too risky, so they agreed to head to the cabin, get G'noch, Steph and Mila and then cross over and find them.

"That one." Samuel said pointing at a large pickup truck. The old, red pickup truck looked to be about twenty years old, had extremely large tires and spots of rust covering it here and there.

"Well, you ain't one for style Samuel, but there's no way that old thing has GPS on it, and it shouldn't have a problem making it through the snow. Let's go." Vic said, as he took off jogging across the parking lot.

Vic got to the driver's side door, reached into one of the pouches on his belt and pulled out two long thin pieces of metal that looked almost like oversized needles. By the time Samuel arrived at the truck, the tall man had carefully unlocked the door and was beginning to hop inside, when he saw Samuel freeze on the other side of the truck as he heard someone with a thick southern accent say, "Oh hell! You sure did pick the wrong damn truck tonight slim!"

Vic slowly turned around to the sight of a medium-sized man, wearing an old, tattered baseball hat, a flannel shirt, under an open leather jacket and old dirty jeans. The man was pointing a large revolver at Vic's face.

Vic noticed a second man, walking up behind the first, pull a black semi-automatic pistol out from under his shirt as he approached. The second man, was a foot taller and about three feet wider. Despite the cold, he just wore an old flannel shirt, no jacket and also sported a well-worn baseball cap.

The second man pointed his gun at Samuel, who was still standing on the other side of the truck and spoke through his thick beard, with a similar southern accent saying, "Look here. We got ourselves a couple damn car thieves. You know what we do to thieves around these parts boys?"

Samuel completely ignored the man and just stared at Vic, who had his back turned to Samuel in order to face the first man who had approached them. After a moment of silence, Samuel said "We don't have time for this Vic", with a hint of impatience in his voice.

As if on cue, Vic moved with lightning speed, diving into the midsection of the smaller man with the revolver. As Vic's body collided with the man's waist two shots were fired into the side of the truck. Vic wrapped his arms around the man's mid-section as they collided, and as they crashed to the ground he rolled to the side, so that his back struck the concrete first, leaving the other man on top.

The heavy-set man saw Vic tackling his companion and without hesitating shot twice at Vic's back, but before the bullets struck, Vic had rolled the man over so that he took the shots.

As Vic's back hit the concrete, he heard the two shots and felt the body on him go limp, he grabbed the revolver from the dead man's grip, and with the man still lying on top of him like a human shield, he fired the remaining four bullets it into the heavy-set man, who fell to the ground dead.

By the time Vic got up, grabbed the pistols and checked their pockets for more ammo and the keys to the truck, Samuel was already sitting in the passenger seat staring at him impatiently.

"What?!" Vic said. "It's not like I was finishing getting dressed or something, and you know you could've helped, right?"

Samuel's only reply was "We have to hurry, let's go."

Vic let out a loud exhale, then grinned and started the old pickup truck. In seconds they were skidding out of the snow-covered parking lot, leaving the two bodies lying where they had fallen.

Hours later, the old pickup truck roared across the thick snowy landscape that led to the cabin. Relief washed over Vic as he saw the cabin lights, brightening the dark night ahead. Instead of driving to the garage area, he just pulled the truck up in front of the porch. Both men noticed that the helicopter was not on the landing pad, above the separate building that served as their garage, but neither said a word about it.

Seconds after getting out of the truck, they noticed the damage. They saw the front door smashed in and the broken window above it and took off running inside.

Upon entering the broken doorway of the cabin, they saw smashed walls and furniture, blood splattered on the ground and the elevator shaft that was supposed to be well hidden, wide open in plain sight. Without hesitation and with obvious panic, Vic ran up the stairs, his long legs taking three at a time.

The tall man ran down the hallway straight to Mila's room, where he saw the broken window and the large tree branch. Vic searched the other rooms and saw nothing. He ran back to the top of the steps and his eyes met Samuel's. Vic didn't say a word, he just shook his head.

Samuel held up Steph's watch that he had found lying on the counter in the kitchen. The same watch they all wore to track one another.

Vic ran down the steps to where Samuel had the elevator doors open and both men began the descent to the sub levels of the now devastated cabin in silence.

After searching both sub levels and finding nothing, the two men found themselves standing in front of the large screen in the center of the second sub level, watching the camera footage from the events at the cabin. They watched the forced entry, the vicious fight on the main level and the getaway through the tunnels. They watched Roid take off in pursuit and then return. Samuel could feel the fear, frustration, and tension building in Vic, especially as he saw the tall man watch his injured daughter being carried by his son with the creatures in pursuit.

As soon as the video footage ended, Vic took off through the access door to the tunnels and followed what appeared to be an old blood trail, searching for any signs of Mila and Steph. Samuel knew what was next, whether Vic found them or not. He knew they were headed to the 'other side', so he took the elevator back up to prepare.

By the time Vic had returned, the sun was just starting to rise. He was distraught and full of anger and rage. After searching the surrounding landscape, he had hiked back to the front of the cabin and walked in through the shattered remains of what used to be the front door.

Clean clothing for Vic, the same black tactical pants and black sweater with the leather patches, were laid out on the counter and weapons were spread out across the floor of the cabin. Samuel had changed into an outfit identical to his previous one, minus the tears and burns. On top of the black sports coat, he wore a thick topcoat and had a short broad sword strapped to his back. He was drinking a cup of coffee and upon seeing Vic, began pouring one for him.

"There's no sign of them Samuel. They must've got away. The snows come down so much over the last couple days that any tracks they might've left are long gone." Vic said, in an exhausted voice.

Samuel handed his tall friend the hot cup of coffee and said "Between Steph and G'noch, they're bound to be alright. If they didn't come back, then they must've crossed over. Let's get your wife and Halbred, then we'll find them Vic. Get yourself ready."

From the doorway of the cabin, both men heard a young, somewhat raspy voice say, "Holy shit!

What the hell happened here?"

Samuel pulled one of the pistols from the dual shoulder holster he wore as he looked up to see Dante standing in the doorway.

Dante stared at Samuel and Vic, and no one spoke for a long moment, before Dante broke the silence and despite the hateful look in his eyes as he looked at Samuel, he said "I'm not here to fight guys. Samuel, you were right, we're after the same evil people."

"Well, you're just in time kid." Vic said. "We're heading to the 'other side' to get my wife and save my kids."

Dante looked at Vic, who after saying the words began changing clothes and gearing up. Then he looked at Samuel.

"I can't forgive you for what you did Samuel. I'll never forgive you, but unless the Na'gee are annihilated, what happened to both our families will happen to more people. The way I see it, we're the only ones trying to stop them, so you need to live, but that doesn't mean I forgive you. Nor does it mean I'll work with you again." Dante said somberly.

"I understand." Samuel replied, followed by, "If not to help us, then why are you here Dante?"

"I need to know what I'm up against. What was that thing I killed back at the jail? It was like the muscle bound soldier from Halbred's unit, but it wasn't. It was more like one of those creatures that Primo described from the other side or something. Is it with the Na'gee?" Dante asked with obvious confusion.

"Did you cut off its head Dante?" Samuel asked. "What?" Dante replied, shocked at the question.

"If you didn't cut off its head, it isn't dead. They only die if they lose their head or sunlight hits them." Samuel said coldly.

"What?! Am I supposed to believe it's some B-movie vampire or something Samuel?" Dante asked.

"Believe what you want Dante, that's what we know." Samuel said. "As far as we can tell they don't work with the Na'gee, but they're just as bad, maybe worse. If they cross over, this world is in trouble. We're going to the 'other side' to find Vic's family, are you sure you don't want to help?"

Dante hesitated before answering. He looked into Samuel's eyes and then stared at Vic, who was finishing loading himself up with a variety of weapons. Finally, the young man directed his attention back to Samuel and said "I'll fight these creatures and the Na'gee, but I'll do it on my own and I'll do it my way. I can't work with you again Samuel. If you run into too many of them, let me know and I'll come help, but I won't stay with you."

The two men stared at each other for a moment and then Samuel nodded and reached into his pocket, pulling out Steph's tracking watch that had been left on the counter. He tossed it to Dante and said "Take this then. You can see our location with it. If we run into a significant amount of them, we'll alert you through it."

Dante caught the watch, then turned to face Vic and said "Good luck Vic. I hope they're okay." Then he disappeared.

Vic turned to look at Samuel. The tall man was fully dressed and armed with his usual large Na'gee knife and .50 caliber pistol. He had another one of the carbon fiber spears strapped to his back and an assault rifle hanging from his shoulder.

"We ready?" Vic asked Samuel as he began to work the talisman to open the 'blur' or the pathway to the 'other side'.

"Wait." Samuel said as he picked up the large shotgun off the counter and slung it over his shoulder by the strap. "I have a better idea. This time we need to move faster."

Several minutes later, outside near the garage-or the 'hangar' as Halbred liked to call it, they were each walking a large dirt bike through the 'blur', just as the morning sunshine spread over the entire mountain valley.

PART 2: Other Side

CHAPTER 15
Long Journey

Steph gently laid Mila down inside the cavern that the opening of the tree had led them to, and focused his attention on G'noch. The large, black-haired T'kche was sitting on the ground with his back resting against the cavern wall, breathing heavily. He was holding the wound in his side with both hands. The blood had matted the thick hair on his side and a small pool was forming on the ground beneath him.

Steph knew that he had to stop the bleeding, or his large friend would be in a very bad situation. He forced the panic out of his mind and racked his brain, trying to figure out what to do. A moment later he quickly started pulling the stitching out of the hem of his leather vest. Once he had a long piece of stitching in his hand, he reached into one of the many pouches on the leather Na'gee belt and pulled out a small needle.

"G'noch, I need to stitch the wound in your side up. You're losing too much blood." Steph said calmly, as he knelt before the large T'kche warrior.

G'noch looked up and softly growled, showing a mouthful of teeth. The skin on his face looked black and leathery, and his large flat nose and oversized mouth gave him a vicious almost gorilla like look, but his eyes looked very human. In those eyes Steph saw his friend's pain.

Steph didn't wait any longer, he just gently pulled G'noch's hand away from his side, prepared the needle and stitching and began to sew up the wound the best he could. G'noch did not try to stop him or even flinch, he just stared at the wall across from him.

By the time Steph was about halfway through his attempt at playing field medic, he noticed that G'noch's stare had shifted to Mila, who still lay unconscious on the cavern floor.

"We must save Brite, Steph." G'noch said softly.

Steph did not look up; he didn't want to think about Mila right now.

"Focus on one problem at a time." He thought to himself.

After another moment G'noch spoke again, "Brite hurt in the head. We need Ancient Ones. They help. Brite must live or no balance Steph." G'noch's words were growled out as usual, but behind the soft, strained growls was a sense of feverish urgency.

"He's truly concerned." Steph thought. Then he said, "Finished!"

G'noch looked down at his side, and then looked up at Steph and patted the young man on the shoulder with his huge, hairy hand. Immediately G'noch began to stand up, using the wall for leverage.

"Whoa, whoa, big guy." Steph said. "You might need to rest for a little bit before we start moving."

"No time Steph. Brite hurt badly. T'kche can see pain. Must get to Ancients. Long journey." G'noch said in response.

The urgency in the T'kche's voice scared Steph even more than the fact that Mila had not moved. He knew the branch had hit her hard in the head, but he just figured she'd regain consciousness sooner or later and be okay. After hearing G'noch he wasn't quite so sure.

Steph didn't protest again. He walked over to Mila and picked her up gently. She was breathing, but her pulse was weak, and her body was cold.

"We've got to warm her up G'noch." Steph said, now more concerned than ever.

"No time. Long journey. Only Ancients can save Brite." G'noch said, urging his young human friend to follow him.

Steph started walking towards G'noch and the large warrior took off, deeper into the caverns leading the way at a brisk pace, despite the fresh wound in his side.

After what felt to Steph like several miles of hiking through the dank, dark caves, they finally emerged into a thick forest. The trees cast deep shadows across the woods, with sunlight peeking through in small patches. It was hard to tell, but Steph guessed it was about midday.

Despite the sunshine, it was still cold. Frost littered the shadowy forest floor, almost appearing to be a reminder that the cold had arrived, and it would only get colder.

Steph surveyed the forest around him, on high alert. Despite its natural beauty, this place didn't feel safe.

"No, it's not that it doesn't feel safe, it's that it isn't safe." Steph thought. This was one of those things that he just knew about the 'other side' ever since his aging. He didn't know how they implanted this knowledge this knowing or whatever it was into his mind, but it was there and now some things he just knew.

Steph heard the sound of dried, frost-covered leaves cracking, as if being walked on, coming from the other side of the bushes to his right. He slowly eased Mila down to the ground and silently stepped in front of her. The noise stopped.

"Whatever it is, it's watching me." Steph thought. Although he was hyper-focused on the bushes, he did not fail to notice that G'noch had disappeared. "Really, he picks now for his disappearing acts." Steph thought to himself, as he eased his large knife out of its sheath.

Steph still carried the traditional weapons of the Na'gee warriors, a large, oversized knife that looked like a cross between a bowie knife and a machete and a .50 caliber pistol. Since he was aged unnaturally by the Na'gee wise ones, he knew how to use these weapons. They were like part of him. The past three months of training with his father Vic, and Halbred, had served to fine-tune these skills even more.

He felt the air change, and knew whatever was stalking him was about to strike.

Suddenly a crude small, axe came flying towards his head. Steph held his large knife firmly with his right hand, but used his left to quickly snatch the flying axe out of the air and send it flying back into the bushes where it came from. A loud thud came from the bushes, followed by a low grunt and the grayish-green Ragu fell out of the bushes onto its face, with the small axe sunk deep in its chest.

Steph had seen a Ragu before and this one looked eerily similar. It was about four feet tall, had grayish-green skin, large pointy ears and did not appear to have any hair on its body whatsoever. This particular Ragu wore a dingy loin cloth around its midsection, wooden bracers over its forearms and shins and had what appeared to be an intricately designed collar of small bones covering its neck. Thick greenish-black blood oozed from the small creature as it lay dead on the cold forest floor.

Steph felt the rush of air from behind him and instinctively ducked just in time to dodge another flying axe. The axe soared right over him, where his head had been seconds before and sunk deep into the trunk of a large tree.

As Steph flipped around to see its source, he heard a high-pitched roar and another Ragu, who appeared very similar to the one lying dead next to him rushed at him, with a crude spear in its hand. Steph stepped over Mila, towards the smaller creature and with a quick spinning move to his right, he was able to dodge the charging spear and come down with his large knife on the back of the Ragu's neck. The creature's head separated from its body and rolled across the forest floor.

Steph didn't have time to inspect his victim, as three more Ragu squealed and leaped from the bushes off to his left, rushing at him with long crude spears. Steph braced himself, still choosing to use his knife over the large pistol he carried. However, before the creatures cleared the halfway point to him, G'noch appeared next to them, seemingly out of nowhere. The large T'kche moved with incredible speed, appearing to be nothing more than a giant black blur of motion.

With one mighty swing of his club, he caught the closest two Ragu across their midsections, sending a splattering of grayish-green body parts flying everywhere. The third one squealed and tried to flee, but G'noch never slowed down and delivered a mighty kick to its chest before it could even begin to get away. The kick sent the smaller creature flying into the trunk of a large tree, visibly crushing the Ragu upon impact.

G'noch looked over at Steph and said, "Ragu hunting party. More will come. Ragu camp close.

Must go. Long journey to Ancients." And with that, the large T'kche began hiking ahead.

Steph sheathed his large knife, picked up Mila and continued following G'noch, paying close attention to his surroundings as he went.

He hurried to catch up to G'noch, which was much easier said than done, especially while trying to carry Mila as delicately as possible. When he finally got near G'noch, Steph asked "Why did the Ragu attack us G'noch?"

Without slowing down or looking back at Steph, G'noch said "Attack you, not us, Steph." Steph thought on the large T'kche's reply for a moment and then asked, "but why?" "G'noch mighty T'kche. Little Ragu scared of G'noch." G'noch said in response.

At this point Steph entertained the thought that his large friend might be messing with him, G'noch had a strange sense of humor, but he still had one and he sure enjoyed picking at the group from time to time.

Despite his thoughts, Steph's curiosity prevailed and he asked again, "No, not why didn't they attack you. Why did they attack me G'noch?"

"Steph little human, why not?" G'noch said, followed by a strange gurgling growl, that Steph had learned was G'noch laughing, or as close as he got to it anyway.

"Really G'noch... I'm trying to learn here. Help me understand." Steph said in exasperation.

At this the large T'kche warrior stopped and turned around to face Steph. There was a hint of compassion in his eyes as he looked at Steph and then he calmly spoke in his growling voice. "Na'gee vest. Na'gee pants. Na'gee weapons. Na'gee hunt Ragu. Na'gee eat Ragu, young Steph. G'noch know Steph not Na'gee, but everyone else only see Na'gee."

The words hit Steph like a ton of bricks. He hated the Na'gee, but G'noch was right, he looked like he was one of them, even still dressed like them. He cursed himself for choosing to keep wearing the garments he'd gotten from the Na'gee, but he knew there was nothing he could do about it now.

G'noch watched his friend digest what he had said for a moment, then leaned closer to Steph and said, "We must go. Brite hurt. Long journey. Very quiet Steph, Ragu camp close." Then G'noch turned and began walking again.

Steph noticed that the T'kche moved a little slower this time, and seemed much more focused on being silent as he went. Seeing the huge T'kche warrior so concerned about stealth, unnerved Steph a little and he followed the example and moved as silently as possible. The further the two of them went into the woods, the closer the noises in the distance became.

"Is he planning on walking us right through their freaking camp?!" Steph thought as he followed his friend.

Before long, Steph could clearly hear the squealing sounds of Ragu talking and yelling on the other side of the thick trees. He caught a glimpse of a massive clearing that had about thirty large boulders which looked to be strategically placed the same distance from one another. Each boulder was about the size of an igloo, and some had small streams of smoke coming from the tops of them, creating a very peculiar scene.

The clearing itself was surrounded by thick forest, that could not be seen through. And in the clearing around the oddly placed boulders were tall weeds and clumps of dirtmaking it look almost like a checkerboard with the boulders being large, oversized pieces on the board.

Steph fought the urge to stop and stare at the strange setup, but the dozens of Ragu running around squawking at each other as they carried baskets from here to there and shuffled about busy with who knew what, was a reminder that he needed to keep moving. It was hard to tell from the forest, but if he had to guess, he thought that there must be fifty or sixty of the small grayish-green creatures down there.

"There's an army of these weird things that look like goblins from a fairy tale and here I am dressed just like the people who eat them. This is great." Steph thought as he hurried through the woods behind G'noch.

Suddenly, G'noch stopped. He held a hand out behind him to stop Steph as well. As Steph peered around his large friend, he quickly saw what had stopped him.

In front of the large T'kche was a pit about five feet deep and four feet wide with crude pointed sticks sticking up from the bottom. It was covered loosely with large leaves, but the cover-up job was done very poorly.

"Whoever had been tasked with hiding that trap, took no pride in their work." Steph thought. "It's almost like they wanted us to see it."

Just as the thoughts went through his mind, he noticed G'noch walking around the pit to the right, which was the only way to go, since a tree blocked the left side. Just as the T'kche stepped in the clear spot on the right, a net wrapped around G'noch and hauled him twenty feet into the air, where he hung upside down.

G'noch let out a vicious roar that echoed through the forest, and Steph heard the sounds of horns being blown from the clearing.

He started to set Mila down to free G'noch, but his friend yelled "No Steph! You look like Na'gee, Ragu kill you! Must save Brite! G'noch meet you outside forest. Go! Quick!"

The urgency and panic in G'noch's voice was something that Steph had never heard before. It startled him and he took off, leaping over the pit and running silently through the woods in the same direction they had been heading.

He was scared, because G'noch seemed to be scared for him, but he also felt terribly guilty for leaving his friend. Steph kept running, as fast as he could run, holding onto Mila tightly, while wondering if he had just left his friend to die at the hands of those strange creatures.

CHAPTER 16
Ragu Camp

Steph didn't know how far he had run but guessed that it had easily been at least three or four miles. He had cleared the edge of the forest and now stared at a large stretch of gigantic boulders and rocks. The landscape ahead of him looked like the remnants of a crumbled mountain that stretched for miles ahead of him and to each side. There didn't seem to be any places to rest without being exposed to whatever might be lurking amidst the sea of rubble ahead.

After staring for several minutes, Steph used his free hand to engage the talisman with the appropriate sequence of movements to open the 'blur' or pathway to his world. While still holding Mila with his other hand, he stepped through the path and looked around.

Steph had no idea where he would end up, so he had prepared himself to quickly jump back through the 'blur' if needed. To his surprise, he was in a large frost covered pasture that seemed to stretch as far as the eye could see. There were dozens of large hay bales scattered about the field and about a half mile away he could see an old barn. There was nothing else in the pasture, which comforted him.

For a brief moment he thought about heading to the barn and then had a change of heart. Instead of heading to the barn, he approached the nearest hay bale and set Mila down gently. The hay bale large and circular, just like several others that were scattered about the pasture. Steph reached into the middle of the hay bale and carefully hollowed out the haystack until he had made an opening that was plenty big enough for his little sister.

Then Steph took off his leather vest, thinking, "It's not much, but it's better than nothing", and wrapped it around Mila, before carefully placing her inside the hollowed-out hay bale.

"I have to save our friend G'noch, Mila. I can't leave him to those creatures, and I can't find these so-called Ancients to help you without him. I'll be back soon." Steph said gently to his still unconscious sister, then he slowly covered the hole in the hay bale with some of the loose hay on the ground. He used his knife to cut a large 'X' in the ground in front of the hay bale and after one more look around to ensure that no one had seen him, Steph activated the talisman, opened the "blur," and crossed back over to the 'other side'.

"Ok Steph. Can't leave her for long, but at least she's not hidden over here waiting for a giant snake or something worse to eat her. Time to save G'noch", he said as he turned and began jogging back into the forest.

After a few miles of jogging Steph found himself nearing the encampment and instead of going the way he had come, he carefully circled back around the large Ragu camp on the far side, keeping an eye out for any of their crude traps along the way.

When he was close enough to the camp to see through the trees, he quickly leapt up grabbing the lowest branch of a large tree and pulled himself up. Once on the branch, Steph made short work of climbing high into the tree to get a good look at the entire encampment.

What he saw did not make him feel better about his mission of 'quickly saving G'noch'. The large T'kche warrior was still upside down in the net, only now he was hanging from a large wooden beam that stretched out like a 'T'. Beneath G'noch, at least a half dozen Ragu were stacking wood for what could only be a large bonfire.

"The little monsters are planning to cook him," Steph thought in horror.

His discomfort about the situation only increased when he noticed that dozens of other Ragu were all gathering around to watch, making an odd sort of festival out of it all. He noticed that many of the Ragu creatures were climbing up out of the dirt patches in the ground that were in front of each of the large boulders that had streams of smoke coming out of the top. It instantly all added up for Steph.

"Somehow they're tunneling through the ground and living inside what must be hollow boulders", he thought.

Steph diverted his attention back to his friend and stared, thinking how he could get to G'noch without having to take on the entire army of little grayish-green creatures.

After what felt like forever, he decided that the longer he waited, the more Ragu would be gathered around and the more likely it would be that they would start the bonfire beneath his trapped friend. So, Steph decided plan or no plan, it was time to act.

It wasn't that he didn't have a plan, it was just that he didn't feel great about it. The only thing he had been able to come up with was pretty much a distraction and then a mad dash.

"Well, it's better than leaving him to get cooked… I guess." Steph thought, as he lowered himself back down the tree, quietly.

Once he hit the ground, Steph snuck close to the large smoking boulder that he now realized was a Ragu homes and eased towards the far end of the camp, opposite from where they had G'noch hanging.

He surveyed the forest edge and found what he was looking for. It was a very tall tree, at least thirty feet tall, that was not nearly as big as most of the larger trees in the forest, only about as big around as a steering wheel. It rested right on the closest edge of the tree line and from what Steph could tell, if it fell just right it would land on at least three or four of the stone Ragu huts.

He darted over to the tree, silently pulled out the oversized Na'gee knife that he carried and as quickly and quietly as possible, he began to chop away at a section of the tree, pausing every few swings to look around and make sure he had not been discovered.

In no time, the tree was teetering dangerously and looked like a strong wind would be enough to send it crashing down onto the Ragu homes beneath it. Steph stepped back, assessed the tree, then nodded to himself in satisfaction and took off jogging back to the other tree that he had previously climbed.

Steph jumped up, grabbed the same branch that he had used to pull himself up earlier, and swiftly made his way back up the tree. Once up to his previous spot, he eased himself out onto a large branch that overhung the edge of the encampment. From the branch he had a good view of the tall tree he had been chopping and G'noch's perilous situation.

"Ok, Steph. Speed is key." He thought, followed by, "My friend needs me, and my sister won't survive if I don't succeed. I cannot fail."

The last thoughts steeled him, as he pulled the large .50 caliber pistol from his belt's holster and aimed it carefully. With one quick squeeze of the trigger, he shot the tree right at the center of the spot he had chopped away. It was more than enough to send it crashing down onto four of the Ragu huts.

The result was better than Steph had hoped for, as the tree crashed through the hollow stone structures. It created an incredibly loud booming noise that drowned out the echo from the gunshot blast and sent clouds of stone and dust into the air, creating an instant sort of fog over that corner of the encampment.

The Ragu went crazy! Half of them scrambled for spears or axes and took off into the clouds of dust, while the other half seemed to cringe and freeze.

Steph didn't hesitate. He leapt from the branch, landing on top of the closest stone hut, and leapt from hut to hut with incredible grace and speed, born of determination. Despite the distance between the stone huts, Steph didn't miss a step, instead seemed to gain momentum as he smoothly leapt from one to the other. By the time Steph was bouncing off the stone Ragu hut closest to G'noch, he was moving at an incredible speed. He turned the last leap into a vertical dive and cleared the ten feet between the hut and G'noch with ease, spearing his large T'kche friend in the mid-section and firing his pistol at the top of the rope that held the net all in one quick diving motion.

The gunshot hit true, the net broke loose, as Steph's arms wrapped around G'noch and the net he was trapped in, sending them both flying to the ground about halfway between the encampment and the tree line to the forest.

Steph didn't slow down when they hit the ground, instead he nimbly rolled off G'noch, pulled his large knife with his free hand, and sliced through the side of the net, while spinning around with his pistol still in his other hand, aimed toward the encampment.

Steph saw the remaining Ragu, shaking off the shock and grabbing spears.

"I'm glad the brave ones already took off after my distraction," he thought with a small feeling of pride as he began to pull the trigger.

G'noch scrambled to get out of the net and by the time the large T'kche was on his feet, Steph had shot down eight Ragu, sending the remaining ones running for cover. G'noch reached out and lightly touched Steph's shoulder, "We go Steph. Quickly," G'noch said.

Steph seemed startled at the presence of his friend and had to snap himself out of the battle fury that had seemed to overtake him. He turned his head and looked over his shoulder at G'noch. When their eyes locked, Steph saw gratitude in his friend's eyes, but also urgency and concern.

Without a word, he turned and took off running into the forest. G'noch followed closely, the two of them gaining speed as they ran, leaving the angry screams of the Ragu farther and farther behind them.

Before long they had run miles through the thick forest and slowed to a stop before the sea of stone and rubble that Steph had come to before.

As they both struggled to catch their breath before the vast plain of broken stones, G'noch spoke the first words that had been said since their run had started.

"G'noch say leave forest. G'noch find Steph later. Why you come back?" The growling words didn't sound angry, but more like genuine confusion.

"Sorry, Bud. I know what you said, but I couldn't leave you to those nasty little creatures. I had to save you," Steph said.

"G'noch not need saving. G'noch mighty T'kche warrior." The large T'kche said loudly, as he stood a little taller with an obvious show of pride.

Steph seemed oblivious to the posturing and simply replied, "It looked like you were about to be a mighty T'kche barbecue, G'noch. Now instead of trying to thank me in your awkward bigfoot way, why don't we go check on Mila before those little monsters catch up to us." Steph grinned as he said the words that obviously disturbed his large friend and waited for a response.

The playful look in G'noch's eyes disappeared when Steph mentioned Mila, and he took on a look of almost panic, as the large T'kche surveyed the sea of rumble and stone before them.

"You leave Mila here?! This place not safe Steph! Home of guardians!" G'noch half roared.

G'noch's panic seemed contagious, and Steph hurriedly worked the talisman he wore around his neck and opened the 'blur' to the pasture on his world.

"She's not here G'noch. She's safe on the 'top side', let's go," Steph said as he stepped through the pathway to the 'top side' world. G'noch followed him through, and as the pathway closed, Steph was already getting Mila out of the bay of hale that they stood before. Once he got her out, he carefully laid her on the hay that he had pulled out and piled onto the ground, and then he used more hay to make a small fire next to her. G'noch sat down by Mila, and the fire and looked at the unconscious girl with concern in his large eyes.

Steph watched for a moment and then sat down and joined them by the fire. After a few moments of comfortable silence, he looked at G'noch and asked, "So G'noch, what are these guardians you looked so worried about and how are we supposed to get past them?"

G'noch looked at Steph for several long moments, staring into the young man's eyes. Finally, the large T'kche reached out and laid his massive hand on Steph's shoulder in a caring and compassionate way. No words were said, but the feeling of the bond between them growing was undeniable to Steph. He didn't know how long they sat like that, but at some point, G'noch removed his hand, leaned back against the hay bale, closed his eyes, and appeared to go to sleep.

Steph stared at his strange friend for a moment and then thought to himself, "I guess we'll talk about it tomorrow."

He added more hay and some small sticks he found lying about to the fire and then looked at the sky as the sun started to set, thinking to himself, "guardians, ancients… for all the things the Na'gee taught me, there sure is a lot I don't know about the 'other side'," before slowly nodding off to sleep himself.

CHAPTER 17

Eva

Eva had been hiking through the cold, wild landscape all day. She had decided early on to abandon following the trail that seemed to have been left from the dark ones dragging off Halbred, and transitioned to hiking through the thick trees and brush off to the side of the trail. Although this approach made her traveling more rigorous, and significantly slowed her down, she felt it was necessary to be less exposed.

"Too many dangers on the 'other side' to risk traveling along a path, out in the open." she thought when making the decision.

She reflected on those thoughts and was glad she had made that decision earlier as she crouched in a thick patch of bushes. She had heard them approaching earlier and had eased herself into the thick brush that she now used as cover, while she watched them.

There were six Na'gee warriors, slowly searching the area and closely inspecting the path. They had come from the direction that Eva was heading, the same direction that Halbred had seemingly been dragged off in and they appeared to be searching for something or someone.

"Probably trying to figure out what happened to their companions that never came back." she thought to herself.

She didn't know if it was mid-afternoon or late afternoon, but she knew that she was well into the day. She watched them inspecting the trail and the surrounding landscape as they got closer and closer to where she hid.

Eva tightened her grip on the assault rifle she carried. "There's no way I can take them all before at least a couple of them get to me.

They're just too fast." she thought as she watched them get closer and closer.

Then, a grayish blur swept across the path, taking the Na'gee warrior who trailed behind the others with it.

"What the hell was that?!" Eva thought, amazed that the last warrior seemed to silently be swept away without any of the others even seeming to realize it.

Again, she saw the blur sweep across the path, only this time it was brown in color. It came from the same direction and seemed to try to sweep the Na'gee warrior in the last position with it. This warrior wasn't swept away like the other, though. At the last second before the blur hit the warrior, he dropped to the ground, in almost a seated position with both legs sticking out and spinning in a circle. To Eva it looked like a cross between breakdancing and some form of martial arts.

"Whatever it was, it worked," she thought as she saw the blur trip and fall after the spinning Na'gee feet. As the blurry color of brown, was hit and fell, it was clear that it wasn't a blur or apparition of any sort, but a monstrous beast covered in brown hair. Its body was somewhat shaped like a man, but it was much larger, not quite as large as G'noch's but much larger than a human. It had a massive head that protruded out in the front with a mouth that looked like some form of canine or wolf, huge teeth and massive claws on both hands and feet.

The beast was tripped, fell on it's back, but almost immediately leapt to its feet to face off against the Na'gee who had tripped it. The Na'gee warrior, flipped up to his feet facing the beast as well. The other warriors turned, as the commotion alerted them to battle in their midst, and then all hell broke loose.

Eva held her breath and gripped her assault rifle tightly, careful not to make a sound or a move, still crouching, hidden in the bushes while she watched.

The huge wolf-like man-creature leapt at the Na'gee with its claws out, just as the Na'gee pulled his large knife with one hand and the large .50 caliber pistol with the other. The warrior crouched to duck below the leaping beast, and raised his pistol to fire into its midsection.

A bullet struck the flying monster in the gut, just as it flew over the crouching Na'gee and swung both viciously clawed arms down. The claws caught the back of the Na'gee's neck, ripping the Na'gee's head clean off in the process.

As soon as the creature had leapt at the warrior, two other blurry shapes, that Eva now knew were these beasts, came speeding across the path from each direction-one grayish, one brown. They both seemed to catch a Na'gee with each one of their extended arms and in seconds all four Na'gee were missing heads or on the ground with their entire midsections ripped open.

The scene before her was horrific, and Eva struggled to watch. She had no problem with violence, but this was something different; these creatures dismembered the Na'gee hunting party in a matter of seconds and now stood on a path littered with body parts and covered in blood.

One of the creatures leaned over the injured one and seemed to inspect the wound, while the other one, with grayish-brown hair sniffed the air and started to circle the path.

It went around the entire path and started to slowly approach Eva's position, still sniffing the air. She didn't move a muscle, didn't even breathe, as she watched the large canine creature, who stood on its legs like a man, get closer and closer.

"It's coming straight for me; there's no way I can get out of this unnoticed." Eva thought, trying to figure out what to do.

Just then, out of nowhere the creature dove into the bushes where Eva was hiding. Its claws were fully extended, and its momentum had it heading straight for her. With almost no time to react, she simply jutted the butt of her rifle into the air as she dove to her left.

The creature came crashing through and took the butt of the rifle directly in the neck. It dragged its claws into the ground as it crashed, and Eva knew that if she had tried to duck, she would've ended up like one of the Na'gee in the path.

She rolled to her feet and turned to face the creature quickly, raising her assault rifle. The beast gagged and held its throat while it slowly turned to face her.

Out of the corner of her eye, Eva saw the larger brown-haired beast, who had been tending to its injured companion, rise to its feet and stare at her.

"I can shoot one of them before the other gets me, but I can't shoot them both before one of them tears me to pieces" she thought in a panic. "I have to try something else."

"Stop! I am not with these Na'gee scum. I hunt them!" Eva yelled with feigned confidence and authority.

The beast holding its neck, slowly began to circle her, forcing her to begin to turn her back on the other one if she wanted to keep the rifle aimed at it. As it did, it replied in a growling voice that was similar to G'noch's but more sinister sounding, like scraping something metal across gravel.

"You are human, you are the same!" the beast growled.

Eva had her response ready, playing the only hand she thought she had to play, knowing it was a long shot at best.

"I gave the orders for my people to free three of your kind from these Na'gee just yesterday. I am owed a blood debt. Is this how you repay your debts, beast?!" Eva yelled, hoping that she had remembered the similar creature's choice of words from the previous day correctly.

As soon as she said the words, she noticed that the monstrous canine creature's face changed - not for the better. It looked angrier and more vicious than before, if that was even possible. The beast stared at Eva and then said, "We owe you nothing, human!" and it lunged towards her.

"Damn!" Eva thought, but before she could pull the trigger, the brown-haired creature that had been behind her shot past her with incredible speed and intercepted its companion, crashing into the gray-colored beast and sending it flying to the ground.

"Do you not recognize her scent?! She was the human watching us from the tree when her companion freed us fool! She speaks the truth. We are in her debt." The creature with the brown hair growled at its companion, who was picking itself up off the ground.

"I am in no human's debt, Grifter!" the gray colored beast growled. "Let us kill this human and bring these Na'gee heads back to the pack to restore our honor."

"Roken are not like the Na'gee, Luca. We will honor our debts. It is this human that freed us from slavery." Grifter said firmly. Then Grifter turned to face Eva and said, "I thank you for commanding your companion to free us. We owe you and your companion a blood debt and shall honor it. Until we meet again, human." Then the large Roken, bowed and walked past her.

He began picking up the heads of the dead Na'gee. His companion walked past Eva and growled viciously before joining Grifter in gathering the heads.

To Eva it appeared that they were just going to leave. At first the thought relieved her, but then another struck her.

"What good is your honor and the blood debt you owe, if you choose to leave rather than repay it, Grifter?" Eva asked boldly.

Both creatures stopped what they were doing and turned to face her, with somewhat astonished looks on their faces.

"You dare to question our honor human?" Grifter growled, sounding a little more like his angry companion, Luca, than he had sounded earlier.

"My name is Eva, Roken, and my companion has been taken. I am going to save him. If you owe a blood debt then pay it and help me free him, like we freed you and your companions." Eva said firmly, despite the fear boiling over inside her. She knew that these creatures could kill her in a split second, but she also knew that trying to face countless dark ones alone might be just as dangerous. She waited and stared at the creature that called himself Grifter.

"Who has taken your companion, Eva?" Grifter asked, with what sounded like forced calmness. "I don't know what you call them, but my T'kche friend calls them dark ones," Eva said.

If the creatures looked surprised before, it was nothing compared to the looks they gave her before exchanging glances with one another now.

"You are friends with a T'kche, Eva?" Grifter asked.

"Yes. His name is G'noch and he is a mighty T'kche warrior. We hunt and kill the Na'gee together with my companions." She replied, feeling a hint of pride as she made the statement.

"You truly are an odd human. We will honor our debt, but we cannot attempt to free your friend from the dark one's temple now. We will need the blessing and the support of the pack. Come with us and we will honor it." Grifter said.

"Grifter! This is madness! We cannot attempt to attack the dark ones at their temple! A blood debt is not worth it. Let nature take the dark ones and we will rise as we always have." Luca growled, then he added, "besides, if the dark ones took her friend, then it's already too late."

Grifter appeared to heavily consider his companion's words, so Eva chimed in quickly.

"It is not too late. My friend's skin is hard like the steel of that Na'gee blade. The dark ones cannot bite him or kill him. That is why they took him. If it was any different, they would've killed him right there, would they not?" Eva said.

Grifter looked at Eva and then back at Luca. After a long moment, he finally said, "We are Roken. We will not shy away from our blood debt because we cower at the thought of facing dark ones Luca. Eva, you must come with us to the pack, then we will repay our debt and rescue your friend."

Luca growled loudly, making his displeasure clear, then gathered the remaining heads and wrapped them in a battered tan cloak. He carried them in one hand and then threw his injured companion, who appeared to be unconscious and bleeding heavily, over his shoulder with the other hand.

Without looking back at Grifter, Luca began walking off into the woods.

"Follow me, Eva," Grifter said as he began to walk into the woods behind the angry Luca.

Eva couldn't believe what had just happened. On the one hand she felt that she had somehow recruited creatures that seemed like they could take on the dark ones and help her save Halbred. On the other hand, if this so-called pack was more like Luca than Grifter, then she might be the one in desperate need of saving.

"Oh well, no choice now, Eva." She thought to herself as she began walking off into the woods behind the large wolf-like creature named Grifter.

CHAPTER 18
The Pack

As Eva followed the two large beasts through the dense forest in the late hours of the afternoon, she considered everything about her situation and everything that was said, thinking of ways to strengthen her case for support. The more she thought about it, the more concerned she became that this, 'Grifter' could be heavily opposed by his pack. Regardless of honor or debt, she realized she was asking these creatures who had been enslaved by humans to risk their lives attacking the dark ones to save a human.

"Not sure if I would help me, if I were them," She thought to herself many times over the course of the hike.

She also kept thinking about something that Luca had said: "Let nature take the dark ones and we will rise as we always have".

"What could he have meant by that? What could nature do to these dark ones, and what does a 'rise' of these creatures look like in comparison?" Eva thought to herself.

When they finally broke through the last of the trees and she laid her eyes upon what could only be the home of this pack, all of her thoughts were instantly washed away. Without even realizing it, she stopped and just stared at the structure ahead of her.

It was a large stone castle, nestled into a clearing in the middle of the dense forest. The fading sunlight glinted off the old gray stone fortress, giving an eerie, shadowy glow of sorts.

The outside walls were covered with mold and moss, as was the large metal grate in front of the huge double doors at the entrance. She saw a small tower at each corner of the walls and noticed two men, not beasts, in thick, rough tan cloaks standing on top of what must have been a walkway behind the tall walls. The men were clearly looking at them, and in the eerie light of the setting sun she could easily see their bright red eyes, even from the distance of the tree line.

Eva didn't know what she had expected, but she surely didn't think it would be a castle. She had no idea that any creatures on the 'other side' even built structures like this. Based on her experiences, she just assumed that they all lived in caves, mountains or inside the strange doorways that led into rocks and trees when activated. This was new and completely unexpected.

"Eva! The sun is setting, we must go. Come." Grifter growled back at her.

His words snapped her out of her frozen state of staring in amazement and she realized that they were almost half the distance to the fortress ahead of her.

Eva broke into a jog and quickly caught up to them just as they were approaching the large steel grate in front of the massive wooden double doors, thinking to herself "That's a bad start Eva. You're standing there staring at their castle, like you've never seen a structure with walls before."

As soon as they stopped in front of the castle fortress, a loud screeching and grinding noise rang through the air, and the metal grate slowly began to raise up, seemingly into the massive stone wall above it. As the last of the grate disappeared, a loud clanking sound seemed to signify it locking into position and then the massive double wooden doors began opening at the same time.

Eva saw two more men, in similar rough tan cloaks, each of them pushing one of the mighty doors open. She made a mental note of the size of the doors and the fact that it only took one of these strange men to push each door open, realizing they must be incredibly strong.

Once the doors were open, Luca handed the bag of heads to Grifter and marched off with their injured companion, still over his shoulder.

The same two men in cloaks, closed the double doors behind them, while Grifter and Eva stood there, not moving, and silent. Once the doors were shut, the men picked up a huge log and placed it into brackets on the inside of the door, locking it shut.

Eva looked at the size of the log secured behind the massive wooden doors and thought, "A semi-truck couldn't even crash through that."

The two men then approached Grifter, eyeing Eva warily the entire time, one of them handed Grifter what appeared to be a folded rough, tan cloak, identical to the ones they wore. As Grifter took it in his free hand, his body started to change.

Eva watched as his massive shoulders and back, began to shrink, his long claws started to retract into his fingers, which also started to get smaller and the thick brown hair that covered his entire body, started to seemingly grow backwards into his skin.

Eva, who still stood behind him, watched the transformation and in seconds she was staring at the back of medium sized, albeit well-built human male in place of the large wolf like, man beast that stood before her an instant before.

Grifter threw the rough cloak around him and seemed to tie the front of it shut with a tattered rope, then turned to face her.

He had the same red eyes, but his face was clearly human now. He had messy short brown hair thick bushy brown eyebrows, and a thick short beard that matched both, underneath a strong, well defined jaw line. For a moment he just stared back at Eva without saying a word, seeming to be assessing her, just as she was assessing him and then he spoke.

"We are Roken, Eva. We are man and we are beast, yet we are also neither. The Roken are a link between man and beast, and the original rulers of both. Very few humans have laid eyes on a Roken changing in many generations and even fewer have seen our home in that span of time. Weigh your words carefully here Eva, as all of the Roken are not as kind to humans as Luca and I." Grifter seemed to pause for effect.

"Many are not as kind to humans as Luca? He wanted to kill me," Eva thought with concern.

Grifter seemed to know her thoughts and said, "I am honorable, as is my pack. We will pay our debt and save your friend Eva. You are safe, but there are also generations of justified prejudices against humans with many of my kind, so choose your words wisely. Now come. It is time to address the pack."

With that Grifter began walking forward towards another set of double doors that seemed the access the one large building in the middle of the castle walls. These doors were already open, and torches hung from either side of the entrance, providing the light that the setting sun had taken from them.

Eva followed, not knowing what to expect and the two other silent, strange men, or Roken fell in behind her.

The four of them passed through the doors and entered a mighty hall that looked like it came straight out of medieval times. There were strange axes, swords, and other bladed weapons that Eva didn't recognize hanging on the walls and in between them were large tapestries depicting mighty battles. The tapestries were done with intricate detail and showed bloody scenes of what appeared to be soldiers and all sorts of different beasts fighting, epic wars.

There were long, narrow tables lining each side of the hall, that appeared to be made of rough wood, with benches tucked underneath them. Lined up in front of the tables, were several of these strange Roken men, all appearing to be human, except the red eyes, and wearing the same rough, tan cloaks or robes.

"Monks. That's what they look like in their robes, or cloaks or whatever. A gathering of monks." Eva thought to herself as she followed Grifter up the center of the hall. As she walked, she counted, about twenty of them gathered, all standing on either side of the main hall, in a kind of formation that made a tight row for Eva and Grifter to walk through towards the front of the hall.

At the end of the hall, where it looked like they were heading was a large, square wooden platform about the size of a boxing ring. Eva noticed the large wooden block in the center of it and then noticed what appeared to be bloodstains all over the floor of the platform.

As they approached the platform, Grifter reached a hand backwards, stopping Eva just before it. Without turning, he said,

"Wait here." Then he proceeded to the large block and stepped up on it as he turned to face the gathered Roken.

Eva was left standing in front of the wooden square platform, with the two men from the front gate, one on either side.

Grifter stared at the crowd of around twenty male and female Roken gathered and waited. Heavy silence created tension in the room, Grifter seemed to intentionally let it build. Finally, he raised the bag of Na'gee heads and upended it, dumping the six of them onto the platform in front of him.

There was shuffling amongst the gathered Roken and some growls here and there, but nothing was said.

Grifter waited another moment and then addressed them.

"These are to be the first of many! The Na'gee will pay for daring to attack and enslave the Roken. We have let them carry on too long and they have forgotten our lineage! They have forgotten who was intended to rule these lands and all their inhabitants! We will make an example out of these foolish humans! Your Prince, your Alpha, has returned!" Grifter roared.

Eva didn't know what she expected to happen or how she expected the gathered Roken to respond to Grifter's speech, but the response she witnessed definitely wasn't it.

One Roken man, slightly taller than the others, stepped out into the walkway and yelled in a rough voice, "You say 'Na'gee' Grifter, but it was the humans and now you have brought one into our midst. What of this human's head? Did you break free of bondage and return with a human mate? You say you are the packs 'Alpha', but you let these Na'gee enslave you. What do your words mean?"

Grifter's eyes narrowed, and he stared at the man for a long awkward moment, then he stepped down from the box in the center of the wooden platform and said, "Have I been gone so long that you forgot your place Runak?"

"I led the pack while you were enslaved by those weak humans! Now you return bringing a human into our midst and one of our own near death's door, and you want us to celebrate a few human heads?" the large man named Runak shouted as he took a step forward.

Grifter noticed the rumbling in the ranks of gathered Roken and knew that Runak's words reflected the feelings of others as well. He fought down the anger rising inside him which urged him to tear Runak limb from limb and chose his words carefully.

"You led while I was gone. That is why there was no attempt at rescue Runak? You mock our capture and enslavement, call these humans weak, yet you were either too cowardly to face them and free us or you wanted to be alpha and were too cowardly to face me and earn it? Tell us, Runak… which cowardice best describes you?" Grifter said in a loud growling voice that hushed the rumblings in the crowd.

The larger Roken, referred to as Runak, ripped his cloak off and stood in the center of the aisle naked, then his body started to shift and grow even larger. Hair sprouted all over, creating a thick coat of black and gray fur. His face grew outward into a muzzle that resembled a giant wolf and his fingers and toes grew into long thick claws. In seconds, he stood fully transformed into a huge version of the man wolf creatures.

Eva watched in wonder, shocked that the creature seemed to have grown as large as a T'kche with a less primal and yet more savage animal look to it. She was startled when a large clawed hand, covered in brown hair gently grabbed her arm and moved her to the side.

It was Grifter. Eva had been so mesmerized by the sight of Runak transforming, that she had not even noticed Grifter transforming behind her.

The two beasts stared at each other and then Grifter stepped backwards into the center of the wooden platform, kicking the box out of the way. Runak took off charging straight for him with incredible speed. As the larger Roken leapt through the air with claws extended, obviously intending to destroy the smaller creature with sheer size and force, Grifter ducked and spun, gaining momentum and then came from an immensely low position to a type of twisting uppercut, right under the leaping Runak's chest. The impact was powerful and sent a booming thud echoing through the chamber.

Runak went flying backwards landing on his back. As soon as his back hit the platform though, he quickly leapt to his feet, but it was only to catch the swinging right claw of Grifter across the side of his face. Blood splattered onto the watching Roken, now gathered around the platform. Before Runak could react Grifter came back with his left claw, this time jumping up and coming down with his claws across the top of Runak's head and slicing down through his face.

Runak's head slammed down onto the platform, sending another wave of blood into the crowd. Instead of continuing his vicious attack, Grifter jumped back and watched Runak closely. The larger Roken barely moved at first,then rose to one knee and bowed his head.

Grifter nodded and the gathered crowd roared and howled.

After a few moments two men approached Runak and helped him to his feet, carrying him off the platform to one of the large benches. Runak sat bleeding, but did not transform back into his human shape.

Grifter, on the other hand, transformed back almost instantly, but didn't bother putting his cloak back on. He stood before them without clothes and didn't seem to notice or care, as he raised his arms and by doing so hushed the crowd.

"We will destroy these Na'gee! We will wipe them all out so that no Roken are ever enslaved again. This human is part of a band of humans who are also hunting the Na'gee and her companion freed us from our bonds. We owe her a blood debt. I intend for us to repay it. Her companion is held captive at the dark ones' temple. I will free him from his bonds, just as he freed me from mine." Grifter said it all slowly and clearly in his deep authoritative voice. When he finished the room was silent for a very long time. No one moved and no one spoke.

Finally, after what felt to Eva like twenty minutes, Grifter continued. "I understand that this is no small feat, but we are Roken-honor-bound, and I will NOT shy away from a blood debt out of fear of the wretched dark ones. For generations, we have waited for nature to shift the balance of power in the land. We have waited our turns. I will wait no more. This blood debt is a sign, a sign that it is time we take control, not wait for nature to deliver us some brite and give us our chance to rule. I intend to free this human and wipe out the dark ones, then I will wipe out the Na'gee! It is time for the Roken to rule once again!" Grifter got louder as he spoke, roaring the last part and getting roars and cheers in response.

After a moment of passionate growls, roars and cheers, he raised his arms once again and the gathered Roken became silent. "This will be no easy task-you have tomorrow to prepare yourselves, we leave at dawn the following day and will strike them while the sun is at its peak-." As Grifter said his final words, he reached out his arm and someone in the crowd threw him a cloak, which he nonchalantly wrapped around himself.

He then walked up to Eva and said "Follow me. I will show you to your quarters. Do not leave them tonight- it is not safe for you here if you are not with me."

Eva looked up at his red eyes and saw this man or beast or Roken differently for the first time. He wasn't so different from her or any of her group. He had suffered at the hands of the Na'gee, was seeking vengeance and trying to lead his people at the same time. She didn't understand half of what he had said to the gathered pack, but she did understand that this creature was honorable and she respected him.

"Thank you Grifter," Eva said.

"I see you, Eva. I will free your friend, as I am honor bound to do so, but you must fight with the pack when the time comes to attack the dark ones. My pack sees all humans the same, your bravery in combat can make them see you different. Prepare yourself in the time you have." Grifter said in a kind sort of way.

Eva nodded and then followed as Grifter turned and began walking away, leading her to her quarters.

"Prepare myself? To attack a temple of freaking dark ones with a pack of giant wolf men?!" She thought as she followed him. On the way to her quarters, she checked her watch, knowing that if any of her party had crossed over, they would show on the tracker. "Still nothing. Something must be wrong. They should be here searching for us," Eva thought to herself, as worry slowly began sinking in.

CHAPTER 19

Late Night Visit

Grifter stopped in front of a pair of double doors at the end of the long hallway that stretched off from the main room. They passed several sets of doors on either side of the hallway, before stopping at the ones they stood before now, closer to the end of the hall.

"This place is way bigger than it looks from the outside." Eva thought.

Grifter did not say a word, he simply pushed the doors open and stepped aside. Eva walked into the room and was shocked by what she saw. She didn't know what to expect, but this wasn't it. The room was large, with what appeared to be a king-sized bed in the middle of it. There were red and yellow tapestries hanging on the walls filled with more battle scenes and most of the wooden floor was covered in a red and yellow rug that had intricate designs sewn into it. The bed itself was covered by a thick red and yellow comforter and had tall wooden posts sticking up from each corner. The top of each bed post ended in a carved wolfs head. Across from the bed was a small wooden table with a mirror on it and a small, wooden chair in front of it with a red cushion on the seat.

While Eva was surprised at how nice the room was, she did not fail to notice the fact that there no windows or other doors.

"Only one way in and out." Eva thought.

She turned to look at Grifter who still stood in the doorway, staring down the hall, seemingly deep in thought. When she turned to face him, he did the same and said, "Lock the door and keep it locked. Do not leave your room. It is not safe for you here Eva. I will come get you in the morning."

Once Grifter finished, he pulled the wooden double doors shut, leaving Eva alone in her 'quarters'. She thought about his words, slightly unnerved, checked the chamber on the assault rifle she still carried and had the with her the entire time and then locked the doors.

Eva walked over to the bed and sat down, marinating on all that had happened over the course of the last two days. She was exhausted, she worried about Halbred and she worried about Vic and her children. After a moment of worrying, she stood up, threw the rifle over her shoulder and began to initiate the sequence on the Na'gee talisman that she wore.

"I should've already crossed over and checked on them, but I was afraid I'd lose Halbred's trail, or maybe I thought they'd just show up looking for me. Doesn't matter, now is as good a time as any," Eva thought. Then she stepped through the 'blur' that had appeared in the middle of the room.

Eva walked through the 'blur' and appeared in a snow covered field. She saw mountains in the distance, but no lights, no buildings, no civilization. There were trees scattered about leading into nearby woods, but little else.

Eva looked around a little more, hoping to catch a sign of anything that would give her an indication of where she was. Finally, after she realized she didn't know this place and that no one was around, she looked at the watch and zoomed in on the blinking dots that indicated Vic and Samuel's locations.

"This shows they're at a jail not far from the warehouse we ambushed." Eva thought confused. "Well, if those idiots went off and got themselves locked up then they're on their own for now. If I leave this place, I'll never find my way back to the 'pack' and right now that's the only chance of saving Halbred." Eva's thoughts haunted her. She never in a thousand years would've expected that her husband would've ended up in jail.

"Dammit Vic! I really need you right now! What the hell happened to you?!" Eva muttered.

Then she looked up Steph's coordinates and zoomed in to see the location. "Well at least it looks like he's at the cabin", Eva thought.

When Eva zoomed in on her own location, she saw that it looked like she had crossed the northern border and was in literally the middle of nowhere. She surveyed her surroundings once more and then stepped back through the 'blur', which led her into the warmth of her quarters.

Eva looked at the bed and felt the exhaustion of the last two days wash over her. Moments later, she was under the comforter sound asleep with the rifle leaning next to the bed and her pistol held tight in her hand.

"Click. Click." The sound was faint, but it was enough to break the silence and wake Eva. She sat straight up and looked at the door closely.

"Click. Click." She heard it again, only this time she could see the round doorknob slightly moving.

She silently eased out of the bed, slid her boots on and picked up her rifle. Then Eva stealthily moved towards the door, without making a sound.

She could just barely hear faint whispering outside her room saying "Hurry up. He may come check on her during the night." A different, deeper voice whispered back "Almost got it Runak, you just watch the hallway."

Eva stifled a gasp and quickly moved across the room towards the bed as she worked the pattern on the talisman she wore. The 'blur' appeared in the middle of the room, and just as she was stepping through, she reached out and grabbed the comforter off of the bed.

She stepped back out onto the snow-covered field and let the 'blur' close behind her, letting out a deep exhale when she did. She looked around and knew that she'd never find this exact spot again if she left it, so she began to dig a hole in the snow to hold out the night.

Seconds after the 'blur' disappeared from the room, there was another "clicking" sound and the door to Eva's quarters opened. Luca stepped inside in human form, holding a long thin blade in one hand. Runak, in human form as well, stood outside the door in the dark hallway. Both Roken in human form were wearing the monk like thick tan cloaks.

Luca silently approached the bed and then stopped within arm's reach. He saw it was not only empty, but that the blanket was gone. He quickly surveyed the rest of the room, then seeing nothing, he dropped down and looked under the bed.

"Nothing. Where the hell could she have gone?" Luca thought in frustration.

He motioned to Runak to come, and the larger Roken man quickly stepped inside the room and quietly closed the door behind him.

"Where is she?" Runak asked.

"I don't know. She's not here. There's nowhere she could go. Her scent wasn't in the hall, so she didn't sneak out that way. It smells like she was right here." Luca said in puzzled frustration.

"Grifter must've hid her somewhere else. It's the only thing that makes sense." Runak said. "Maybe, but it doesn't smell right." Luca said as he peered around the room, trying to see if he had missed a clue.

"Doesn't matter now Luca. She's not here. Let's get out of here before someone comes to check on her." Runak tapped Luca on the arm and headed for the door. Luca followed slowly, looking around with a confused look on his face as he left. They closed the door behind them and the room fell silent once more.

"Finally! Almost dawn." Eva muttered through chattering teeth. She had spent the entire night curled up in the comforter, inside a small hole she had dug out of the snow. It had kept her from freezing to death, but she sure didn't get any sleep. She had decided that despite the cold, it was too risky to go back before dawn as Runak and whoever was with him could still be waiting for her.

"So much for enjoying that cozy room." Eva thought.

With her watch indicating that dawn was near, she crawled out of the hole, dragging the thick blanket, that was now damp from the snow, behind her.

She dropped the blanket and readied her rifle initiating the sequence on the talisman once more. The 'blur' appeared, and she eased through it, into her quarters, with her rifle at the ready.

"Empty." She thought in relief. She rushed to the door and found that it was unlocked. Knowing that it locked from the inside, it confirmed what she already knew, someone had been there and had been looking for her.

Eva quickly locked the door and then ducked back through the 'blur', coming back into the room a second later with the large comforter. She let the 'blur' close, hung the damp comforter over two of the bed posts to dry and then heard the light knocking at the door.

Eva aimed her rifle at the door and remained silent.

"Do not fear. It is I Grifter. The night has passed, the day begins. Come Eva. We will feed you and then prepare for the battle to come." Grifter's voice was unmistakable. Eva was relieved to hear it, but she had also hoped she might get a few minutes of sleep before it was time to 'prepare', whatever that meant to these creatures.

"Oh well. Better cold and tired, than dead." She thought as she walked to the door and opened it. Grifter stared at her in an odd way that made Eva feel like he was reading her mind, almost like he knew she hadn't slept, but he said nothing. Instead, he just waved her along with his arm and began walking down the hall.

Eva followed, holding her rifle tightly while thinking, "I sure hope these creatures drink coffee."

CHAPTER 20
The Monarch

Roid's large black eyes slowly blinked open. He felt confused, not knowing where he was or what had happened to him to cause him to blackout. He tried to move and found that his abnormally large, muscular arms and legs were bound. Roid pulled harder, but could not break the bonds that held him.

Instantly angered, he quickly began to survey his surroundings looking for a way out. He felt a panicked need to escape, like a wild animal stumbling into some hunter's trap. As Roid took in the details of his situation, his concerns increased.

He was held in the air about ten feet off the ground by some form of chain. There was one wrapped tightly around each of his limbs, leaving him suspended stretched out in some kind of 'X' formation. The room he was in was incredibly large, with what appeared to be large ancient stones for walls, that angled up towards the ceiling. It was dark, very dark, but Roid's eyes were meant to see in the dark, so he clearly saw the forms of dark ones lurking about on the floor beneath him. From what he could see, there were about six of them, scurrying from here to there, but he couldn't make out what exactly they were doing. To his left the wall appeared solid, with what looked like an oversized stone doorway or walkway in the center of it. To his right there appeared to be some form of platform overhanging another identical doorway. Roid found it odd, that despite his eyes being made to see in the dark, he couldn't make out what was on the platform. It was as if it was shrouded in a black cloud of some sort.

What he could make out though, was the figure directly in front of him. Twenty feet across the large room, suspended in the air by chains, just like him was Halbred.

Roid's anger grew even more as he laid his eyes on his old commander. The man he had been hunting for so long. The man he blamed for his transformation into the monster he had become. As the thoughts flooded Roids mind, he heard the voice that spoke to him in his head say "If you had listened, they would have helped you hunt him down. Now you are at the mercy of the monarchs. You must beg their forgiveness and swear to serve."

The voice had been with him since his transformation, almost like another mind or another entity all together riding in his head. Early on, it had helped him, although it constantly warned him that it would eventually take over his being altogether.

So far, that hadn't happened and Roid had learned to listen to it, but often chose to ignore its directions.

"I'll beg to serve no one. I'll find a way free, destroy these monarchs for daring to put me in bonds and then tear Halbred limb from limb." Roid thought angrily.

"Wait… is he smiling at me?" Roid thought as he squinted, straining to see the expression on Halbred's face. "He is smiling! I'll destroy him!" Roid thought enraged, and began to squirm and struggle, helplessly trying to free himself.

"What's the matter Roid? You decided to join these cockroaches and they in turn choose to treat you far worse than anything you ever got from me? Thought it would be different?" Halbred shouted out. Then his smile faded, and his face took on the stoic look that seemed to be the old soldier's default expression and he shouted out, "You should've let me help you. We could've figured out a way to save you."

"You left me to die Halbred! You left me to this fate! You had your chance to save me and instead you chose to run away with Samuel. Now it is both of you that will beg for saving. This is nothing more than another delay." Roid hissed back, as he hatefully stared at Halbred across the room.

"Enough!" A powerfully loud crackling voice roared. It sounded like a radio station that wasn't coming in quite clearly, but the words were still clear enough and the sound was overpowering. When the word was spoken a strong wave of cold dusty air swept across the room from the direction of the platform, sending both captives bodies and the chains holding them into an eerie swaying motion.

The scurrying dark ones on the floor immediately disappeared through the doorway on the opposite side of the room from the platform.

"Now you get to see who you chose to serve Roid. He's not a fan of me; something about my impenetrable skin makes his attempts at torture ineffective. I don't think he likes it. Wonder how you'll fare?" Halbred said.

While Halbred's words infuriated Roid more than he already was, in this moment he was much more interested in whatever this thing was that Halbred was referencing. Especially as he noticed the thick darkness getting closer. It was almost like a dark cloud that moved off the platform and slowly advanced on Roid. He couldn't make out anything else, just blackness getting closer and closer, until it was inches from him.

Roid stared at the blackness. He smelled decay and dust, but also something else he couldn't make out, like a foreign herb of some sort. Then the blackness retreated towards the platform, leaving a huge figure standing in its place, right next to Roid's suspended body.

The figure stood on the floor and was still eye level with Roid, making it at least fifteen feet tall, considering that Roid's feet were about ten feet off the ground. It looked similar to the dark ones that Roid was familiar with, but its black eyes were more of a bluish color. It was like a giant dark one, but outside of the eyes, there was a different aura about it all together, it was one of their species that was for sure, but it was also something very different.

"You have not come to the temple. You have not chosen to follow. You have crossed to the other world. These things are forbidden." the giant said in the same crackling voice that echoed throughout the room.

"Your place is to serve. You are to remain at the temple until the transformation is complete," The giant said as it leaned in even closer to Roid's face.

Roid stared at the large head in front of him without fear and responded boldly, "My transformation is complete. I serve no one. Free me now and hand over my prey that I have been hunting, and I will leave you and your servants alive." Roid hissed.

In response the giant dark figure raised its huge left hand and placed one clawed finger on Roid's neck, right above his chest. The giant let its finger linger there for just a moment and then dragged it down from Roid's neck to his waist, peeling a long patch of Roid's translucent skin off with it.

Roid was shocked at the pain he felt. It was more than just being skinned alive, which would've been painful enough, it was also like the creature's claw left a strange burning sensation that inflamed and burned his insides.

"We have only begun. You have killed your own kind, and you ignore the being growing within you, that you are to become," The giant dark one said, as it placed its claw on Roids left shoulder, just below the neck, leaving a long patch of skin from the previous torturous movement, hanging over Roids waistband.

The creature repeated the movement, dragging its claw from Roids shoulder down past his elbow, stopping at his forearm that was wrapped in the chains. Once again it left the skin hanging over the chains.

"I am of the monarchs. We rule our kind. You will follow our rule, or you will not survive. I feel your rage, your hate, and your… power. You have physical gifts unlike the others. You could be valuable if you survive." The giant said as it placed its claw on Roid's right shoulder and repeated the skinning motion, leaving another long patch of skin hanging over the chains.

The wounds hurt, but the burning pain that the touch of the claw ignited on his insides was almost unbearable. He had never felt any pain like this, it was like it was searing him from the inside out. The pain began to cloud his thinking, it began to override his anger and his stubborn pride.

Finally, Roid yelled out, "What do you want?!"

The giant creature leaned in and said, "tell us how you crossed over to the other world". "It's the talisman I wear. Free my hands and I will show you." Roid said in a pain-filled hiss. "Use your words" the giant replied in its loud crackling voice.

Roid began trying to describe the movements that initiated the talisman, the movements that created the 'blur' or pathway to the 'top side' world. The giant dark one listened closely and then yanked the talisman off of Roid's neck. The creature looked at the strange stone talisman that looked tiny in its massive hands and then it began to go through the motions on the talisman that Roid had described. Moments later a 'blur' appeared in the center of the room. The 'blur' was not like the others that Halbred and Roid had seen before, it was huge. The 'blur' stood at least fifteen feet high and was much wider than any they had seen before, it seemed that it was made to accommodate the size of the person who opened it, in this case a giant.

Halbred gasped from across the room, thinking to himself "that pathway is big enough for an army to cross over at once. An army of these things could destroy our world."

The giant dark one stuck its head through and then seconds later pulled its head back out. "How does it close?" It asked Roid.

Roid provided the instructions, and the giant monarch closed the 'blur'. Then it directed its attention back to Roid and placed the same claw on Roid once more, this time under his right arm on the side of his chest. The monarch repeated the peeling of skin, with its face hovering just inches above Roid's face.

"The smell of your pain is as sweet as blood," It whispered to him.

The torture continued over the course of several hours, before the monarch finally turned and walked away, back towards the platform without a word. As he moved away, the black cloud seemed to surround him again, making him appear to completely vanish in darkness by the time he was just a few feet away.

As the black cloud moved back onto the platform, several dark ones poured back into the room. They took positions on either side of the large chamber and began working levers along the side of the walls. As they did a huge stone section of the floor began to open up in the center of the room. When the stone slab stopped moving and the loud grinding noise had stopped, there was an opening in the center of the room's floor about the size of a garage door.

Two of the creatures moved down the wall to a large stone looking wheel with two handles and they began turning it, while two other creatures positioned themselves beneath Roid. As the dark ones turned the wheel, Roid began to slowly lower to the floor of the large room.

He wanted to prepare himself to fight his way free, to rip these creatures apart, but his body was overwhelmed with the internal burning from the strange torture that he had endured from the giant monarch. As his body hit the floor, it collapsed. The dark ones scrambled to remove the chains and then hurled him into the opening in the floor. Roid felt himself falling for what seemed like too long. His mind was clouded with pain, but it still seemed to him that he must've fallen at least one hundred feet or more, before crashing down to a cold, damp, stone floor.

He could barely hear the grinding of the stone floor closing above him as he slowly drifted out of consciousness.

CHAPTER 21
Guardians

Steph and G'noch stood motionless side by side, just staring at the horizon. The light of the sun was just starting to break through the darkness that covered the frosty pasture like a dark blanket. The two companions patiently watched and waited for the sun to peek its nose out over the horizon in the distance.

As soon as it did, Steph looked at G'noch and the large T'kche nodded. Steph immediately engaged the talisman and the 'blur' appeared. G'noch promptly stepped through, while Steph gently picked up Mila. With Mila over his shoulder, he stomped out the remains of the small fire and then stepped through the 'blur' himself, leaving his world behind.

As Steph emerged from the 'blur' into the 'other side' he took in the scenery around him. The thick forest, that he knew was crawling with furious Ragu, was behind him and in front of him lay a sea of boulders ranging in size from enormous to small. It was truly like looking at an ocean of rock and rubble. Steph took it all in and for the first time he realized that to him, this world felt much more like home than the world he was from. He felt this savage, mystical land that was full of dangers was where he really belonged. Steph embraced the thoughts and felt a sense of peace wash over him, he would not fight it any longer, there was no more confliction in his heart and soul, this was his land.

He was standing next to G'noch with Mila over his shoulder, lost in his thoughts as they both stared out over the sea of rubble, when the line of trees far off in the distance, on the other side of the sea of rock caught his attention.

"G'noch, what is that on the other side of this rocky mess? It looks like trees," Steph asked, still staring out over the sea of rocks trying to make out more details of what looked like trees on the other side.

"Ancients, home, Steph." G'noch replied. "We must go. Guardians will try to stop us."

Steph turned from gazing at the landscape and looked at G'noch closely. "G'noch, you've got to tell me more. If the ancients are the only ones that can help us, why would their guardians try to stop us? And what are these guardians? Are they T'kche?" Steph asked it all with as much patience as he could, but his concern was growing. It frustrated him that his friend seemed to know so much more than he did about what they were walking into.

"Ancients help Brite. Guardians let Brite pass. Mila no look like Brite now, Steph. Guardians will try to stop." G'noch said.

Steph pulled Mila off his shoulder and held her out in front of him in his strong arms, looking at her. "He's right. She just looks like a normal little girl, who's unconscious. Her glow is gone." Steph thought.

"Ok G'noch, what are these guardians and what do we do?" Steph asked.

G'noch turned from Steph and looked back out over the sea of rock and rubble. After a long moment of silence, he said "We go. When guardians try stop, we fight. We go to trees Steph." As he finished speaking, the large T'kche pointed out at the trees many miles in the distance, on the other side of the rocky plain.

G'noch then turned back and stepped closer to Steph, staring down into his much smaller human friend's eyes and said, "We must get Brite to ancients Steph. Brite more important than G'noch or Steph. Brite save world. Without Brite, this world die."

It was more than Steph thought he'd heard his large T'kche say at one time before and it definitely more passionately said than anything he'd heard from G'noch before. Steph didn't understand it all, but he understood it was important and that was all he needed to know.

Steph simply nodded in response and G'noch took the first leap off of the cliff face, landing on the closest boulder. Steph shook his head from side to side, gently positioned Mila back over his shoulder and leaped off the edge too, landing right behind G'noch on the same boulder.

G'noch looked back at him with eyes that were excited and alive. There was no more worry, concern or passion in the large T'kche's eyes, instead there looked to be excitement, and maybe a little fondness for his young human friend that seemed intent on keeping up with him.

Steph saw the look in G'noch's eyes and felt the same. The planning and worrying were over, now it was time for action, and he could do action. The two shared a half grin and G'noch leapt off the boulder, landing gracefully onto another, slightly smaller boulder a few feet away. Once again, Steph followed and off they went, leap frogging from rock to rock, slowly making their way across the sea of rubble.

The two went on like that for several miles without slowing down. As they went Steph noticed several creatures running and slithering on the ground between the rocks, but their leaping across the tops of the highest rocks kept them far from the floor of the sea of rocks. Steph figured that G'noch had come up with this approach, knowing good and well the dangers that they would face if they had attempted to walk across the floor of the rocky terrain.

"Either that, or he knew that we'd likely get lost in the maze of rocks if we weren't high enough to see our destination." Steph thought as he leapt once again.

When he landed this time though, G'noch did not move and leap to the next rock. Steph was shocked. After half a day of rhythmic leaping from rock to rock, the sudden change alarmed him. It alarmed him even more when G'noch reached back with his right arm and pressed his open hand on Steph's shoulder, gently pushing him down onto the boulder, while the large T'kche lowered himself into a crouch at the same time.

G'noch stared out ahead, and Steph tried to follow his gaze, wondering what had alarmed his friend, seemingly out of nowhere.

Then Steph saw it. He almost ran his eyes right past it without noticing, but the movement gave him pause. Twenty or thirty feet ahead, a huge boulder, much larger than most of the ones they had leapt between, was slowly shifting.

"No, it's not shifting, it's standing up," Steph thought as he watched what had appeared to be a large boulder just moments before, seem to stretch and move. In a few minutes, the rock form seemed like it had been nothing more than this large creature leaned over in ball. When the shifting had finished, the thing stood well over twenty feet tall. It had rocky brownish, gray color skin that blended in with the entire rocky sea of rubble so well, that it was almost hard to distinguish it from its surroundings. Well, almost hard if it wasn't standing twenty something feet in the air.

The creature appeared to have no neck, just a boxy, rocky-shaped head that went straight down into massive rocky shoulders and gigantic arms and legs. Its body was built like a gorilla, only covered in thick rocky type skin. The thing looked up and its gaze landed right on them.

Steph stared at the massive rock creature's face. It had a large wide nose that protruded out boldly from its face. A wide mouth, with thick rocky lips and jagged teeth that stuck out here and there. Its eyes were big and cold, and even though they were made of rock, its eyebrows still appeared bushy. The thing also had huge rocky looking ears that seemed a bit too big for its gigantic head. As Steph soaked in the strange features of the thing before him, he couldn't help but think of stories of strange creatures from fairy tales like golems or mountain trolls, but he never had heard a story of one made of rocks or of rocks coming to life.

"It almost seems like everything in this world has some twisted, distorted storybook version of it in our world," Steph thought to himself, wondering who and when was involved in the original crossing of worlds that started the stories and how they got so much of it so wrong.

He was snapped out of his thoughts as he saw another of the large stone creatures standing up about ten feet out past the first one, and about fifty feet past that one, a third one was standing up.

"Guardians," G'noch said in a hushed tone, as if the thing wasn't staring directly at them.

"So, these are the guardians," Steph thought. He instantly understood G'noch's concerns and asked G'noch, "How do we fight creatures made of rock?"

G'noch glanced back at him for a split second and growled, "Fight fast. Fight strong. We must get Mila to trees." Then G'noch slid off the front of the boulder they were both perched on, dropping ten feet to the ground before taking off running through the maze of rocks.

Steph knew his T'kche friend well enough to know that he wasn't running away, but he also knew that there was no telling when and where G'noch would decide to join back in on the battle.

"So, I'm on my own for now, and I need to get Mila to the trees." Steph thought. Instantly he decided that fighting these giant stone creatures might be the T'kche's game plan, but he thought getting past them as quickly as possible might be the better plan and that's exactly what Steph planned to do. Childhood memories of his father watching sports games flooded his mind and he looked out at the field of rocks and the three giant creatures and saw a field, opponents and destination. Steph tightened his grip on Mila, who was still over his left shoulder, and took off, cutting left, but still heading forward towards the trees.

Despite its size and its rocky appearance, that somehow made Steph think it would be slower, the creature took off to its right moving fast to cut Steph off. Steph had too much momentum to switch directions, but knew that this thing was moving way too fast for him to evade it, he knew a collision was about to take place.

As Steph leaped onto the fifth boulder from when he had started to try to pass the creature, it was upon him. The large stone guardian came rushing towards him, swinging both hands downward, in what appeared to be an attempt to crush him.

Steph saw it coming and leapt off the boulder to the ground beneath him. As soon as his feet hit rocky dirt, the boulder he had just been on exploded as the guardian's fists hit it. Steph was already running through the maze of huge boulders and rocks when the boulder was crushed.

"Great. They can't see me now, but I can't see them either," Steph thought as he ran as fast as he could through the rocky maze. He thought he was going in the right direction of the trees, but had no way to know for sure.

He turned the corner around another large rock and saw the guardian swinging down just in time, to slide under the creature's legs as it smashed another boulder in the path. Steph kept running with everything that he had in him.

The creature had him spotted now and the chase was on. It quickly gained on him and Steph realized that attempts at outrunning these things were probably not going to prove successful.

"What else can I do though?" Steph thought as he came running around the side of another huge rock in the maze he was navigating and barely stopped himself from running into the leg of another guardian.

"Oh shit!" Steph yelled as he scrambled to turn around and run backwards, only to see the first guardian running right at him. Then out of nowhere, he saw G'noch leaping off the top of the boulder that the pursuing guardian was passing. His large T'kche friend was holding a huge rock with both hands over his head as he jumped right at the guardian and smashed it right into the side of the stone creature's head.

The blow knocked the creature off its feet and sent it crashing to the ground, with G'noch on top of it, smashing the huge stone he held with both hands over his head into the side of the guardian's face over and over as they crashed to the ground.

Steph had no time to be amazed at the brave heroics of his friend, for he felt the rush of air behind him and instinctively leapt to the side, just in time to dodge a giant stone fist slamming into the ground where he had just stood.

In that moment, the last words G'noch had said to him, rang out in his mind... "Fight fast. Fight strong. We must get Mila to trees," His friend had said.

Steph raced around another rock and reluctantly set Mila down on the stone floor of the path, leaning her back against a large boulder. "Sorry Mila, but I can't fight this thing with you. Please don't get eaten while I'm gone." Steph said hurriedly and then he leaped up on top of the boulder that he had leaned her against.

He saw the creature coming for him, fast. He leaped from boulder to boulder, leading the large stone guardian away from Mila's location was his primary goal. Once he had gotten several boulders away from his sister, he turned and faced the rapidly approaching guardian. In a split second the thing was on him, swinging down its mighty fist. This time, however, Steph didn't jump away. Instead, he jumped towards the fist, landed on the creature's arm and ran up it, while he pulled his .50 caliber pistol.

Steph began firing into the creature's face with the large pistol, and when the creature tried to swat him away with its other hand, Steph jumped onto that arm and from there onto the guardian's neck, still firing at the creature's face.

Each bullet seemed to take a large chunk of stone out of the creature. The stone beast roared and turned in circles as Steph hung onto its neck with his legs and free hand, still shooting the guardian's face at point blank range with his other hand.

Suddenly, something rough and powerful grabbed Steph's neck from behind and yanked him off the guardian. It was the third stone giant, and it held Steph in the air, with its giant stone hand wrapped around his neck and shoulders. Steph squirmed, trying to break free, but knew it was hopeless. The grip on him slowly tightened and he frantically thought of any way to get out of this situation. It didn't help that he couldn't see the creature, as it was behind him and holding him out in front of it.

What Steph could see was the guardian in front of him that he had been attacking. The stone creature had huge chunks missing from its face and one of its eyes looked completely gone. It staggered from left to right, rubbing its face.

Steph watched, thinking that it may fall and then out of nowhere, again, G'noch leapt through the air holding another huge rock over his head with both hands. Once again, G'noch smashed the rock into the creature's head and the two of them went crashing to the ground. G'noch swinging the entire way down.

The guardian holding, and slowly crushing Steph, roared out and Steph heard the roar echo strangely. He lifted his eyes and saw at least six other giant stone guardians not far from them. One of them leaped over a nearby boulder and grabbed G'noch with both hands, ripping the large T'kche off of the guardian that G'noch had been beating with the huge stone.

It rose and held G'noch out with both hands, as the other guardians slowly advanced. Steph felt the creature holding him tightening its grip and he felt the life starting to slip away from him. He was facing G'noch and saw clearly that his friend was being killed the same way.

"We can't die like this. Not like this. Not before we save Mila." Steph thought, and with the last of his breath, he screamed out, "Mila!!!"

A split second later, blinding brightness flashed and for a moment Steph thought it was death welcoming him, then he saw Mila hovering shakily above a large boulder not far from him and G'noch.

When she spoke, her voice was weaker and shakier than Steph had ever heard it before, but it was still loud and in the same ominous echoing voice that had become hers. Shaky or not, her otherworldly words rang out across the sea of rubble.

"Just as you guard the ancients, they guard the Brite. Free them and take us to the ancients, for the time of the Brite has come!" Mila said, hovering about two feet over a large rock, with brilliant bright white light emanating from her.

The grip loosened, and the next thing Steph knew, he was being set down gently next to where Mila hovered, as was G'noch.

Mila lowered herself onto the rock and stood between them. Her eyes and her body shined bright white light that Steph had become so accustomed to during their time at the cabin, only now it was fainter than it had been before her injury.

They all watched as two of the larger guardians picked up a huge flat piece of stone that was about the size of a school bus, and carried it between them. Each of the two guardians held a side of the flat rock as they walked up towards Mila, Steph and G'noch. The guardians held it out in front of them and Mila said, "Come. I cannot hold my light much longer". She said it softly, seemingly meant for G'noch and Steph's ear only, but it still came out in that ominous voice.

The three of them stepped onto the flat rock, and the guardians began walking them across the sea of rocks, towards the trees.

Steph looked around as they were carried and noticed that the other guardians were crouching and curling into balls again, making them appear to be just another boulder. As he watched them turn back into large boulders, he wondered if every boulder in the vast sea of rocks was actually one of these guardian creatures. The thoughts unnerved him and sent chills down his spine, so he chose to push them out of his mind and focus on his sister.

"Mila! You're okay. I was so worried." Steph said as they were being carried to the thick tree line in the distance.

Mila's body and especially her eyes were still glowing that bright white light, when she turned to face Steph. She showed no signs of emotion when she replied and simply said, "We will be with the ancients soon, they will help, and then it will be my time Steph. Please stay with me until then."

CHAPTER 22

The Ancients

As they approached the far end of the vast sea of stone and rock, the tree line became more visible. Although Steph told himself that nothing on the 'other side' should surprise him anymore, he was still surprised at what he saw before him.

It was a tree line, that much was still obvious, but it was unlike any line of trees that he had ever seen before. Steph strained his eyes, thinking that he must be missing something.

"There are no gaps between the trees. It's not a tree line at all, it's a solid wall of trees." Steph thought to himself. What stretched out before him, as far to the left and right as his eyes could see, was a solid wall of some sort of hardwood trees. They still had thick trunks spanning in ranges from what appeared to be five feet in diameter, up to over thirty feet in diameter, but there were no spaces between them. It wasn't just that they were close together, it was that they were touching so tightly against each other that streams of light couldn't even find a gap to sneak through. It was a solid wall of trees that stretched as far as the eye could see.

As the guardians continued to carry them towards the mighty wall of trees, Steph transitioned in his inspecting gaze to the tops of the trees.

"Surely there are at least gaps towards the tops, where they thin out and spread into branches," he thought to himself.

At the top, the trees seemed to do the opposite of thinning out though. Sure, their trunks got gradually smaller, but the thick branches intertwined with one another making what one would think was an airtight seal, based on how tightly they seemed to weave together. It almost created a green ceiling of leaves and branches that reached at least one hundred feet in the air.

Steph was blown away by the structure or fortress that nature had seemed to build. He turned to G'noch and Mila to see if they seemed to also be experiencing these wild feelings of shock and awe, but he found no comfort in their expressions.

G'noch stood staring in the direction of the trees, but he seemed not even to see them, as if staring right past them. The large T'kche seemed to be lost in his thoughts, and his expression gave the clear impression that the thoughts weren't pleasant ones at all.

As Steph took in the body language of his strange friend, his feelings of wonder were replaced with a sense of readiness and anticipation. He had stopped trying to understand everything about his friend, choosing to accept that the T'kche were naturally a mysterious species, but he also knew G'noch well enough to know that he looked like something worse was yet to come.

"Not sure what he's worried about now, but if he looks more concerned about facing these ancients, than the guardians, we're not out of the woods yet." Steph thought. Ironically, despite the tense situation, he found himself chuckling to himself at the thoughts and muttered under his breath, "Not out of the woods, ha. We're headed straight for them."

The guardians stopped about twenty feet from the wall of trees and slowly set the large flat stone, that had served as the companion's chariot, down on the ground. Then the two of them turned and began walking away, the same way that they had come from.

Steph looked around and took it all in. If the massive green and brown wall of trees appeared big from the stone chariot, it appeared gigantic from the ground. The twenty feet between the sea of rocks and the tree line that they faced seemed to smooth out into a fine bed of gravel leading up to the trees.

"Huh, if that is an ocean of rocks and stones that we just crossed, then this is like the gravel shores of the beach leading us to land." Steph thought.

Then a loud groaning noise echoed across the gravel expanse between them and the tree wall and the trees before them seemed to open up. Their thick, immovable trunks seemed to slide through the ground and spread out to the left and right, creating a ten foot wide opening or entrance to whatever the wall of trees guarded.

"Come." Mila said and she began to walk forward towards the opening. Steph and G'noch followed. As Mila walked, she staggered or wobbled twice and without a word, Steph and G'noch rushed to each side of her and gently grabbed her arms, helping her along.

As they walked through the opening into the fortress of trees, they heard the groaning of the opening closing behind them. Steph glanced back over his shoulder to confirm what his ears told him had happened and thought, "No getting out of this place now."

It was only then that his surroundings really struck him. Steph lost his breath for a moment and missed a step. He even heard G'noch gasp at the sight before them.

It was like a magical forest from a fairy tale. Everywhere the eye could see was life. Flowers and trees and plants of all shapes, sizes and colors exploded into view. There were streams and creeks, flowing between it all, and streams of beautiful sunlight rained down everywhere, adding to the magical look of the land. It stretched out forever, or at least appeared to. They saw strange small shapes fluttering around and small animals or creatures of some sort running here and there. Everything was moving so fast, that it was hard to make out what they all were or maybe it was that all the colors and scenery had drowned out their senses. Regardless, Steph could think of no other way to describe it than 'beautiful life' everywhere he looked.

In the distance ahead, a large grass covered hill seemed to rise up above everything else around them. As they took it all in, they continued walking ahead, letting Mila guide their direction while they each still held her arms and assisted her along.

Steph didn't know how long they had walked, as time didn't seem to exist in this strange place, but before he knew it, they were slowly walking up the grassy hill. As they came to the top of the hill, they saw three figures facing them, apparently awaiting their approach.

Each figure appeared more tree than man. They stood at least fifteen feet tall and appeared to be made of thick strands of bark or tree roots. They had patches of what appeared to be moss here and there across their tall, thin bodies. They each had a pair of legs and arms, shoulders, torso and heads, but that was as far as any similarity to a human went.

Steph noticed that their feet seemed to end in a large circular spreading out of vines on the ground and that their long, thickly braided arms of roots or brownish-green vines ended in hands that had strange versions of fingers that looked more like vines which hung down almost touching the ground. Their heads were drastically elongated compared to that of a human, or even a T'kche for that matter, and looked strangely like the tops of trees, each having different colors of leaves forming a sort of hair on top of their heads. Steph noted that the one on the far right had leaves of yellow and orange that seemed to cover the top of its head and spread down onto its shoulders, while the on the far left had strange blue and purple covered leaves that spread out in a huge circular expanse like an explosion of color fanning out on top of it's head, while the one in the center had what appeared to be a thousand different shades of green leaves that were short and low to its head, but spread all over it. Their eyes were hollow black holes and what appeared to be mouths were gaping black holes under their eyes that seemed to have thin vines stretching down from top to bottom.

They had a powerful and majestic ambiance about them, and it felt strange to be in their presence.

Mila stopped several feet before them and faced them without a word. Steph and G'noch still stood by her sides, but they let go of her arms and let her stand freely before these magnificent tree people that had to be the ancients.

"We have awaited your arrival, Brite one. We welcome you here," The one in the center said. Its words flowed softly, like the gentle babbling of creek waters flowing.

"As have you guardians. You have delivered the Brite one to us. You have our gratitude." The ancient tree-like being in the center continued. As it spoke those words, Steph felt a sense of calm flood through his body, and also a sense of pride. To have this amazing being extend gratitude to him, was unreal and breathtaking.

The tree-like being on the far right with the flowing leaves of yellow and orange, moved forward towards them slowly. It didn't really step forward, it was more like the outcropping of vines from where each leg touched the ground seemed to crawl across the grass-covered hill, while the rest of the things body remained completely motionless.

It stopped within a foot of Mila and then it spoke, its soothing voice sounded like the sound of a breeze rustling leaves when it said "You are injured. I will help you." As the tree being spoke, it extended an arm towards Mila. The vines at the end of the arm slowly wrapped around her and lifted her in the air. Then the tree-being slowly backed away the same way it approached and kept going off the far side of the hill, taking Mila with it.

Then the tree being on the far left, with the explosion of purple and blue leaves fanning out on top of its head, neared G'noch and Steph, in the same way that the other one had moved. It too, stopped within a foot of them and said, "Come guardians. Rest, eat and drink. You have delivered the Brite one to us, but that is just the beginning. The time of the Brite has come, and you have been chosen as the Brite's guardians. You have much to do. I will help you understand, while you replenish your energy. Follow." This tree creature's words were not soothing like the other two, they sounded more like old wood creaking, in a dark sort of way. It did not reach out for them or back away, as the other one had done, instead it clearly turned around and moved off towards the left over the side of the hill.

G'noch looked at Steph for the first time since they had arrived and said, "We must go, Steph.

We are now chosen. We must save the world from more than Na'gee now."

Steph didn't say a word, he didn't even know what to think, he just knew he needed to follow the strange tree being. As they walked away, Steph glanced back at the green-leafed being that had stood in the center of the three. It stood motionless on the top of the hill, appeared to be nothing more than a strange tree.

Once G'noch and Steph cleared the left side of the hill they saw a large stream running before them. Next to the stream were two large stones, that sunlight shined directly on. Smaller stones were next to the large ones and on each there was a large wooden cup and a variety of fruits and vegetables spread out. The blue and purple leaf covered being stopped before the stones and without turning back around to face them said, "Come. Drink, eat and rest while. I tell you what is to come"

Both G'noch and Steph walked over and each sat on one of the large stones. The sun had warmed the stone and it immediately began to warm and soothe them as well. Steph noticed that the large wooden cup was full of water and he drank it down, not realizing how thirsty he'd been until he started drinking.

G'noch did the same and in seconds both of them were devouring deliciously ripe fruits and vegetables that were spread out on the smaller stones next to the ones they sat on. They were so caught up in eating and drinking that they seemed to forget about their host's presence, until he began to speak in that creaking wood voice.

"The time of the Brite has come. It is a time of cleansing and a time of change, like the shifting of seasons. Just like the seasons, the Brite wipes away some things and ushers in others. This is the way of life and of balance." The creaking wood words seemed to sink into their souls. They didn't spark questions and thoughts didn't wander through the various potential implications of the words, they were more soaked up like the warming rays of sunshine that poured down upon them and they listened earnestly soaking it all up.

"Seasonal change brings about the most bountiful produce when caretakers tend to the earth. When the ground is turned, the crops flourish more. It is the honor of the Brite's guardians to turn the ground. Your efforts decide how bountiful the crop will be. You have been chosen." The tree being said, before growing silent.

It was the first time since the being had begun speaking that questions came to Steph. He calmly turned on the warm stone to face the blue and purple leaf-colored, tree figure and asked, "How do we 'turn the ground'?"

He felt warmth emanating from the tree-like being when he asked it, and then the thing responded, "The Brite brings light to cleanse the land of darkness and to usher in a new crop for a time. Just like turning the ground breaks up the soil to make way for new life, breaking up the places where darkness hides, makes way for the light. The more diligently you turn the ground young guardians, the more the light will cleanse this season and usher in the next. Just as the farmer destroys the tough land to usher in life, the guardian must destroy the strongholds of darkness to usher in the light. Eat and drink your fill, rest your fragile bones, and when you are ready choose whatever tools you like from the forest and prepare yourself. The Brite will be with you soon and the work will begin." As the final words were said, a kind of chill seemed to come from the being and it took on the look of a motionless tree.

As Steph and G'noch ate and rested, they noticed the sunlight shift to a path in the forest across the stream from them. G'noch looked at Steph and then said, "G'noch ready. Come, see what tools the tree gives." The large T'kche stood up and stared at Steph, obviously waiting to be joined.

Steph stood and followed G'noch as he stepped from stone to stone and crossed the stream. Once across, they walked to the path that was strangely lit up by sunlight and entered the forest, not knowing what to expect, but feeling a strong sense of peace and calm, nonetheless.

CHAPTER 23
Time of the Brite

Steph and G'noch once again found themselves standing on the top of the grassy hill. They were joined by the ancient treelike being with the blue and purple leaves fanning out over the top of its head. It was this same ancient being that had seemingly appeared in the forest and ushered them up here hours earlier.

Steph didn't know how long G'noch and he had been in there, time was funny in this strange place, but he knew they had definitely taken their time. When the tree being had told them to choose their tools, Steph assumed that maybe there would be wooden clubs or quarterstaves, after all, they were in a forest being ruled by tree people. As soon as the path opened into the large clearing, he realized he couldn't have been more wrong.

It had been a large circular clearing with what appeared to be a large stone in the center that seemed like a huge table. The clearing seemed to have the same solid tree wall that the outside of this entire place had, except the one opening where the path fed into it. Hanging all over the tree wall were weapons of all shapes and sizes. There were no firearms or explosives, but there were certainly steel blades, clubs and war hammers galore.

Steph and G'noch had made their way around the clearing eagerly, testing the weight, feel, and balance of countless weapons before the purple and blue leafed ancient had appeared out of nowhere and ushered them back up to the hilltop. In the end, Steph had chosen a huge sword that he now had strapped on his back. It looked like a mighty two handed weapon, but the strange metal was so light that it could easily be wielded with one hand.

G'noch on the other hand had chosen a massive club, which was no surprise to Steph whatsoever, but it was far from a normal club. The thing was about six feet long, got progressively larger from the handle to the massive end and was covered in large spikes. It appeared to be made of the same metal substance that Steph's sword was made of, making it incredibly lightweight, despite its massive size. G'noch now rested it over his huge shoulder while he stood next to Steph on the hilltop waiting.

Before long, the other two ancient tree-like beings appeared and between them was Mila, glowing that bright white light from all over and hovering in the air at a height that made her level with the heads of the fifteen-foot-tall tree like beings.

"The time of the Brite is upon us." Said the ancient tree being with the short cropping of multi shades of green leaves on top of its head.

Then Mila spoke in that same ominous other worldly voice, "Steph, G'noch, I thank you both for guiding me here. It is my time now; this world needs the Brite and I will need you both once more. Will you help me save this world?"

The scene felt overwhelming to Steph, there was a heaviness to the air and her statement seemed to encompass much more than a request to travel with her. No, it felt more like she was going to some final battle that she didn't expect to survive and wanted to know if they were willing to fight and die with her. He didn't know how to respond or what to do, so he did what G'noch did and simply nodded his head.

Mila nodded back, still shining brilliantly and it almost looked like the ancient tree people all nodded too. "How in the world does G'noch know exactly what to do?" Steph thought.

Then Mila spoke again and this time it rang out even louder, "We will travel to the dark temple, the heart of this season's darkness, and I will cleanse this age and usher in the next season. You will escort, protect, and then engage the darkness lest the cleansing be incomplete. Your diligence will dictate the next season of this world."

This time Steph couldn't just nod, despite the tension in the entire forest around him, it was time he spoke up. "Brite or no Brite, Mila's still my big sister," he thought.

"What do you mean engage the darkness? I understand, or really I don't, that you're something different now Mila, but if we are to play a part in all this you've got to give me a little more than that. I'm with you, no matter what. Just tell me what we're going to do and what you need from us," Steph said, getting louder as he spoke. He expected to get awkward glares from G'noch and the tree people, but instead they all seemed oddly pleased by his response and his questions.

"You will need to ensure that my light can reach them Steph. Shatter their temple, lead them out, whatever you do and how you choose to do it, are up to you. It is your responsibility as a guardian to decide and act, but the light must reach them all or my time has been for nothing, and the world will be stuck in the same season." Mila said in response.

"Wait, so me and G'noch have to tear down a fortress or lure a bunch of what, dark ones outside? And why are you talking like you're going to die or something. Just light them up and we'll move on," Steph said with growing concern.

"Steph, it is my time. I am the Brite of this season, like a star that will cleanse the land of darkness and usher in the next season, my light will encompass all of this world and when it does, I will be no more. It has to be done," Mila said it all with authority, with honor and with dignity. Steph was crushed by the words, but he couldn't find his voice to argue.

In that instant he knew, somehow just knew deep down, that it had to be done. Somehow, he knew that the dark ones would spread like a parasite and ravage this world if she didn't do it. Somehow, he knew this was how it always happened, they were wiped out and slowly they spread again until the next … "the next what? The next season?" he thought to himself.

As he dwelt on the words, a strange sense of understanding seemed to wash over him. "This world's seasons are not like the weather seasons of our world, it has seasons of creatures that come and go, that rule the land and then are wiped out only for others to rule in their place. Weather is geographically driven here, but it is not seasonal like the 'top-side' world. Here seasons are with species and otherworldly forces or something like that." He thought through it all and just knew that he was right, he knew that was exactly what it was. He didn't know if this was something implanted in his mind from the aging or something else, but he knew he had to help Mila and that he would never see her again after.

When Steph snapped out of his thoughts of realization, he noticed the ancient tree being with the short green leaves on its head staring at him, and he had the eerie feeling that this being might have more to do with his sudden understanding than anything the Na'gee wise ones had done to him.

Then the ancient tree being, with the yellow and orange leaves flowing down from its head to its shoulders spoke, "You have been here longer than you know, it is time. Follow the sun's path out the far side of our forest and you will be close to your destination. Good luck guardians. Serve the Brite well."

Then the blue and purple leafed tree being spoke in the deep voice that sounded like creaking wood, "Turn the earth well and the crops of the next season will be bountiful."

In an instant all three of the ancient tree beings seemed to be gone. They still stood on the hill, but they were motionless and seemed like nothing more than strange trees. Their presence wasn't felt the same as it had been moments before.

Then sunlight appeared to shine in a straight line from where they stood on top of the hill, down the backside of the hill, and through a path that appeared on the far edge of the forest.

Mila turned, still floating in the air and began to float along, following the path of light down the backside of the hill. G'noch patted Steph on the shoulder roughly, but lovingly nonetheless, and began walking behind her, following the sunlit path.

Steph stood a moment longer and then pulled himself together. "I always knew she was special," He thought. "If this is her purpose, to

save this world, then I will see to it that nothing stands in her way."
Feelings of pride, obligation and a sense of honor seemed to make
him feel taller and stronger, as he hurried to catch up to G'noch and
begin his journey.

CHAPTER 24
Preparation

After a crude, yet rather tasty breakfast of various cuts of meat in the Roken's makeshift dining hall, Grifter led Eva out of the great hall and around the building. As they circled the large great hall that sat in the center of the castle walls, she saw three large circular rings behind the hall.

Each ring was on the dirt and was made from large stones placed in the shape of a circle. There was a small wooden shack with double doors next to each ring. Each of these shacks had their doors wide open and a variety of medieval weaponry was inside and hanging on the inside of each door. This was no doubt a training yard.

Other than the two of them, the yard was empty. Grifter once again seemed to respond to Eva's thoughts by saying, "I instructed everyone to clear out of the training yard today, Eva. I am sure you have noticed that many of my kind strongly oppose having a human around, let alone helping one, regardless of debts of honor." Grifter looked disgusted as he said the last part. Eva could tell that this creature, this Roken, cared for his people and was greatly disturbed that any of them would consider taking a dishonorable approach to anything, ever. Grifter paused for a moment and then continued, "Humans do not have huge favor in my eyes, but I understand that not all of a species can be judged by the actions of a few. You and your friend freed us from captivity, even when we arrived with your enemies, and I am in your debt and intend to repay it. Regardless, we are going to battle dark ones, who are formidable foes. I need to know you are prepared to battle them. I will help you prepare, but my people do not need to see your skills." As Grifter finished speaking he stared at Eva, seeming to gauge her level of understanding. After several seconds it got awkward, so Eva responded by saying, "I understand."

"Good," Grifter said. "Now, choose your weapon."

In response, Eva simply patted the assault rifle slung over her shoulder and said, "This is my weapon of choice." Grifter eyed the assault rifle, pointed at a large square column of wood across the yard, one that Eva had failed to notice earlier, and said "Show me."

Eva looked at the large wooden column coming out of the dirt. It was covered in claw marks and gouged from some sort of blades all over. The column stood about ten feet tall and was a solid square piece of wood that looked about eight feet by eight feet in width.

After staring at her target for a moment, Eva quickly raised the assault rifle and fired several rounds into the center of the column. Every shot hit the same exact spot, which Eva was quite proud of.

"Yeah, all that training with Halbred has really paid off," she thought to herself.

Grifter stared at her, then calmly walked over to the column and inspected the area that the shots had hit. After a moment, he walked back over to Eva and asked, "Do you know why the cursed Na'gee all wear those large blades on their sides?"

Eva shrugged in response.

Grifter continued, "It's because these metal propulsion weapons won't kill the dark ones. They may slow them down, but you have to remove their heads to kill them." Grifter once again paused for effect and then pointed at the closest wooden shack of weapons and said choose one. We will work until we find what best suits you, Eva."

Eva didn't like this at all but figured it couldn't be worse than training with Halbred, plus she didn't really want to die fighting dark ones, so she went to the shed and surveyed her options. There were axes of all shapes and sizes, swords, scythes, and a variety of other bladed weapons to choose from. After careful consideration and the realization that she'd never fought with anything like any of these weapons, she finally chose a long sword that resembled a katana.

With sword in hand, Eva turned to face Grifter who had moved over to the center of the closest ring and was holding a large wooden stick. He was still in human form and while muscular, he wasn't that large of a human and didn't seem that intimidating to Eva. She stepped into the ring and Grifter simply said, "Attack".

Eva hesitated for only a second, but it was oddly familiar to how Halbred started a sparring session, so she did as she was told and attacked.

Eva came in swinging the large katana downward aiming to swipe Grifter from his left shoulder to his right waist. Grifter effortlessly leaned back, just enough for the blade to barely miss him and then reached in with the large stick he held and slapped the blade forward adding to its momentum. The effect made Eva lurch just slightly in the direction the blade was going and feel the gentle touch of Grifter's stick jab her in the neck.

"Again," Grifter said.

This time Eva didn't bother resetting, she just swung up from the leaning position she was in, aiming to slice Grifter across both legs. He jumped back this time and Eva followed him with another wild sideways swing, aimed at the center of his body.

Grifter stepped into this swing and holding his stick with two hands, whacked Eva in the neck, again.

Eva fell backwards this time, landing roughly on the dirt behind her.

"Do your people not know how to battle with their hands? Can you only throw things from afar with your firearms?" Grifter asked, not trying to hide his disappointment and ridicule.

They had only just begun, and Eva had enough already.

"Sure, we know how to fight, just not with your ridiculous stone age weapons. This isn't the damn crusades, Grifter!" Eva roared as she jumped to her feet and threw the sword down onto the ground.

"Show me," Grifter said.

Eva roared and rushed at Grifter. Despite her rage, Eva had been trained well and she took everything in, instantly. She noticed that

Grifter still held the large stick. She noticed that Grifter stood with both hands towards the center of the stick, which he held out in front of him, and that his left leg was slightly in front of his body, while his right leg was slightly bent behind him. The slightly sideways stance told Eva that he would likely rear back away from whatever attack she threw at him and then lunge forward, leading with the right hand and using the bent right leg behind him to provide the power behind the lunge.

Eva processed it all in seconds, like Halbred had taught her to and decided to knock his plans out from under him, almost literally.

She lunged up and reared back with her right fist as she rushed him, feigning like she would swing at him. As he started to lean backwards, like she expected, she dropped onto her right side, still rushing forward and swept his left leg away with her left foot, while colliding with his back, right leg with her right foot that was sliding across the ground.

The move caught Grifter off guard and sent him falling forward as Eva slid out from underneath him, planted her feet and jolted upright. She turned and swung down, fast enough to catch Grifter in the back of the head as he fell.

The result of her flurry of moves was Grifter's face crashing hard into the ground, sending blood splatting out from each side of his head when he hit.

Eva backed up and prepared herself for his counter.

Grifter slowly got up and turned to face her. Blood was streaming from his nose which Eva thought might be broken, but the man had a smile from ear to ear.

"You are no soft human, Eva. I am impressed," Grifter said, in a more jovial tone that she'd heard him use before.

"I expected him to be enraged and attack me with everything he had, but instead I bust his face and he looks pleased. This is just like training with Halbred," Eva thought to herself.

"You are right, Eva. You are far too advanced for swords, a formidable weapon for our ancestors with far less skill. I have just the thing for you," Grifter said, with a hint of excitement in his voice, and he dashed off to the wooden shack of weapons by the sparring circle furthest from them. When Grifter came back he was carrying two fairly small metal gauntlets.

"Try these on, Eva," Grifter said, still appearing to be holding back excitement.

Eva shrugged and took the gauntlets, putting them both on. To her surprise, she could move her fingers and her hands. They were thick and made of some sort of metal, but they let her hands move like wearing well-fitting leather gloves.

"I like them, Grifter, but it still doesn't help me cut off heads," Eva said as she gave Grifter a questioning look.

"Squeeze your thumb against the knuckle of your forefinger," Grifter said.

Eva did as Grifter asked, and a long blade came out of the top of each gauntlet. Each blade was the size of a small machete, but slightly wider. Even with the long blade sticking out from the top of the gauntlets, Eva was amazed at how light they were. She immediately shared the excitement that she had sensed with Grifter.

When she looked up at Grifter, with excitement in her eyes, she watched his grin get replaced with a more serious look and then he took off the tan cloak he was wearing and threw it outside of the sparring ring and his body began to change.

A moment later, Eva was not staring at the smaller man that had been sparring with her, but a huge wolfman-type beast that was almost as big as G'noch.

"Now, Eva, I will teach you how to fight dark ones and Roken alike. Attack!" Grifter roared.

The two had fought all day. Eva had lost many, but by the end she felt that she had been holding her own. More importantly, she had learned many moves that were specifically designed to take your opponent's head. By the end of the day, she absolutely loved the gauntlets and planned on never taking them off.

Evening had come and Grifter walked her to her room again, now back in his human form. She thought of telling him about the attempt on her life the night before, but she thought that it may cause turmoil in the ranks and that if so, it could potentially delay their departure to rescue Halbred, so she chose to remain silent.

As she entered her room, Grifter said, "We leave at first light. Be ready… and Eva, remember do not leave your room. I fear it may not be safe for you here."

"Yeah, you think?" Eva thought to herself, but instead of sharing her thoughts, she simply said, "I understand."

The door closed and Eva locked it. Then she walked over to the bed and grabbed the thick blanket off of it. Standing in the middle of the room, Eva once again used the talisman to open the 'blur' or pathway to the 'top side' world and stepped through onto the thick snow. She was pleased to see that the hole she had dug and used to sleep in, or try to get some sleep in, the night before was still there and hadn't been covered up. Exhausted from the day of hard training, Eva wrapped herself in the thick blanket and crawled into the hole in the snow, intent on getting some sleep before having to face the following day.

Several hours later, Eva's eyes popped open. She knew it was time to go back. Her internal clock told her that it was almost dawn on the 'other side'. Despite the cold she felt in her bones and the stiffness she felt all over, she felt better overall. Exhaustion had ultimately prevailed over cold and discomfort, and Eva had gotten some sleep.

As she climbed out of the hole in the snow, dragging the frozen blanket behind her, Eva thought "After not finding me the first night they probably didn't bother coming back. I probably froze in this hole in the snow for no reason."

Her thoughts sparked feelings of frustration and she grumpily used the talisman to open the 'blur' or the path back to the 'other side'. As the 'blur' appeared, she stepped through with her frozen blanket.

As soon as Eva crossed through the 'blur' and into her quarters, she saw him. He appeared to be a fairly large human male, wearing a tan burlap-looking cloak or monk's robe. Eva knew better, she knew this was a Roken. His hood was pulled back and he had thick, wild grayish-brown hair.

As Eva entered the room, he jumped, obviously startled, and turned to face her, staring at her with those red eyes. She had no doubt that this was Luca. Her eyes quickly shifted to the long thin knife in his hand, and then movement in her peripheral drew her attention to the much larger man in a similar rough, tan robe, standing just inside the closed bedroom doors.

"Runak", she remembered him from the night before, and she noticed that he too carried a long slim knife.

The sun was just starting to rise, she thought it would be safe to come back now, but apparently, they had decided to wait for her.

"Makes sense." Eva thought. "This is their last chance to stop the raid on the dark ones. Grifter said we'd be leaving at sunrise today. If I'm gone there's no point in going, or at least they'll have a good argument to not go."

As the thoughts were running through her mind, she was already easing back into the 'blur'. She stepped back with one foot, and both men took off for her. She was less worried about Luca, as he was across the room from her, but the large one, Runak, who stood by the doors, was not far from her at all.

She dove the rest of the way through the 'blur', her body hitting the snow, and while laying in the snow, quickly used the talisman to close the 'blur' behind her.

She exhaled deeply, rolled over in the snow, and saw the knife coming down at her. Eva instinctively rolled to the side, dodging the stabbing blow, and leapt to her feet.

She turned to face her opponent and saw Runak. He stared at her for only a split second, showing no emotions whatsoever, and then he lunged forward, attempting to stab her in the gut with the long slim knife.

Eva sidestepped the lunge, and swung hard with her right fist, delivering a powerful right hook to the side of Runak's head. The large Roken in man form stumbled and then turned to look at her and snarled. Blood trickled from his eye and the side of his mouth. The damage her right hook had done to this large man shocked Eva, until she realized that she still wore the gauntlets that Grifter had given her. She had never bothered to take them off.

Runak threw the knife down in the snow and tossed his cloak aside. His form was starting to change as he spoke, "You would let him lead our people to death. You are no different than all the other humans. You plot with the Na'gee and use Grifter's sense of honor to lure us all to death. You want us and the dark ones to kill each other. I will not let it happen. You do not fool me!"

He roared the last words as the transformation was almost complete.

Eva instantly realized that he thought he was saving her people by killing her and would do anything it took to end her. She also realized that she had a much better chance of maybe living through this if she attacked while he was still changing. Then the next thoughts flooded her mind, and she leapt into action.

"I just hope this works." Eva thought as she engaged the blades on her gauntlets and spun towards the transforming Runak. She spun past his right side and sliced him open just below the arm with both gauntlet blades. The spin sent her past his side behind him. Once there, she grabbed the talisman with one hand and used the other hand to slice the back of his right leg open, just behind the knee.

Runak roared and fell slightly forward towards his injured right side. Just as the 'blur' appeared next to Eva, she stepped backwards through it and quickly closed it, just as she saw the fully transformed Runak turning around to face her.

Eva closed the 'blur' as quickly as she opened it, and then immediately looked around. She was standing in the hallway outside her quarters, looking at Grifter who was about to knock on the outside of her bedroom door.

"Eva? How did you get out here?" Grifter asked.

Out of breath and panicked, she blurted out, "Open it! He's in there! He's trying to kill me!" Without hesitation, Grifter kicked in the door and darted into the room.

Eva stood in the hall huffing and puffing, blood dripping from the blades on her gauntlets.

Moments later, Grifter emerged from the room with a curious look on his face.

"There is no one there, Eva. Who attacked you? Whose blood runs down your blades?" Grifter asked.

Just then three more Roken came walking up the hall behind Eva, at a brisk pace. There was a thin, shorter man with his hood pulled low, on the left, a stocky, dark haired woman with her hood thrown back on the right and Luca walked in the middle.

Luca's hood was thrown back as well, and he called out, "Grifter, what is it? We heard commotion from the hall". As Eva saw them approaching, she retreated back towards Grifter.

"It was Runak" she whispered to Grifter, "and him".

Grifter looked at her surprised, when he heard her last comment. He studied her eyes for a moment and then looked up at Luca and the two Roken with him.

"Where is Runak?" Grifter asked.

"We haven't seen him all morning, Grifter." Luca replied. "What has happened, Grifter? Whose blood does the human wear?"

"Runak tried to murder the human. Were you not aware of his intentions, Luca? Were you not with him this night?" Grifter asked sternly.

Luca's red eyes lit up in immediate anger. "I have been open about my feelings regarding helping humans, Grifter, but I am still honorable. Of all the time we have spent together, I have followed. Why would you doubt me now? Why would you accuse me of sneaking in shadows to challenge your commands?!" Luca got louder as he spoke and stepped closer. The man and woman on either side remained where they had initially stopped, but their eyes were locked on Grifter and glanced at Eva here and there.

Grifter remained silent for a moment, staring at Luca. He appeared unaffected by the man's words and seemed to be contemplating whether he believed him or not. Finally, he looked past Luca and asked, "How long have you all been in the gathering hall this morning?"

The woman spoke first, "We have been there hours before sunrise as is the custom before a day of battle. Luca has been with us. We have not seen Runak."

Grifter stared at the woman, and she stared back. Finally, he said, "Thank you, Lerra. Eva must have been mistaken about who was with Runak. Go see if you can find him and see if anyone else is missing." The woman nodded and took off. The slim man left with her, but Luca stayed, still staring at Grifter.

"You are right, my friend. I mean you no dishonor. Hatred of the humans can provoke even the most honorable of our kind. Eva is not like the other humans, but I still fear everyone sees her that way. I was wrong to accuse you, Luca." Grifter said.

Luca stared at him a moment longer and then nodded, before saying, "I understand, Grifter. My claws are yours today and forever. I do not like these humans, but if you say she is different, then it is so. If you say we will slaughter dark ones and free her friend on this day, then dark ones will die."

Then Luca looked past Grifter, directly at Eva and said, "You have nothing to fear from me, Eva. I am with Grifter no matter what. You will not be hurt by my claws or anyone else's while I'm around."

With that, Luca slightly bowed his head and started to walk away. As he walked down the hall, he said, "I will find Runak the betrayer and bring you his head, Grifter".

Grifter looked at Eva and said, "It could not have been Luca, but I have no doubt that Runak was involved. Where did he flee to and how did you get into the hall with the door still locked?"

Eva looked at Grifter and thought about telling him he was wrong about Luca, but then decided it wouldn't help anything. "It may even delay things." She thought.

"I tried to escape him, by leaving this world and going to mine, Grifter. He followed me. I wounded him and came back here, leaving him in my world." Eva said.

Grifter looked at her curiously, then grabbed her by the arm gently and pulled her into the room that she had stayed in. He looked at her intently and said, "Show me."

Eva triggered the talisman, the 'blur' appeared, and they both stepped through. A moment later Eva and Grifter stood on the thick snow. Eva saw her hole and saw blood splattered all over the white snow just past it. The blood streaked off into the distance.

"He is gone. We will hunt this traitor down after we free your friend." Grifter said as he surveyed the landscape. Then his eyes rested on the hole in the snow, and he looked back at Eva. He did not say a word, but his look told her he knew where she had spent the night.

"This is the other world that the Na'gee travel too?" Grifter asked. "Yes, but much of it looks very different than this." Eva replied.

"I will have you show me and teach me more once my debt is paid. Is that agreeable to you, Eva?" Grifter asked.

"Yes." Eva replied.

Grifter nodded and then he grinned, "So, you have evaded one of the more powerful Roken warriors for what looks to be two nights" he said eyeing the hole in the snow that Eva had slept in, "and then wounded him and left him stranded in another world. You are definitely not an ordinary human, Eva. I am proud to have you with the pack that I'm leading to battle." Grifter said with a degree of pride as he and Eva stepped back through the 'blur'.

As they closed the 'blur' behind them and walked out of the room and into the hall Grifter said, "It is rare to see a human so formidable, Eva."

As they walked, Eva mumbled, "Wait'll you meet my husband and we're not even the ones with powers."

Grifter raised an eyebrow, but only said, "Let us go. It is time for the pack to begin our trek to battle. We have a full day of hiking, if we move swiftly, we should arrive at the dark temple by evening."

CHAPTER 25
"It Doesn't make sense"

Vic skidded his dirt bike to a stop next to Samuel, kicking dirt and frost, covered leaves up into the air around them. When he killed the motor, silence washed over them like a wave.

They had been riding for several hours, headed in the general direction of Eva and Halbred. They had seen a few strange creatures, but so far the dirt bikes had served them well, allowing them to maneuver through the wild forests of the 'other side' at a fast enough pace to be able to avoid any encounters. This was their first break since they had crossed over and started riding that morning. They needed to stretch their legs and refuel the bikes.

Both Samuel and Vic had killed the engines of their bikes, refueled them, left them leaning on their kickstands in a small clearing in the cold woods, and were stretching their legs a few feet away, when Vic broke the silence.

"I'm going after Eva," Vic said. He didn't add anything else to it, didn't ask Samuel if he was coming, he just simply stated his intention and stared at Samuel.

"It doesn't make any sense, Vic." Samuel said.

Vic was slightly surprised at Samuel's response, thinking that Samuel would offer to go with him after Eva or at least split up and go after Halbred, while Vic went to his wife. He did not expect Samuel to challenge his intentions to go after his wife.

"What the hell is he even thinking?!" Vic thought.

Samuel watched Vic, considering what he had said, and then saw Vic slowly remove his pistol and raise it towards him. "Whoa, what are you doing, Vic? Just listen to me, it doesn't make any sense." Samuel said.

Vic's only reply was "Fuck that and don't move," as he aimed the large .50 caliber pistol directly at Samuels head. Vic paused for just a second longer and then squeezed the trigger.

BAM!!!

The sound of the gun blast echoed through the cold forest and through Samuel's head. It took only a split second for Samuel to realize he hadn't been shot. He quickly turned and saw a huge hairy spider of some kind squirming on the ground behind him.

The spider was at least the size of a large hog, and it was covered with thick black hair. Green ooze or blood was squirting from its mid-section, as it shook and rolled on the ground.

Samuel quickly pulled his two 9mm pistols from his hidden shoulder holsters and looked up. Slowly climbing down the trees circling the clearing were, several more of these giant spiders. Vic obviously saw them too, because he fired again, blowing another one off a nearby tree.

Samuel joined in, unleashing gunfire from both of his pistols at two different spiders, both fell from the trees to the ground.

Without a word, and while still firing, both men slowly moved towards the center of the clearing and stood back-to-back, firing away at spider after spider. The creatures seemed to keep coming and coming. Despite at least twelve dead, there seemed to be at least twenty more that had actually made it to the ground and were slowly advancing on the two men. It didn't seem to matter how many they shot, more joined the ranks and the slow advance continued. Vic and Samuel were cut off from their bikes, which were not only their escape route, but also where Vic's assault rifle and Samuel's shotgun were stashed.

"They're getting close! We're about to have to start squishing these damn things with our hands Samuel. You think you can freeze spiders?" Vic called out.

Before Samuel could answer, the spiders stopped their advance. For a moment they didn't move, then suddenly they turned and took off back to the trees, climbing up them much faster than they had climbed down them just moments before.

Vic and Samuel exchanged concerned looks, and both simultaneously took off running for their bikes. No words were needed, both men had the same thought running through their minds, "If the spiders took off that fast, something worse must be coming".

Vic hopped on his bike, as Samuel did the same, and then he called out to Samuel, "Go help Halbred. I'll go to Eva. We can't call on these damn watches, but I can make it alert you if I need your help!" Vic started up his bike, not waiting for a response, right when the beast came crashing through the woods.

It was as big as an elephant, was running at them on all fours, and had a long tail. The beast was covered in gray skin, that also looked very much like an elephant's skin, and had a head shaped almost like a huge hairless dog. It had enormous tusks and rows of jagged teeth between them.

The beast was running at them fast, and Vic didn't wait around for Samuel to respond to his suggestion, he just took off on the dirt bike.

Samuel yelled, "Wait Vic! It doesn't make sense!" as he took off on his bike, heading right or further northeast, towards Halbred's location, while Vic headed left, or North west, towards Eva's location.

The creature chose Samuel and was quickly in pursuit.

Samuel saw the beast gaining on him, unable to go full speed as he navigated through the thick trees of the cold forest. The creature behind him didn't have the same problem and seemed to be speeding up. Samuel could feel it gaining on him and knew he'd have to find a quick way to put some distance between him and the large beast. With that in mind, he yanked his bike hard to the side and skidded around a tree he was passing, turning around it back towards the way he had come and pulling the shotgun from the bike's side holster as he turned.

Samuel almost crashed into the side of the beast, which had obviously not expected its fleeing prey to turn around and come back at it. To avoid slamming into the side of the pursuing beast,

Samuel had only one option; he laid the bike down and slid across the ground with it, directly under the creature. As he slid under the beast, he fired the shotgun at the creature's huge legs.

By the time Samuel and the bike came sliding to a stop on the other side of the large creature, it was laying on its side with its two back legs blown to pieces.

Samuel stood up stiffly, left his bike lying on the ground, walked over to the wriggling beast and shot it in the head with the shotgun, putting it out of its misery.

"This place is never boring," Samuel thought, as he stared at the newest reminder that humans were not anywhere near the top of the food chain here.

Then he heard the faint scuffling and noticed the large spiders scrambling back down the trees all around him.

"Not this time. Vic will catch on soon enough," Samuel thought as he rushed over to the dirt bike, picked it up off the ground and took off.

After several miles of riding, Vic skidded the bike to a stop. He looked up, before he bothered looking around, just to make sure nothing was dangling above his head.

"It's bad enough we gotta look around every damn tree for who knows what kind of monster or damn dino beast is lurking, now we gotta worry about giant insects too. This sure ain't a place to get a vacation timeshare." Vic mumbled as he checked his watch to pinpoint Eva's location.

"What? That's not where she was earlier. She's moving at a steady pace and I'm heading in a big circle towards where she was earlier today." Vic looked up at the sky and then back at his watch. "Midday, huh? She keeps moving at this pace in a straight line like she's been doing then she's likely to end up…" Vic paused as he zoomed out on the watch's map.

"Damn. Right where Halbred is. She should be there by this evening. That's why Samuel kept saying it doesn't make sense." Vic pulled up Samuel's coordinates. "I can still catch back up to him if I really push this thing." He thought.

Vic started the bike back up and took off, as he went, he muttered, "I damn sure hate it when he's right."

Vic pushed the bike hard. He moved it as fast as he could, darting in and out of the trees, cutting through the forest at extremely high speeds. Part of Vic thought that one wrong turn could end with him dead in a bike wreck in this weird world, but the other part of him loved it, loved the adrenaline rush and that excitement that came with it.

He didn't bother stopping the bike again to check Samuel's coordinates, he figured he had a general sense of where he was going and that he'd never catch him if he stopped again, so on he went.

An hour of riding later, Vic saw Samuel ahead of him, zig-zagging around the trees as he rode through the forest. Vic pushed the bike even harder, and in no time, he was riding right next to Samuel.

Samuel glanced at him and gave him a little nod.

"He's right again, and the bastard doesn't even rub it in with a cocky smile or anything. It almost makes it worse," Vic thought as he rode on next to Samuel. He glanced up at the sky and thought, "If we keep up this pace, we should make it to Halbred's location right around sunset. Great. Sunset in weird world, that'll be loads of fun."

CHAPTER 26
What's y our plan?

As Steph, G'noch, and Mila walked through the thick forest, they noticed that the clear, defined path slowly faded away. As the path seemed to disappear into the frost-covered forest floor, the trees and life of the forest around them seemed to change as well. Not a drastic change, a change almost felt more than seen, but a change nonetheless. A shared glance between G'noch and Steph was all the confirmation they needed to know it wasn't just them. They knew that somehow, they were not in the forest of the Ancients anymore.

As if on cue with their thoughts, a large snake slithered across their line of sight in the distance ahead. Its exact size was difficult to tell because of the distance between them and the snake, but Steph guessed that it had to be at least fifty feet long and eight to ten feet in diameter at its thickest section.

G'noch eyed the large snake and turned his head to follow the direction the snake was heading through the woods, despite it disappearing from sight. A moment later, G'noch reached out one of his large hands and grabbed Steph's shoulder, while simply saying, "Stop".

The large T'kche warrior then turned and faced behind them, easing his massive spike club off his shoulder and holding it to the side of him, at the ready. Steph grabbed Mila's arm gently and said, "Wait, Mila, there might be trouble". As he said the words, he noticed that the glowing white light faded away from Mila. It just went away, leaving her standing there looking more like a normal young girl than she had in months. Mila looked at Steph and nodded, with a sense of 'knowing' in her eyes, then she stepped back a few paces.

Steph turned to face, whatever was coming up from behind them had gotten G'noch's attention, and when he did, he saw the large black snake easing out of the trees to face them. It was bigger than Steph had thought from a distance. Its head was larger than G'noch by far, each of its black eyes was larger than their heads.

The snake flicked its long-forked tongue out, flashing its massive fangs when it did and kept slithering towards them. Steph was reminded of stories of giant dragons that his father told him about at bedtime, as the creature before him dwarfed anything that was ever described as a snake.

"One thing is for sure, this thing is looking at us like we're its next meal," Steph thought. Instinctively, he pulled the large two-handed broadsword from the sheath on his back and held it before him. Once again, Steph marveled at how light the huge sword was in his hands.

The snake was within ten feet of them, when it stopped moving and stared at them both.

G'noch glanced at Steph and nodded, just as the snake raised its head as if preparing to strike… then it did!

With lightning speed that didn't seem to fit a creature of such enormous size, it darted its giant head towards them with its jaws opened wide and its fangs flashing. G'noch did not wait, nor did he dive to the side or run for cover, he simply leaped into the air straight at the snake's massive head. Without thinking, Steph took three quick steps towards the snake and leapt into the air as well.

G'noch swung the club in the air and caught the snake on the side of the head with such incredible force, that the snake's head went flying towards the left, directly in front of where Steph was leaping. Steph came down with the two-handed sword in midair, swinging with all of his strength.

G'noch landed first, then the snake's head that was no longer attached to its body, and then finally Steph's feet hit the ground. The two of them watched the gigantic snake's body twist and thrash, while the head rolled off in the woods. Steph felt an incredible rush, washing over him.

"That thing was huge, and we killed it in like two seconds, G'noch!" Steph blurted out as he turned to face his large, hairy friend. When he did, he saw the second snake of equal size, in mid-strike, coming straight for G'noch, who was facing him.

With no time to think, Steph rushed his friend, shoving him to the side, raising his sword over his head, and dropping to his knees as he slid forward, just when the snake was striking downwards at them.

As the snake came down and Steph slid forward across the ground on his knees, below it, his sword sliced through the center of the snake's head. It cut through the beast without even slowing Steph's slide, like a knife through hot butter. By the time the momentum that carried him through his sliding motion stopped, Steph had sliced the snake's head and about six feet down into its body directly in half through the middle.

Each half of the snake's body fell to either sides of him, while he sat on his knees, blood rained down upon him, and he stared ahead at the wriggling seventy feet of snake that was still in one piece.

No rush washed over him this time, Steph sat on his knees in a daze, shocked at what had just happened and what he was able to do without even thinking. He felt a rough pat on his back and turned his head to see G'noch's outstretched hand. Steph took the offered hand and G'noch hauled him up to his feet. He was snapped out of his daze, by the gurgling growling noise that he knew to be G'noch's laughter and looked at his friend questioningly.

G'noch took his massive hand and wiped chunks of blood and who knew what else off the top of Steph's head, then patted him roughly on the side of his arm and walked off towards Mila, still carrying on with his growling laughter. Steph figured he'd never understand the strange humor of his T'kche friend, as he slowly followed along.

When they got over to Mila, who seemed to have been watching them the entire time, she stared at each of them for a moment, then the white light emanated from her once more and she began to hover about a foot off the ground. Without a word, she turned and began to glide forward over the ground. G'noch and Steph followed closely, on foot. Before they had made it a few feet, Steph noticed another large snake in the woods, but it was turning away from them, seeming to slither away in a hurry.

The change in behavior was odd to Steph, and for a moment he thought that he and G'noch had scared off the other creatures by their heroic actions, but then his eyes took in the bright glowing light emitting from Mila and another thought occurred to him.

"Is your light scaring them away Mila?" Steph asked as he walked along behind his gliding sister.

Without looking back, he heard Mila respond in the strange otherwordly voice that was apparently hers now, "The light sweeps away all forms of darkness Steph" she said.

"Wait, why did you just step back and turn the light off or whatever it was, when the giant snakes attacked us earlier then?" Steph blurted out the question loudly.

"Your task ahead will not be easy, young Steph. Practice and proficiency will be critical. As you were told by the ancients, the guardian's ability to till the earth will largely dictate the change in the seasons." Mila said while still gliding ahead. Then she added, "We do not have much time, we must make the most of it while we travel towards our destination. Do you know yet what you will do?"

Steph was struck speechless by the response and the question. "So, she let those things attack us to what give us practice?!" He thought, followed by thoughts of the question that she had asked, "Do I know what I'll do yet, huh? Does she expect me to come up with a plan? I thought we were just here to protect her, and she had the plan." Steph's mind wandered through all these thoughts and then he began to think through all that the Ancients had said to him and G'noch. He walked along replaying every interaction with the ancients, over and over in his head.

Steph had no idea how long they had been walking when it hit him. He stopped in his tracks, earning a curious look from G'noch, who also stopped.

"Do you have a plan G'noch? If not, I think I might." Steph said quietly. "G'noch plan kill dark ones. Protect Brite. What Steph plan?" G'noch said.

"The ancients told us we had to get them all outside, in the open, or something like that so she can do her thing. That means we'll have to attack them when it's dark, we don't know how long we'll have to hold them off to lure all of them out, or for Mila to do the Brite thing, so…" Steph stared at G'noch with excitement.

Without waiting for him to finish, G'noch patted Steph on the arm and said "Steph sound like little foot Halbred. You plan. G'noch fight. Come." With that the large T'kche started walking again, following the glowing, gliding Mila.

Steph began walking behind his friend, but his mind was elsewhere. He decided he'd have to cross over to get what he needed. He hoped he'd find what he wanted but had a couple of ideas regardless. "One way or the other, we'll get the fire going and even out the odds. If we're lucky, no not lucky, if we're good enough we should be able to last as long as it takes." He thought to himself.

Later that afternoon, Mila came to a stop and stepped out of the air and onto the ground. She sat cross-legged on the ground immediately and silently and stared off at nothing.

Steph realized this was his time. "She might even have stopped on purpose just to give me time" he thought to himself. "It doesn't matter. Like Mila said earlier, we don't have much time, we need to make the most of it. This is my chance."

"G'noch I need you to watch her, keep her safe. I have to cross over to the 'top side'. I will be back soon. Wait here for me." Steph said.

G'noch nodded, but did not reply. It was good enough for Steph, who immediately began to work the sequence on the stone talisman around his neck, making the 'blur' appear. Steph stepped through and disappeared.

As he stepped out of the 'blur' and into the 'top side' world, Steph closed the 'blur' or the pathway behind him. Once he finished closing it, he took in his surroundings.

He was standing in the middle of a large parking lot. There were tons of cars, trucks and SUVs all scattered about in various parking spaces in front of a large strip mall of stores. He noticed people were stopping in their tracks, whether on foot or in their vehicles to point and stare at him, but Steph didn't care.

"After the things I've faced on the 'other side', this is nothing. Let them stare." Steph thought, as he began walking through the strip mall towards the shopping center. After he walked a few feet, he turned back to look at the spot he had initially appeared at. Looking for some way to identify the location so he could easily rejoin G'noch and Mila after collecting supplies.

He saw certain cars but noticed them pulling in and out of the spaces, even while he watched. "That won't work." He thought. Then Steph's eyes landed on a shopping cart return, mixed into the adjacent row of cars and decided that would be as good as it got. When he looked from left to right though, he noticed several shopping cart returns scattered across the large parking lot.

"I guess I need to mark it, so it stands out." Steph thought as he began approaching the shopping cart return. He slowly pulled the massive two-handed sword from the sheath on his back as he neared the spot, earning him a couple screams of 'he's got a sword' from across the parking lot.

Steph ignored them and swung his sword at the sign above the cart return, slicing the metal sign in half. "There, no way to miss this one now." Steph said to himself, as he re-sheathed his weapon and turned back towards the strip mall.

The store directly ahead of him looked like a large grocery store. Steph noticed there were at least a dozen more stores in the large strip mall, but figured he'd start with this one. His only experience at stores was when he was six years old, being towed along by one of his parents, which was long before the Na'gee had aged him. He had learned much since then but mostly around combat techniques and strategy, nothing about where to shop for what. From what Steph could remember of his childhood, which was less than a year ago, you could get anything you wanted from a grocery store.

"Sounds like just the place for explosives and fire-starting stuff. I couldn't have arrived at a better spot. Grocery stores have everything!" Steph thought excitedly to himself.

CHAPTER 27

Clean Up on Aisle 10

As he walked into the huge grocery store, he noticed some people pointing at him with panicked looks on their faces and others grabbing their belongings or their children and hurrying away from him. While Steph didn't really care much, after all he was a 'Guardian', he had to protect Mila, so she could save the world, these people didn't matter, he still wondered what was so terrifying about his appearance.

Steph turned to look at his reflection in the automated sliding glass doors that he had just entered through and instantly understood the reactions around him.

He saw himself in the same black leather pants and thick brown fur jacket, sure, but that wasn't the noticeable part. What was noticeable and unnerving even to himself, when looking at his own reflection, was that he was still covered in blood from the giant snake, not to mention he had a huge pistol on one hip, an oversized knife on the other hip and a large two-handed sword strapped to his back.

"Wow! I do look scary. No wonder they're all freaked out." Steph thought, slightly amused.

Without a second thought, he began to wander through the grocery store looking for explosives and fire-starting materials, ignoring the random screams and squeals as he entered various aisles.

After several rows of searching, Steph had managed to only come up with a large bag of chips that he casually munched on while he continued to search. He was beginning to grow concerned at how long it was taking, so he decided he needed to speed things up and went back towards the front, in search of someone who worked at the grocery store.

"Excuse me." Steph called out the first person he saw, wearing a green shirt and name tag. The person looked at him, gasped and took off in almost a run, in the opposite direction.

"Really?!" Steph yelled out.

He noticed some people checking out and he decided to approach a cashier for help. Steph walked up to the closest one, who was a short elderly lady.

"Excuse me. I need some help." Steph said.

The old lady kept on ringing up groceries and said, "Go find someone on the floor, I'm busy."

"I tried ma'am. They keep running away from me. I just need help finding a few things and then I'll leave." Steph said in the nicest voice he could muster.

The old lady stopped and turned to look at him, then she gasped "Oh my! Of course they're running from you young man, you're covered in blood and carrying a gun, and what is that on your back… a sword?!"

"Yes ma'am. Like I said, I just need some help finding some things and I'll leave." Steph said.

"You need to get cleaned up, is what you need to do. What are you thinking coming to a grocery store like that? You're old enough to know better." The old woman said in a scolding voice.

"If only she knew how old I really was." Steph thought.

"Well, let's go. Let's get you what you need so you can leave and quit scaring these poor people." With that said the old lady walked away from her register and headed for the aisles, leaving the people in line just standing there.

Steph hurriedly followed her.

"Well, what is it you need?" the old lady said gruffly.

"I need explosives and fire-starting stuff." Steph said, relieved to finally get some help. "Explosives?! What? Are you some terrorist or something?! We don't sell explosives here you fool! We sell groceries!" The old lady yelled at him.

"No, I'm not a terrorist. I have to save someone; it's a matter of life and death. What about fire- starting stuff?" Steph pleaded.

"Well, there's barbecue cookout supplies on aisle ten, but they've already called the police on you, young man, and now that I know you're looking for explosives, I think they did the right thing. I won't help you anymore, terrorist." The old lady said it like she was lecturing him and then stomped off, as she went, she started yelling, "He's trying to make a bomb! He's a terrorist! Everybody run!"

"That's just great," Steph mumbled to himself, as he watched people start screaming and running for the exits.

"I guess I better get what I need and get out of here before the police come, but I didn't break any laws, so they can't do anything to me," Steph thought as he began looking for aisle ten.

Moments later, the grocery store had fallen completely silent, and Steph stood in front of a variety of charcoal, wood chips, lighter fluids, and other barbecue supplies. After a couple minutes of surveying his options, Steph decided this was not the best store he could've chosen.

He stuffed about four jugs of lighter fluid into his jacket pockets, unwrapped a couple of long grill lighters and stuffed them into one of the various pouches on his belt and then thought through his remaining options.

"Well, I could take the empty gas cans down there and go find a gas station to fill them up, I guess, not I'm sure how long that will take though." Steph thought. Then memories of his father grilling in the backyard when he was young filled his mind. "Dad always made huge fires come out of the grill, maybe I just need charcoal?" Steph thought.

He reached down and picked up the two largest bags of charcoal he could find, which to Steph looked bigger than what the shopping carts looked like they were made to hold.

"Freeze right there!" shouted the two police officers at the end of the aisle.

Steph jumped in surprise. He had been so busy 'shopping' that he had not even noticed them approach, let alone draw their guns.

"Whoa! I didn't do anything wrong. Why are you pointing your guns at me?" Steph said calmly to them, thinking that there was no way he could get in trouble if he didn't do anything wrong.

"I said FREEZE! Put down the bags and slowly put your gun on the ground NOW!" one of the officers screamed at him.

"You can't yell at me like that, I haven't done anything wrong!" Steph yelled back.

"We can yell at you any way we damn well want to, and we can shoot you too, if you don't do what we say. Now I won't tell you again… drop the bags and then slowly lower your gun to the ground. Do you understand me, freak?!" The officer roared.

Steph's entire demeanor changed. He thought police officers were there to help people. He thought you couldn't get in any trouble if you didn't do anything wrong. Then Steph thought of Mila, who was counting on him, and made his decision.

"Okay. Okay." Steph said, starting to lower the huge bags of charcoal onto the floor, but instead of setting them on the ground when he leaned down, he hurled them up and at the two police officers. Gun shots rang out, echoing in the grocery store and the bags burst into clouds of black smoke or dust that filled the air before they collided with the police officers.

As soon as Steph threw the bags, he took off running low towards the officers and then dove between them, grabbing one of each officer's legs, while they fired their pistols at the bags of charcoal that he had hurled at them. He yanked them off their feet as he dove between them, by the leg he held in each hand, sending their faces crashing into the floor hard enough to break the tiles and leave the men motionless.

He didn't bother to look back, he took off running for the door, realizing that this was a terrible idea. As he burst out of the front doors, he saw three police cars parked sideways in front of the grocery store. The doors on the cars were open and officers with guns drawn were positioned behind each of the doors. Steph ducked right back inside, as they started yelling for him to get on the ground.

He looked around the entry way of the grocery store for anything he could use to help him escape. There was a video rental machine and a drink vending machine on the opposite side of the entry way. On the side he was on, there were several rows of empty shopping carts, and on the back wall was a large metal cage full of propane tanks.

Steph opened the cage and grabbed a propane tank with each hand. He didn't really know what they were, but he knew they were big, heavy, and still light enough for him to throw them.

"If I throw these at the front two cars, maybe I can dart past them and get to the spot in the parking lot," Steph thought.

He jumped out of the entry way doors and hurled the propane tanks at the closest two police cars. The officers immediately opened fire on the flying propane tanks. The tanks exploded in midair shattering all the glass windows and doors of the front of the grocery store and sending Steph flying backwards, crashing into rows of grocery carts.

"Wow! I thought they didn't have explosives here?" Steph thought as he picked himself up from the ground. "A little bigger than I hoped for, but it will have to do." He thought.

Steph loaded four propane tanks into a large shopping cart and pulled it up behind him. Then he grabbed two more tanks and prepared himself to attack.

"I guess it's them or me. If I don't get past them and get back to G'noch and Mila many more people will die." Steph thought, steeling himself for the violence to come. He peeked around the corner and looked at the officers, then he looked past them at the cart return that marked his way home.

"I just have to take them out and make it twenty or thirty feet," Steph thought to himself, then just before he lunged around the corner and began his assault on the officers, he thought, "Wait, it's just twenty or thirty feet."

Steph stepped back, set down the two propane tanks he was holding, and began to work the sequence on the stone talisman that he wore. The 'blur' appeared, and Steph went through, pushing the shopping cart full of propane tanks.

Moments later, Steph came walking out of the woods into the clearing where G'noch and Mila sat. He was roughly pushing a shopping cart, full of propane tanks, over the frost covered-forest floor.

Mila, slowly stood up from the cross-legged position she had been sitting in and said, "It is time to proceed, Guardians." With that, her feet slowly came off the ground, hovering inches above it, and she began to glide ahead, through the forest.

G'noch rose to his feet, looked curiously at Steph's shopping cart, and began to follow her. Steph wheeled the cart around and tried to keep up, while pushing the old shopping cart over the rough forest floor. It was not fun at all for Steph, and he dreaded hauling the cart through the forest terrain for the rest of their journey, but deep down he felt confident about his plan.

"This is actually better than what I hoped for," He thought to himself, followed by, "I wonder if I can talk G'noch into pushing this damn thing?"

PART 3: Crossing

CHAPTER 28
Dark Season Forever

Halbred had no idea how long he'd been chained up hanging in the dark temple. He felt his body severely weakened from a lack of food and movement in general. They had tried to torture him physically, but like so many other enemies he'd faced in his world, they found torture ineffective on someone with impenetrable skin like Halbred's.

"Still, lack of food is torture enough," Halbred had thought to himself many times.

He had tried to wrench his hands and legs free, but it was useless, they were wrapped far too securely around his arms and legs. On his arms, the old chains wrapped from his wrists to his elbows and then extended tightly in opposite directions to old, rusted pulleys mounted on the ceiling of the large temple room. His legs were similarly secured, from ankle to knee, and each one extended up to a similar set of pulleys on either side of him. The result was Halbred suspended in midair with his body in an X shape.

While he had given up on freeing his hands or feet from the chains themselves, he continued to rotate his arms and legs, jerking them back and forth over and over. Some of it was just to keep some sort of blood circulation flowing through his body, but alternatively he thought he just might be able to crack one of the old, rusted pulleys loose.

"All it takes is one arm free and I'll rain hell on these blood thirsty demons," Halbred had thought many times. He knew he didn't have his pistol or his hatchet, but his belt was still on him, and his pouches still felt full. He had thought through his plan of attack many times during his captivity. With at least six small explosives in his pouches and a long dagger in the back of his belt he figured he could blow a hole in a wall or two and take out at least a handful of the nasty creatures.

"At least two explosives are going right at the big bastard hiding over there in that damn black cloud," he had thought many times.

Halbred didn't know if the giant dark one was always sitting and watching him in that cloud or if the thing vanished and went somewhere else altogether when the dark cloud appeared, but either way, he had decided that the thing was definitely in charge, and when he got free, he was taking its head off even if he had to chew it off with his teeth.

His thoughts of vengeance and violence were abruptly interrupted when he felt his right arm jerk loose. He instantly looked up and saw that the old, rusted pulley had snapped loose from the ceiling and was hanging there. The chain still ran through a large O ring, but it was no longer secured. Halbred, didn't immediately try to pull it all the way free, but he did pull a little, and just as he had thought, he could now pull as much of the chain to him as he wanted to.

"It's on now," he thought. Halbred sat still for a few minutes, contemplating if it was better to pull his arm free and use it to try to snap the other pulleys, or if he should go straight for the explosives and hurl them at the other pulleys.

"I've only got six explosives, if I use them to destroy the other pulleys, I'll be down to three. I don't like that." Halbred thought to himself.

As he continued to contemplate the best way to break free and conserve his resources for the battle that would come next, he saw the creatures pouring in from the large doorway. There had to be at least thirty of them and more were flooding to the room. The dark cloud on the other side of the room started to move towards the center and Halbred didn't move an inch, holding very still and hoping they didn't notice the pulley hanging from the ceiling.

"As long as my arm is still in an upward position, the damn things will probably think I'm secure even if they notice the pulley hanging," he thought.

As the creatures continued to gather and flood into the room, the dark cloud dissipated, revealing the giant dark one who stood before the platform on the far side of the room. It stared at the gathered creatures for several long moments and then it let out a loud hissing noise that seemed to echo through the large chamber.

All the gathered dark ones stopped moving and fell silent, staring at their large leader. The giant dark one paused for another moment and then began to speak in that strange hissing voice.

"The time of the Brite will be coming soon; the voices have warned us. Past generations could only hide or die, and in the end most died. We have other options; we can continue to thrive, to feast, to continue to live on while the world cringes in fear." The giant paused and stared at the huge gathering of dark creatures. After several moments of silence, it continued, "We will leave this world until the time of the Brite has passed. While we are gone, we will begin to crush the other world. The world where this strange being is from." The giant pointed at Halbred.

Halbred held his breath, thinking, "Shit, don't look at me. Look at the big guy and listen to his bullshit. Nothing to see over here, especially not a pulley hanging from the ceiling."

The giant dark one continued, "We do not have the safety of the temple there, so the first night will be key. We must forego the hunt and prepare our new temple if we are to survive the sun of the new world. Tomorrow night we go. We will convert human shelters to temples until a more appropriate location can be established. The voice will tell us when it is safe to return. Our generation will not be extinguished like past generations! We will rule two worlds, the dark season shall last forever!"

The dark cloud slowly surrounded the giant dark one as the last words were spoken, and the gathering of dark ones, hissed and howled strangely. They continued with their rally until the dark cloud had shifted back to the platform on the far side of the room, apparently taking the giant with it, then the creatures began to disperse.

Halbred let out a long exhale and thought through what he had heard. "These damn creatures are going to try to take over my world. If they're able to cross over, the world will never be the same again. I can't let that happen." Concern and determination flooded through, Halbred and he began working twice as hard to yank his left arm loose.

"If I can break all the pulleys loose, it's on. If I can't by tomorrow, I'll use the explosives. Either way, I've got to take this roof down before the sun sets tomorrow. These dark vermin can't be allowed to cross over." Halbred thought, and then he began to count in his head, using it as his only method of timing himself, while he doubled his efforts to break the other pulleys loose like he'd done with his right arm.

After several long moments of tugging and pulling to break the other old rusty pulleys free, like he had done with his right arm, Halbred's patience ran out.

"Enough of this shit, I'm getting out of here now!" Halbred said quietly to himself as he jerked his right arm forward, pulling the loose chain, and the pulley that had broken off the ceiling, to him. He continued these movements, until all the excess chain had pulled through the O-ring. As soon as the last of the chain came through and it dropped downward beneath him, it unwrapped around his arm and fell loudly to the ground.

Halbred was left hanging in midair, with his right arm free, his left arm still stretched upward wrapped in a thick chain, and both legs stretched outward, similarly wrapped in chains. He quickly used his free right arm to grab onto the chain wrapped around his left arm and began yanking as hard as he could. Halbred pulled and pulled, filled with growing concerns that the loud sound of the chain hitting the floor would bring the creatures in to check on him.

"Or worse, it could bring the giant one in the black cloud," he thought.

Suddenly the pulley holding the chain on his left arm in place, broke off of the ceiling. He had pulled with such force to break it free that it immediately brought all the chain through the O-ring with it, and it clattered to the floor, slipping off his arm in the process.

The noise was much louder than when the other chain had fallen, and Halbred knew someone would notice this time. On top of that, with both of the chains holding his arms in place having broken free, Halbred's body flipped upside down, leaving him hanging in the air by his legs.

Halbred hung upside down and stared at the door to the large room, waiting for a barrage of dark ones to pour in, but none came. Then his peripheral vision caught a glimpse of the dark cloud starting to move from the platform across the room. The dark cloud was slowly moving towards him and Halbred knew what that meant.

"Damn, here comes the big one. Well, no point in waiting now." He thought as he reached into one of the pouches on his belt and pulled out two small circular explosives. Holding one in each hand, and still hanging upside down, Halbred threw them both at the same time. Each explosive went towards the pulley holding the chains to the ceiling and each one was a direct hit.

When the explosives hit, the ceiling erupted, sending Halbred flying to the floor along with huge chunks of stone from the ceiling, and behind the chunks of stone, where the ceiling used to be was bright, beautiful sunshine.

Halbred hit the floor hard and immediately covered his head, trying to do what he could to protect himself from the chunks of stone raining down from the giant hole in the temple's ceiling.

When the stone seemed to stop falling, Halbred dug himself out. He was already holding another explosive in each hand, prepared to be tackled by a dozen dark ones or grabbed by the giant dark one. As he stood, he saw them. There were far more than a dozen, and they were standing across the room in the shadows.

Before Halbred could wonder why they weren't attacking, he noticed the ring of sunshine around him, coming from the hole that his explosives had blown in the ceiling.

He looked across the room and saw that the dark cloud had retreated back to the platform.

Feelings of relief and confidence, followed quickly by anger, flooded through Halbred as he looked at the massive gathering of creatures staring at him from the shadows across the room.

"What's the matter bloodsuckers?! Scared of a little sunburn?" Halbred yelled at them.

He noticed them easing towards him slowly and cautiously, and then looked around and noticed that the ring of sunlight he had been standing in had shrunk in just the few minutes of him standing there. Halbred quickly took a step backwards into the center of the shrinking circle of light and looked up. He could tell right away what was happening.

"Of all the times to break free, I choose to do it when the sun is setting." He thought.

He looked at the horde of dark ones easing closer and thought, "and they know it too. I've got maybe a minute or two and they'll all be on me."

Then, just as the last of the sunlight began to fade, a deafening "BOOM" rang through the temple, and the large stone door that had secured the front of the temple came flying through the main room, wiping out a row of dark ones in the process.

Halbred and the gathered dark ones, well the ones that hadn't just been knocked across the room by a giant stone door flying through it anyway, all stared at the opening that the door had come flying through.

"What in the...?!" Halbred muttered, as he saw a shopping cart come rolling in through the doorway. It was rolling fast, and it was full of what appeared to be propane tanks and bottles of lighter fluid. A split second later, he heard the gunshot and covered his face just before the entire room exploded.

CHAPTER 29
Come Out & Play

As Steph and G'noch topped the hill, they saw the long open plain before them and the massive pyramid that seemed to be in the middle of it. Past the pyramid a good hundred yards in each direction, the landscape sloped upward steeply, creating hills that almost seemed like sheer mountain faces. On top of these cliffs, if you will, were thick forests and woods.

"It looks like this entire plain was just dug out of the land to make way for the pyramid," Steph said. G'noch nodded in agreement, as the two kept walking towards the pyramid. Then Mila spoke.

"It was Steph." Mila said, in her dark, distant voice. Then she said, "This is as far as I go. Bring them out, bring them all Guardians and I will usher in a new season for this land."

Then Mila's eyes changed from the bright glowing light to almost pupils, although they appeared to be made from a fainter shade of light, and she looked at Steph. "Make sure they know it was my purpose. I was destined for this, long before my birth, that is the way Steph. Tell them I love them and tell them not to mourn me." Once she spoke the words, her eyes immediately changed back to bright lights and her entire body glowed brighter than it had before.

Mila's body slowly rose a few feet off the ground, and she looked at both Steph and G'noch, saying, "When this work is done, protect the land Guardians. You have also now been changed and it's your destiny to instill balance in this world throughout the new season."

As soon as she made the last statement, she flew straight up into the air at least two hundred feet and then hovered there motionless, looking like a star shining above the plain.

Steph and G'noch looked at each other, obviously both soaking in what she had charged them both with, and somehow both of them could feel the truth in her words. They knew that somehow the forest of the ancients had changed them, they knew they were not the same, but neither had spoken of it.

"I guess it's up to us to protect the land after all this, huh G'noch?" Steph said, trying to lighten things up a little.

"First, kill dark ones. Next job if we live Steph." G'noch said.

"What? Come on G'noch! We're guardians now, man, of course we're gonna live." Steph said. G'noch looked at him for a long moment before saying "Where are last guardians then?"

Neither of them said a word after that, but both of their faces took on more serious looks as they resumed their hike towards the temple, Steph still pushing the old shopping cart full of propane tanks. They knew G'noch was right. They knew that this could go a lot of ways and the odds weren't on their side. They also both knew that they had to do it, so they kept on going, staring at the temple that appeared to get darker, the closer they got.

By the time they got to what appeared to be the only door to the large pyramid, the sun was setting. They looked at the huge stone door before them and then looked up at the setting sun. As they were preparing themselves for what would come next, the sounds of explosions filled the air and the temple seemed to shudder.

G'noch and Steph looked at each other, and Steph said, "Maybe the other Gaurdians got here first".

G'noch snorted, looked up at the sky and said, "Sun gone. Ready?" Steph did not fail to notice G'noch cynical glance at the old shopping cart when he said it.

"Yeah, I'm ready… and G'noch, this will work. Now let's see if they want to come out and play," Steph replied.

In response, G'noch eased the massive spike club off of his shoulder and stepped forward towards the large stone door. He looked closely at the door's edges, the top and the bottom of the door and then turned and began to walk away.

"What are you doing?" Steph asked in shock.

G'noch did not answer with words, but what he was doing quickly became evident, when the large T'kche stopped and turned around about ten feet from the door. He paused only for a second, before he started running at the door full speed. As G'noch neared the door, his speed increased and he flowed into a massive swing of his club, putting his entire body's momentum into it.

The loud "BOOM" that followed was deafening, and the door instantly disappeared into the dark insides of the temple.

Steph didn't waste any time admiring the powerful blow his friend had delivered to the stone door, he immediately ran forward pushing the cart as fast as he could, even going as far as to step a couple feet inside the dark doorway, before letting the cart go with a final shove.

He watched as the cart rolled through the open room and through a large doorway, into what Steph could only imagine was an even bigger room. As the cart started to slow, and was easing out of line of sight, Steph pulled his large .50 caliber pistol from its holster on his hip, aimed, and fired at the cart. As soon as he pulled the trigger, he turned and half ran, half dove back out the doorway.

An even louder "BOOM" filled the young night, as the inside of the pyramid exploded. Flames burst out through the doors at his heels as he dove to the safety of the outside.

Steph hit the ground, rolled, and quickly jumped to his feet. He rushed about twenty feet further away from the flaming temple, positioning himself not far from where G'noch stood. He didn't get too close, keeping a good ten feet distance between them, as Steph had seen his large friend in battle before and he didn't want to worry about 'friendly fire' from the giant club, while he was fighting his own battle.

Both of them stood ready and waiting. Time seemed to stop. Neither knew how long they would have to last before Mila did her 'Brite' thing. All they knew was they couldn't go down. No matter what, they couldn't fail.

Steph didn't know if it was hours or seconds before the first dark-cloaked figure emerged from the flaming doorway. The creature was about his height and wore a tattered black cloak. It had strangely long arms, that extended into elongated hands, with fingers that seemed more like claws. The feet were very similar. The creature's skin was a pale, almost translucent color, and when it turned its head to face Steph, he saw the sinister hairless face, with the solid black eyes.

The dark one flicked out its long black tongue, showing rows of pointed teeth and two enormous fangs in the process. Then another one came out of the door behind it, and then another and another.

In seconds, there were ten of them, with more pouring out. Steph holstered his pistol and pulled the large two-handed sword out of the sheath on his back. In response, the creatures split into two waves and dashed ahead, making hissing noises and flashing their fangs and long black tongues as they ran. One wave of dark ones was heading straight for G'noch, and one was heading for Steph.

Steph twisted his feet in the dirt and found his footing. He held the sword in front of him, feeling like he'd been born with this weapon in his hands. He didn't know how, but he knew somehow, he was one with the blade. Steph bent his knees, dipped low and to the right and then swept back up to the left swinging his lethal blade, just as the first two dark ones got to him. Both heads were removed in the clean swing.

The next pair was behind them and leaped over the headless bodies as they fell. Steph didn't stop moving, he gracefully flowed from the previous swing, back into an overhead downward motion, towards the closest of the two, cutting the creature straight down the middle of its body from the top of its head. As his blade came out between the creature's legs, leaving each half of the beast to fall on either side of Steph, he spun towards the other one and took its head off. Steph kept spinning right past it and crouched as he did, swinging the sword at the next two dark ones' legs. The movement cut their legs off at the knees, and Steph swung his sword backwards, taking their heads as the bodies crashed to the ground.

As he came from the swing, he stopped for the first time, since he began his flows of sword movements. Steph hadn't thought, his mind had been blank, just going through the motions as if he'd practiced them his entire life. As he stopped, he noticed the bodies around him and realized that in mere seconds he had dispatched six of the lethal creatures. Dozens more stared at him, but no more rushed in. They slowly began to make a circle around him.

"Come in from any direction you want, either way you die," Steph said coldly as he found his footing once again and readied himself for the next attack.

G'noch stood still as the wave of dark ones flooded towards him. The large black haired T'kche warrior adjusted his grip on the massive club, growled quietly and swung the club just as the closest two dark ones leaped into the air towards him. Their bodies splattered through the air like confetti and the same happened to the next two behind them, when G'noch swung the club back.

He saw two pairs racing at him from his left and his right and he waited until the last second to leap straight up and come crashing back down with his club as the dark ones collided where he had just stood. Two more dove at him from the front, before he could swing the club back around, so he just held it front of him. They caught onto the club and tried to bite and claw at him around it. G'noch headbutted one of them with such force that the dark one's head splattered. Then he shook the other one off and kicked it in the midsection, sending it flying several feet through the air.

Two more leaped at him from behind, but he saw it coming and swung around with his club, splattering another two dark ones into pieces in the air.

The creatures backed away, forming a circle around G'noch, seeming to wait for the steady flow of dark ones exiting the temple to continue bolstering their numbers. G'noch looked around at the growing numbers for a second, but that was all. He was a T'kche warrior, he would not wait for these dark creatures to attack. G'noch rushed into the forming circle, splattering dark ones to pieces all around him as he roared and furiously swung his massive club.

CHAPTER 30
Sunset or Sunrise

It was late in the afternoon when Grifter halted the traveling pack of Roken with a raised fist. The pack had mostly traveled in human form, with the exception of a few Roken who occasionally seemed to be scouting ahead and around them at all times. These were the ones that had also apparently left a few carcasses of some slaughtered creatures along the path waiting for on the larger caravan a few times earlier in the day.

The carcasses were picked up by the Roken traveling at the front of the large group, ripped into chunks, and passed about, seemingly as snacks to eat along the way. They did not stop to eat or rest; they just continued their hike through the thick forest landscape from sunrise until now.

As soon as Grifter raised his fist, the caravan's hike halted and the large group of Roken began gathering around. The handful of "scouting" Roken in their beast forms appeared on the outskirts of the gathering, close enough to be part of the pack, but still keeping their distance.

When the shuffling of movement had stopped, all of the Roken had gathered together, filling the thick area of the forest in what would look like a massive gathering of monks in thick hooded burlap robes to any passerby. Grifter assessed his gathered pack carefully, looking them up and down silently for long moments, like a drill sergeant inspecting troops. After what seemed like forever, he stepped up onto a large fallen tree and addressed the pack.

"We have arrived! Fifty feet through the woods to the north is where the trees end, and the unnatural plains of the dark ones begin.

We have two choices before us, my brothers and sisters: we can lay siege to these vile creatures at nightfall when they begin to emerge from their holes to hunt, or we can wait until daybreak and raid their home while they sleep and hide from the sunlight. If we choose to wait, we will divide up into two nearby dens that our scouts have found and quickly fortify the entrances to ensure we do not become the hunted throughout the night. I have led you here, I have chosen this course of action to not only pay the blood debt that is owed, but also to rid ourselves of these dark vermin and take our rightful spot as rulers of this land! Now I will let the pack choose to hunt by day or night, but you must choose quickly." Grifter shouted it all to the gathered pack and then stared at them, obviously waiting for the deliberation to begin.

Luca spoke first, "If we are still set on this foolish course of action, then we should slaughter them while they sleep during the day. Although, we still have time to reconsider and allow nature to change seasons with the coming of the Brite as we have always done, Grifter."

Grifter eyed Luca angrily. A low growl seemed to rumble from his chest as he looked at him, but when he responded his voice was level and calm.

"The decision to honor our debts and wipe out our enemies has been made, Luca, and considering you, like me, owe this debt firsthand, I would expect your honor to place you on that side of any debate." Grifter stared at him and watched as others in the pack turned to look at Luca, obviously thinking about Grifter's statement.

"I do not seek to run from the obligations of honor, Grifter, I just cannot help but to place the best interests of the pack above my own honor and obligations. To me they come first." Luca responded.

Eva was impressed and unsettled by Luca's response. She felt like she was watching a political debate, and when she thought of it that way, she couldn't help but understand Luca's point. Sure, she needed the help of the Roken, sure that monster Luca had tried to kill her, but still she couldn't help but acknowledge the risks that would come with them attacking the dark ones.

"A lot of their pack could get killed, hell, we all might die if we attack these dark ones. I don't blame him," Eva thought.

"Enough!" Grifter roared. "We will attack, we will slaughter our enemies, and we will repay our debts because we are Roken! Talk of anything else is fear and cowardice!"

Luca stared at Grifter but did not respond.

Another young Roken male yelled out "I agree, let's slaughter them while they hide from the daylight, it will give us an advantage."

One of the females in the group countered by saying, "Hiding throughout the night, hoping they don't attack us first and then having to go into their home the next day doesn't sound like an advantage to me! I say we wait outside their home and slaughter them when they come out to hunt. I'd rather fight these creatures in the open and see who comes out on top."

Several nods and murmurings of approval followed the powerful statement.

"That is a strong argument, Shirak." Grifter said with approval towards the female that spoke.

Although she hadn't noticed this female Roken at their fortress, she saw immediately that this 'Shriak' held quite a bit of sway and influence over the pack. Almost as much as Luca seemed to, maybe more.

Eva watched and listened as several more arguments were made for both options and some minor debating took place. In truth, she felt impatient and wanted to go now, but she knew this would be a battle and figured she needed to let the Roken decide what plan of attack gave them the best shot to succeed.

The debate carried on, as the sun sank lower and lower. At one point, Grifter sent the scouts to prepare the dens and have the fortifications ready in case they chose to hide throughout the night and attack in the morning.

It was about then that Eva decided, she would hike over to the edge of the trees and see what they were headed into.

"I might as well, my vote here doesn't count. If I spoke up to vote, it'd probably just stir up an argument or another fight. Besides, Grifter said it was only fifty feet or so north," Eva thought as she eased back away from the gathering and headed north into the woods. She knew it might not be a good idea, she knew two of these Roken had already tried to kill her and that Grifter had warned her to stay close, but she told herself that they were too busy debating to worry about her.

"Besides, what good would killing me now do? They're already here. They've already decided to attack," Eva thought, continuing to convince herself that it wasn't as terrible an idea as she felt like it was.

She hiked for what felt like far more than fifty feet, not failing to notice the sun slowly starting to set as she did. She was about to give it up and turn back, thinking that 'fifty feet' must mean something totally different to Roken than it did to her, when she saw the break in the trees ahead.

It was too thick to really make out yet, but it looked to Eva like the edge of the forest. She hurried forward, bursting through the trees and just barely catching herself before falling off the edge of a steep cliff. Eva wobbled at the edge, looking down at the steep drop off.

"Whoa. That's a heck of a drop." She thought. She stared at the drop off for a few minutes and was able to identify a couple ways to climb down, using roots, rocks, and what appeared to be shrubs sticking out of the side of the cliff, but knew that wasn't a now thing.

Having figured out how to climb down if needed, Eva shifted her attention to the valley before her. It was gray dirt and rock that spread out for miles. It looked like it had been dug out of the forest by a gigantic shovel scoop, leaving nothing alive across the plain. There were no signs of any vegetation or life whatsoever, just dirt, rock, and a very large pyramid in the center.

She saw movement on the plain as she looked at the pyramid, but before she was able to figure out what it was, a hand touched her shoulder, startling her.

She jumped and looked back to see it was Grifter who had touched her shoulder. He had two Roken that Eva didn't recognize with him.

"Eva, the sun is going down. In moments the dark ones will emerge from the temple and begin their nightly hunt. It is not safe. The pack has chosen to wait until daylight, come," Grifter said the words gently, but firmly.

Before Eva could reply, an explosion shook them all and the landscape around them. It was evident it came from the temple as they could see flames burst through the top right side and a giant hole in the pyramid's ceiling appeared before them.

Grifter, Eva and the two Roken with them rushed to the edge and peered at the temple.

Eva had trouble seeing that far, but apparently the Roken did not, as one of them said, "I know not what exploded from inside the temple, but look a human and what appears to be a T'kche at the entrance."

"Did you say a human and a T'kche? Is the T'kche black haired?" Eva asked in shock and excitement.

"Yes, and the human appears to be dressed similar to a Na'gee warrior but is taller than most of the Na'gee and has different hair. I haven't seen many Na'gee with hair," The Roken warrior said.

Excitement flooded through Eva. "That's G'noch and Steph, my son! He is no Na'gee! They are my pack!" Eva exclaimed, just as a much more powerful explosion rocked the entire landscape and sent them all back a few paces from the edge of the cliff.

They saw flames burst out from the entrance of the pyramid and saw the human and the T'kche position themselves a good distance away and await the dark ones. In seconds the wait was over, and they watched dark ones racing out in pairs, only to be slaughtered by the two warriors.

Eva gasped! On one hand she was mortified that her son and her friend were facing all of the dark one's on their own, on the other hand she couldn't believe her eyes as she watched them slaughter dark ones after dark one, creating circles of bodies around them as they appeared to dance through the battle with a flowing grace.

Grifter and the Roken, turned and looked at Eva with surprise. "This is your pack?! A T'kche and a human that attack the entire dark ones' horde to save your friend?!" Grifter asked with surprise and a hint of respect.

One of the two Roken with them chimed in before Eva could answer and said, "Grifter, the two of them aren't just attacking the horde, they're wiping them out!"

"We've got to help them! With or without you, I'm going now!" Eva said and she immediately began to climb down the steep face of the cliff.

Grifter watched her take off and then looked at his two companions. "This human's pack shows courage and bravery that makes our pack's debate shameful. We are Roken, no humans should ever be more fearless of bloodshed than our people." Grifter said.

Both of his companions nodded and then one of them smiled sinisterly, as his body started changing and said, "I've always wondered how a T'kche would compare in battle to us. Guess I get to find out."

Grifter and the other companion both started transforming as well, and the other one chimed in and said "They are a strange pack Grifter, no humans, not even the treacherous Na'gee would dare an attack like this, especially with only two of them. It will be an honor to shed blood with these strangers."

Grifter nodded, his transformation complete. Then he looked at his two companions and said, "Cirka, go back and gather the pack. Tell them what you have seen and lead them here. We attack now, while these strangers are helping to thin the enemy forces. Yokan, you wanted to see a T'kche in battle... well let's go help him battle."

The Roken Grifter had addressed as Cirka, took off through the woods without a wordwhile the Roken called Yokan growled viciously and leaped off the edge of the cliff. Grifter leaped off behind him.

Both of their feet hit the sheer face of the cliff twice during their descent, each time, their feet hit and they propelled themselves off again, seeming to bounce the entire way down in seconds.

Eva was a little over halfway down the cliff face, when she watched the transformed Roken fly by her. Determined not to be left behind, she looked down and saw a dirt trench or gap a few feet below her that seemed to go to the bottom of the cliff face.

Eva quickly climbed down to it, slung the assault rifle off of her shoulder and holding it in front of her, she turned onto her back and let go, sliding on her back and hips down the trench, kicking with her feet to keep her on track.

She slid faster and faster and as the bottom of the cliff approached, Eva feared that she may break both her legs upon impact. She was almost there, when she saw a blur of hair and was snatched off of the cliff face and plopped onto the ground at the bottom.

Grifter stood over her, and she instantly knew he had leapt and grabbed her off of the cliff.

"Do not start so recklessly Eva, or you will not last." Grifter growled. Then he added, "That weapon is useless." He pointed at the assault rifle and then continued, "Remember your training, you know how to fight this darkness. I will see you in battle my friend." With the words said, Grifter and Yokan took off across the plain with incredible speed, leaving Eva to get up and jog along on her own, trying to cover the distance as fast as she could.

CHAPTER 31

The Battlefield

Grifter and Yokan raced each other, each one's speed seeming to set the bar for the other as they headed towards their prey. Faster and faster, until the enemy was almost within reach. That's when Grifter roared, "You help the T'kche, I will help the human!"

Without a word or any sign of acknowledgement, Yokan veered right towards the massive gathering of dark ones around G'noch. G'noch swung his club through the masses of dark ones, leaving splatters of blood and body parts in the wake of each swing. Despite the devastation that the T'kche warrior was letting loose on them, the enemies' numbers kept growing. He couldn't kill them fast enough to offset the seemingly endless tide of dark ones pouring out of the burning pyramid.

As Yokan neared the gathering, he saw G'noch swing his club completely through the bodies of three dark ones, while two other dark ones leapt on his back. He reached back with his left, grabbed one of them and hurled it into the crowd of its comrades, while the other bit and slashed at him. He kicked others back, then grabbed the second and threw it into the crowd as well.

Yokan saw the T'kche's back was shredded and caked with blood, just like his arms and legs, and he knew that these weren't the first two to make it past the T'kche's mighty club. Despite the wounds, G'noch fought on, as if he didn't even notice they were there.

Yokan admired the T'kche for but a second, thinking, "I've always wondered what T'kche was like in battle, now I get to fight alongside one." That was the last thought that went through his mind, before bloodlust and battle rage took over. Yokan leapt into the melee behind G'noch, slashing the heads of two dark ones off at the same time, before leaping past their falling bodies to relieve two more of their heads. As the ranks of dark ones flowed in towards him, Yokan leapt straight up into the air, at least ten feet, and then shot down into the swarm with claws outstretched. As he crashed into the dark ones he slashed about, shredding bodies and taking heads.

G'noch swung his club again through the ranks of dark ones. As he did, he readied himself for the next couple to leap on his back, but they did not come. The large T'kche risked a look over his shoulder and saw the large Roken slashing and biting at dark ones, who slashed and bit back, well the ones that didn't lose their heads, slashed and bit back.

G'noch didn't waste time wondering where his new ally had come from, there was too much work to do, too many left to kill. So, the T'kche kept at it, careful to keep the Roken at his back, affording each of them some momentary relief from the dark ones leaping on their backs.

Steph maintained his circle and guarded it well. It was littered with limbs, heads and bodies of fallen dark ones, but it was still his circle. They leapt at him from opposite sides, in twos and threes, but he just flowed through rhythmic movements, dancing with the sword, killing with grace, no dark ones had made it to Steph in one piece.

Despite the thoughtless zone he was in as he danced with the blade, like it was something he had been doing his entire life, he didn't fail to notice that the numbers kept increasing. He felt that he could keep this up all day, but he knew at some point the bodies would interfere with his dance and things could get more complicated.

As Steph flowed through the movements, lashing out with his blade, he noticed dark ones dropping and body parts flying that were not attributed to him. A handful to his left dropped headless. Then a handful to his right had their legs torn off, before their heads rolled from their bodies. He caught glimpses of a blur of hair and claws.

"It's moving too fast to be G'noch, or any T'kche for that matter," Steph thought. Careful not to pay it too much attention, lest he open himself up for an attack.

After a few moments, Steph quit trying to figure it out and just accepted it. He continued to dance with his blade, as dark ones continued to rush him from all sides. He sliced them out of the air, and spun in a low crouching circle taking the legs of their rushing companions, then leapt up and spun taking heads off of others still. The flows consumed his focus, while the hairy blur continued to dart around the exterior of the circle, in and out, in and out, dropping handfuls of dark ones all around him.

This seemed to have been going on forever, or maybe it was mere seconds, time did not exist to the combatants on the battlefield, but all fighting stopped for just a moment when a thunderous roar echoed across the plains. The ground vibrated and dark ones, T'kche and Roken alike paused for just a moment to look up at the dozens of Roken charging their way across the plain.

The sight was breathtaking. They were huge, ferocious, and moved as one across the plains with incredible speed, kicking up clouds of dust and rocks that seemed to serve as their flag, letting everyone watching know that death was on the way.

A tide of dark tattered cloaks and pale clawed figures flowed out to meet them, and the two forces collided like a mighty wave crashing onto the rocks. Blood flowed, there were hisses and roars and bodies of Roken and dark one alike began to fall.

The dark ones outnumbered the Roken at least four to one, but the forces still appeared evenly matched. The mighty battle seemed to enrage the dark ones attacking Steph, as they came at him with intensified speed and power. He heard a roar, and felt something flying at the back of his legs, so he instinctively leapt and swung downward with his sword. Steph stopped his swing at the last minute, shifting it to his right where a dark one was leaping in, when he noticed that it wasn't a dark one at all. It was one of those giant wolfman creatures. The beast was bleeding from a devastating slash across its chest. Steph landed next to it, and glanced at the creature.

"I am Grifter, I have brought my pack to help your pack destroy these beasts." The creature growled, as it eyed the circling dark ones. "I have brought one of your packs with me, Eva. She fights with us. We are here to pay a blood debt and free the one you call Halbred… after we slaughter these vermin!" As the creature finished its statement, it leapt at two charging dark ones, slashing one's chest open with his right claw, and taking the head off the other with his left claw.

Two more rushed at Steph and he fell back into the flow of the sword, spinning and slashing dark ones to pieces, while he thought "My mom's with these guys? And the dark ones have Halbred? What the hell did I miss?"

The pack dove into the battle and Eva was with it. As Roken slashed away at dark ones with claws and tore into them with teeth, Eva used the gauntlets that Grifter had given her, to slash and behead a dark one here and there. She had killed two, when she found herself looking at two more, they dove at her, one from the left and one from the right. The claws and fangs coming at her from the terrifying creatures, started to fill her with panic, but then she remembered Grifter's training and thought of them as opponents, nothing more, nothing less. Nothing else mattered.

She ducked under one's leap, twisting her body and raising her right gauntlet as she did, slashing the dark one from neck to groin, as it flew over her. The other dove at her waist with its claws outstretched, so Eva slashed downward with her left hand. The creature crashed into her, knocking her to the ground, but it did so without the hands that Eva had cut off with her swing. It rolled off her in pain and she relieved it of its head.

She turned just in time to see another one slashing at her and stepped back. Its claws still tore through her arm, but just grazed instead of tearing to the bone, like it would have done if she had not stepped back. It lashed out with its claws again and Eva stepped in towards the creature swinging both of her arms down from in front of her, towards her sides. The move caught the creature off guard and took its arms off, she immediately came back up reversing the same motion and sliced it, almost as if her gauntlet blades were giant scissors. She turned to see another rushing her and continued to fight for her life, wondering how long she would be able to keep up with these otherworldly creatures.

Across the battlefield a dark cloud appeared and seemed to float across the ground towards where G'noch and Yokan continued to fight a large horde of the dark creatures. Suddenly out of the cloud emerged a dark one unlike any of the others. This dark creature had the same translucent skin and claw-like fingers and toes, it wore a tattered black cloak like the others, but it was at least fifteen to twenty feet tall, a giant in every sense of the word.

The creature roared out across the battlefield in a loud hissing voice, "Two of them carry guardian's weapons! The time of the Brite is upon us! Kill what you can, but the crossing must begin!"

As the giant dark one spoke in its loud hissing voice that echoed across the valley, it also began shifting something in its huge hand and then a twenty foot tall 'blur' appeared on the battlefield.

Several dark ones started pouring through the 'blur' as soon as it appeared, while others intensified their attacks on Roken, Human and T'kche alike.

"They're crossing over! We have to stop them! We have to keep them here!" Steph yelled out to G'noch who was by now at least fifty feet away, with dozens of dark ones between them.

Suddenly, the giant dark one turned and caught an object flying through the air at it. When it did its hand completely blew up. Steph looked to see where it had come from and saw Halbred, limping out from the flaming pyramid, looking at the giant dark one.

"Hey big guy! You and me ain't finished!" Halbred roared as he hurled another explosive at the injured dark giant.

This time the creature didn't try to catch it, with its remaining hand, instead it ducked and the explosive blew up in a patch of dark ones trying to flood through the 'blur'. Then the giant moved. Steph didn't know what he had expected, maybe that bigger meant slower, but that was anything but the truth of what he witnessed.

The giant dark one moved faster than he had seen any dark one or Roken move on the battlefield, rushing Halbred and smacking him aside with tremendous power. The blow knocked Halbred literally into the wall of the pyramid. Rock and stone shattered and flew about as Halbred disappeared.

The giant stood pulsing with anger and hatred right outside the hole in the pyramid that Halbred had crashed into. Then something small came flying out of the hole and huge explosion lit up the air just a couple feet from the giant's head. The giant staggered and Halbred came rushing out of the hole, heading straight for the staggering giant. Dark ones rushed in from the sides intent on cutting Halbred off before he could get to the giant, but Halbred threw his last two explosives with both hands and blew up the groups rushing him from either side.

Without missing a step, the old soldier pulled out a large knife and leaped onto the giant.

Slashing and stabbing the monstrous creature, with ferocity that seemed fitting for this violent world.

Steph was startled as blood splattered across his face. He directed his attention back to where he was, not even realizing that he had been staring when he saw Grifter standing there and the headless body of a dark one falling to the blood covered ground.

"Your pack is formidable and fearless young one, but the battle rages on. It is not time for admiration." The Roken growled, before leaping back into a group of four dark ones.

The giant dark one was caught off guard for but a second, before it struck Halbred with incredible force, knocking him to the ground. The creature had spent long enough with the old soldier to know better than trying to use claws or teeth, so instead it stomped. The giant stomped down on Halbred over and over, "boom" after "boom" echoed through the violence-filled valley as Halbred lay motionless, disappearing deeper and deeper into the ground.

During it all, more and more dark ones seemed to flow out of the battered pyramid. The bloody plain was filled with at least two hundred dark creatures and more and more kept coming. Many joined the battle, but dozens and dozens poured through the 'blur' on the battlefield, choosing to fight less formidable foes in the new world that they had been promised.

When Halbred was so deeply impacted into the ground that he could not be seen from a short distance away, the giant dark one stopped its stomping and surveyed the battlefield. As it looked around, its gaze lingered on Steph who was still fighting off a large mass of dark ones that circled him, and he had the help of a large Roken.

The giant scowled and then shifted its gaze towards G'noch, who seemed to be similarly fighting a large circle of dark ones, although the circle around G'noch seemed to keep shifting, as the dark ones all seemed to back away every time the powerful T'kche raced into the edge of the circle swinging his deadly club. He also had a large Roken darting in and out of the circle supporting him.

Then the giant shifted its gaze upward and seemed to lock its eyes onto Mila floating at least one hundred feet above the plains, shining like a bright little star. The dark ones look changed and then it bellowed out across the battlefield in a voice that was clearly heard by everyone there, regardless of how loud the battle around them was.

"The human and the T'kche are guardians! Look at their auras and the weapons of the ancients they wield! Look into the sky! The time of the Brite is upon us! Kill the guardians and then cross over! We will not come back to reclaim this world with guardians roaming about! We'll wipe out the flea ridden Roken upon our return! Their season will not last long!" The battle seemed to stop as all combatants on both sides paused to listen and look at the things the giant dark one pointed out. When it finished shouting its commands, the giant turned and ducked through the huge 'blur', crossing over to the 'top side' world.

Luca heard the giant dark one's words, just like everyone else. He was surrounded by at least a dozen Roken, fighting as one in a sea of dark ones. As the words of the giant sunk in, he shouted to the Roken around him, "He is right, look at the Brite in the sky! Look at the guardian's weapons!" As Luca shouted to the Roken around him, he could see it was catching the attention of other Roken fighting in smaller groups not far from his, so he raised his voice and continued. "Grifter has led us to needless slaughter! Had we waited another day or two, our season would have come to pass without the deaths of so many of the pack! It is time to retreat! Leave these humans to die at the hands of the dark scum and leave the Brite to cleanse the land of them! Roken retreat!"

Luca knew he did not command the pack, he wondered if they would follow his orders, challenge them, or ignore him altogether and continue their fighting. Instead, he heard responses, not challenging, but not following either. "What about Grifter? We cannot leave him!"

Luca responded quickly, "I will take these two and get Grifter" he said referring to the two closest Roken, the same two that had accompanied him in the hall when Grifter had confronted him. The Roken around him seemed to agree and started to pull away from the battle, just as the dark ones began disengaging the Roken, shifting their attention to the guardians and the 'blur' as the giant had instructed.

Before Luca and his two counterparts took off for Grifter, a female Roken shouted "I will accompany you Luca!" She shouted loud enough for all of the surrounding Roken to hear. She was the female that had debated Luca on attack strategy earlier that evening. The surrounding Roken seemed more pleased to have someone who wasn't biased towards Luca's perspective joining the recovery mission and as they murmured agreement they began backing away from the fighting and the valley.

Eva, watched as the dark ones turned their attention away from her and the Roken. She listened to the giant before that and to Luca's words. She eased away creating some distance between herself and the large pack that still remained standing. Eva knew better than to argue against their retreat. She knew that Grifter was the only Roken that cared about human life and that if they were open to Luca's direction, then killing her wouldn't take much convincing.

She thought of rushing towards the battle to help G'noch and Steph but seeing the hundreds of dark ones converging down on them, she knew that she would never make it to them alive.

Luca, his two counterparts and the female Roken took off tearing a bloody path through the dark ones. In seconds they had managed to make it into the shrinking circle that Steph and Grifter still managed to hold.

As the four Roken burst into the circle, they immediately joined in the fight, slashing and biting at the mass of dark ones pressing in on them all. The four ferocious Roken, quickly helped to clear a much larger circle. Grifter, spared them a glance, that seemed to say 'what took you so long' but said nothing.

Steph danced with the blade as if nothing had changed. He noticed the impact the reinforcements had made, but knew the battle was far from over. He didn't slow down or waste any time with foolish thoughts that help in his circle might would change the tide of a battle that seemed to be shifting to favor an enemy with a seemingly endless number of troops.

"Grifter, we are leaving these humans to face their fate. The giant dark one is right, look at who you fight with, he has the scent of a guardian and a blade of the ancients. Look in the sky, the time of the Brite is upon us, our season starts soon, let these humans waste their lives in a meaningless battle," Luca said, while shifting his eyes from his two companions to the female Roken the entire time.

Grifter heard the words, and despite the group still fighting the charging dark ones he did not fail to notice the two male Roken shift to either side of him, while Luca stood near the front of him. He didn't pay attention to the female who seemed to have shifted behind him, where Steph was watching his back.

"No need to worry about her, she openly challenged Luca, but these two are loyal to him and something doesn't seem right," Grifter thought. Then he responded roughly, "You only choose to fight with me in the heart of the battle when you're asking me to retreat?! We will not leave these humans to face our common enemy on their own and we will not wait for some Brite to change the seasons like cowards Luca! You owe a blood debt as much as I do, yet you prove to be more cowardly than honorable!" Grifter was roaring by the time he finished, with more of his attention on Luca and the two Roken on either side of him than on the mass of dark ones.

"Then die with these weak humans! The pack will not die with you!" Luca roared back.

"I rule the pack! You haven't earned the right to be an Alpha. Lead a mutiny and death is the sentence coward! You have to defeat me to rule the pack, is that what you came into the heart of the battle to do?! Do you think you can defeat me coward?!!" Grifter roared in a rage.

Steph heard the confrontation but kept fighting, thinking, "Great. That's all we need, our only support in this fight, turning on each other."

Before Luca could respond, Grifter felt the claws sink into his lower back. He gasped and his body reeked of pain, as he felt the rough claws, that he knew to be Roken claws, wrap around his lower spine. He had no idea how much internal damage was being done, but he knew how much pain he was in, just like he knew if he moved, his spine would be ripped from his body. Then a clawed Roken hand reached over his shoulder and gently pushed against his throat, prepared to rip it out. He felt the hot breath on his ear before he heard the growling female Roken's voice.

"Luca is right and if we listened to him, half the pack would still be alive to rule this land tomorrow when our season arrives. You risk are lives with your foolish talk of honor and we do not have time to wait for someone powerful enough to defeat you to come around. Your time ends now Grifter." The female Roken said harshly.

Luca and his two counterparts shared shocked looks with one another, while they continued to hold back the dark one forces. It was quite clear that this turn of events was not what they had expected.

"I thought I'd have to kill them both, but never imagined this happening", Luca thought.

The female Roken picked up on the surprised looks and said, "Why do you think I came fools? If you came back without him the pack would've suspected foul play, but with me here to testify to your story of the mighty Grifter falling in battle, well… no one will question that." She smiled sinisterly when she said it.

"Kill me then cowards. I am ashamed of your weakness. This pack of humans fights with more honor and bravery than all of you!" Grifter roared.

As he did, the hand fell from his throat and something rolled over his shoulder, down his chest and fell the ground at his feet. Grifter felt the claws come out of his back, leaving his spine intact and looked down at his feet, only to see the head of the female Roken. Grifter kicked it away from him in shock and turned to see Steph with blade in hand.

"Dark one or whatever you are doesn't matter to me." Steph said coldly. "This Grifter, risked his life to fight this evil by my side. I don't know him or you, but he will not die while I live. Flee like the cowards he claims you to be or die by my blade like the dark ones around you." Steph said it all flatly and coldly, keeping his eyes and his head on a swivel, looking all around.

The dark ones, had momentarily paused their attacks, seeming to be watching the altercation with intensity. Steph didn't know if they were waiting for their moment to strike or if they were enjoying watching them shed each other's blood but he appreciated the reprieve.

Then the Roken to Grifters left rushed at him, with incredible speed. The thing moved faster than any dark one Steph had faced. He could barely see anything but a brown blur of motion, yet somehow he knew where it would be. He didn't swing his blade at the movement, instead he swept it upwards in an arch in front of him. The motion was timed perfectly and his blade caught the beast where its neck met its chest, the motion propelled the blade upward from there and split the Rokens head in half. Its body slumped to the floor of the circle.

Steph heard the dark ones, hissing with excitement, but none attacked. His peripheral vision caught the one to Grifters right swinging an extended claw towards him, and Steph stepped in towards it, ducking as he did and swinging his blade from left to right. The movement cut the Roken in half at its waist, sending two separate halves of its body crashing to the bloody dirt.

Steph looked up to face Luca, the only remaining Roken, beside Grifter, and saw the beast grab the female Roken's head and take off, slashing its way through the mass of dark ones.

Grifter slumped to the ground, blood pouring out of the wound in his lower back. He remained on his knees, leaned over and did not move. Then the reprieve ended. Dark ones darted in from every direction and Steph resumed his dance with the blade, fighting desperately around Grifter to maintain the circle and spare this creature's life that had chosen to stand with him.

As he resumed his fight Steph thought, "Come on Mila, whatever you're going to do, do it already. We're not going to make it much longer."

Luca managed to break free from the thick swarm of dark ones, bleeding from a dozen deep wounds, but still up and running, nonetheless. Once he broke free, they did not chase him. It was clear that the giant's directions were all they cared about, 'kill the guardians and cross over' was all that mattered to this army of death.

Luca ran across the plain to a distant part, where what was left of the pack was gathered. Their numbers were depleted, but they stood together. As he approached, he saw the looks of concern and anger.

"Grifter is dead. They are all dead. The human guardian killed him and began killing the rest of them. I only barely escaped to ensure that the rest of you didn't waste your lives going into a hopeless battle to try to save us. The same humans he vowed to help, turned on him and the pack. They are all the same! They are more evil than the dark ones! The next season is ours; we must wipe out all the humans and avenge Grifter and our pack!" Luca roared passionately.

Several cries and several roars followed his speech, but a few Roken stepped out from the rest and neared him. "You wanted to leave this battle before it started, how do we know that you didn't kill him? How do we know that Grifter didn't take out the others and send you running away scared Luca?!" One of them asked.

Luca expected someone to challenge him. He tossed the challenger the head of the female Roken that he carried. As his challenger caught it, Luca said "look at the neck. Does that look like claws took her head or human's blade?"

The Roken inspected the severed head and then nodded. He turned to the rest of the gathered pack and said, "he speaks the truth. This is the work of a human weapon. They have betrayed the pack, when we risked so much to help them! I'm with Luca, they all must die!"

The pack roared in response, and all began to make their way across the plain together. Leaving the bloody battle that still raged on behind them without at second a glance back.

CHAPTER 32

You Worry about the World

Despite the sun setting and darkness enveloping the land around them, they didn't stop. Vic and Samuel still tore through the thick, frosty forest as fast as they could without crashing their motorcycles.

When the sun had just been starting to go down, they exchanged glances, but they didn't stop to discuss it. The look they shared was all the discussion they needed. They both knew the risks of being out after dark, they both had faced the dark ones that lurked in the shadows of this world, and they both saw that Eva's and Halbred's homing beacons had them placed at the same location not far away. So, despite the darkness, they pushed on.

As they burst out of the forest on their bikes, they each skidded to a stop before a steep cliff. Both men had been silently wondering if they would reach their destination before they were attacked by the dark ones or not. Neither man had ever expected to see what they saw before them now.

From the edge of the cliff that overlooked a vast plain, Vic and Samuel saw more dark ones than they imagined even existed. They had both survived a dark one siege on a Na'gee settlement, but even that was nothing compared to the number of dark ones they saw before them now.

Hundreds of the black cloaked creatures swarmed the vast plain of dirt and rock.

"Well, now we know why they didn't attack us. They're all throwing a party in the field," Vic said. "Look! Those ones are different, and the dark ones are just letting them leave," Samuel said,

pointing at the group of Roken in the distance, on the far side of the plain, leaving the battlefield.

Vic's eyes shifted to what Samuel pointed out and then continued to survey the field before them. His eyes landed on the huge 'blur' not far from the burning pyramid, just as Samuel's did.

"They're pouring through the pathway to our world, Vic." Samuel said gravely.

"Yeah, in the biggest damn 'blur' I've ever seen. How the hell did they make it so big and why are only some of them leaving?" Vic responded, squinting his eyes as he tried to make out what the other two large masses of dark ones that were not pouring through the 'blur' were focused on.

"Look! It's Halbred!" Samuel said, pointing once again, but this time he pointed to a spot near the large 'blur'.

Both of them watched the large red-haired soldier, who was obviously Halbred, climbing up out of a sort of hole in the ground near the 'blur'. Despite the distance, they could see Halbred was in rough shape. His clothes were torn all over, half of his shirt was missing, and he staggered slightly as he leaned to pick up what appeared to be a large stone about the size of his head.

They watched as Halbred leaped into the thick lines of dark ones pouring through the 'blur' and began smashing the heads of dark ones around him as he forced his way through the crowd and crossed into the 'blur'. They saw the dark ones claw and bite at him, and saw that he kept moving without acknowledging their counterattacks.

"Yep, that's damn Halbred and his impenetrable skin, alright. Must be nice." Vic said.

"The other groups of dark ones are attacking people Vic, look that's G'noch in the middle of that group. He's fighting, but from the looks of it they'll overtake him any minute." Samuel said. Once he pointed it out, they both noticed that for split seconds here and there, you could catch a glimpse of G'noch swinging some massive club and clearing out a patch of enemies, only for it to be filled with countless more.

"What the hell is he doing here?" Vic mumbled.

Then they shifted their attention to the other gathering a few feet away from the crowd gathered around G'noch. They could see dark ones leaping here and there, and they could tell that whoever fought there was holding their ground in the center of a mass of creatures as large as the one that threatened to overtake G'noch.

Then a slight shift in the ranks of dark ones opened up a line of sight and they saw it. It was Steph, swinging some large sword. He stood, or more jumped and leaped around an injured creature, fighting off incredible numbers of dark ones by himself.

"I'm sorry Vic." Samuel said, as they both saw clearly that the circle of enemies around Steph was slowly shrinking in on him, right before their eyes. "In seconds, they'll both be overtaken. We may still be able to save our world though. It's obvious that's what Halbred is trying to do and Eva's probably with him. We have to try to save the world Vic." Samuel said compassionately. He knew what he was asking his friend to do. He knew that it made sense, but that it wouldn't dull the pain of having to leave your loved one to die. He knew first hand that nothing ever would dull that pain.

Vic turned and looked at Samuel with a strange look in his eyes, it wasn't really sadness, but it wasn't really anger or rage either, it was more like all of those things being ruled by a deep understanding.

"You worry about the damn world, Samuel! I'm saving my son!" Vic yelled, as he revved the motorcycle and rode it straight off the face of the steep cliff. As the bike went over the edge, Samuel heard Vic yell, "Keep Eva safe!"

Vic's bike went straight off of the edge and he rode it down the steep face of the cliff facing the ground below. Just before he crashed head on into the rocky, dirt floor of the plain, Vic yanked the bike up into a wheelie, making both tires land roughly on the ground below. He had the throttle twisted all the way back, making it take off as soon as the wheels made contact with the ground below. Heading straight for the massive gathering of dark ones around Steph as fast as he could go.

Samuel watched Vic go and thought, "Dammit, Vic. Always rushing straight into the middle of the fray without thinking."

As much as it aggravated him, he'd also grown to love it about this man that he now thought of as his friend. If nothing else Vic could always be counted on to be, well, Vic.

"The man fearlessly charges into anything without a second thought, and usually with a few smartass comments," Samuel muttered. In truth, he had even grown to appreciate and admire Vic's sarcastic comments and jokes in the heat of battle and in the most inappropriate of situations. It had a sort of levity effect on everyone around him and seemed to instill a stronger degree of confidence in the group he was with, no matter the odds.

"Vic will be staring down death in his final hours, confident and probably outspoken that he'll come out on top, until the moment he takes his last breath," Samuel thought.

As Samuel watched his friend ride into clearly unbeatable odds, he was shocked at how much he'd grown to care for Vic and Vic's family. He realized he'd even grown a strong fondness for Halbred and G'noch. It seemed to Samuel like only yesterday that he started this hate filled mission of vengeance. Committed to killing Camacho and the Na'gee and anyone else that got in the way, for the murder of his family. He never thought he'd care for anyone, ever again and he was fine with that. Then somehow along the way, he'd grown close to all these people. Somehow, he'd seen that there was more to love in this world and that despite the pain of losing the ones he loved more than anything, he was still capable of caring for others.

The thoughts overwhelmed Samuel for a brief moment, as he thought of Vic and Eva, Steph and Mila, Halbred and G'noch. He thought of them as his family now, and he realized that he was likely about to lose another family.

"If we die, then we die together this time," Samuel thought, as he peered over the edge of the cliff face, choosing not to ride off the edge of the cliff blindly like Vic. When he did, he noticed Eva not far from the cliff but a ways down from him. It was clear she had backed away from the heart of the battle. She was bleeding but did not seem severely injured.

As Samuel's eyes locked on her, he saw that she must've just made a similar decision as he had, because she took off running towards the hundreds of black cloaked dark ones, that Vic was riding the bike into.

"She'll never even make it close enough to see them, let alone help them, before they kill her." Samuel thought.

He instantly made up his mind and following Vic's example, took off down the face of the cliff on the motorcycle.

"Who said any thing about dying?"

Vic pulled on the throttle as hard as he could and watched the needle fly by the numbers on the speedometer. One twenty-five, one fifty, one sixty. Faster and faster, he went, headed straight for the mass of tattered, black cloaks.

As he hit the gathering of dark creatures, he yanked up and sideways on the bike without slowing down, sending it, and him, flying sideways through the ranks of dark ones. The move cleared a path, like swinging a weed trimmer through tall grass and somewhere in the middle of it, while still airborne, Vic flipped off the bike backwards into the air.

As he flipped himself off the bike and into the air, the tall man pulled his large .50 caliber pistol and fired twice into the bike's gas tank. An explosion of flames erupted and wiped away dozens of dark ones. Others caught fire and began running around amok.

Then Vic's feet hit the ground. He found himself standing on an open patch of dirt that seemed to widen the circle Steph was protecting, essentially making it bigger. He looked at the path of destruction that the bike had made and saw that it had cleared a path all the way to where G'noch fought.

"What's the matter Bigfoot, afraid we'll show you up if you come fight in our circle?!" Vic yelled out to G'noch.

He saw the large T'kche look up at him and grin, despite having a dark one on his back slashing away at him and another one, tearing at his leg. Vic knew that was all he needed to say, and that if G'noch could make it to them, he would.

Vic holstered his large pistol and pulled the long staff off his back. He engaged a hidden switch on the staff and a long blade came out of the bottom of the weapon, matching the blade on the top. He began to spin his staff, as he backed into the heart of the circle with Steph.

"I guess your old man's gonna have to bail you out of another mess, huh son?" Vic said to Steph while keeping his eyes on the massive gathering of dark ones all around them.

"Dad?! How in the world did you do that? What are you doing here?" Steph couldn't believe any of what had just happened. He had no idea how his father had somehow hurled a motorcycle through a horde of dark ones, then blow it up, lighting countless enemies on fire and was now standing next to him. Not to mention, he was grinning.

"We're about to get torn to pieces and he's grinning. Of course, my dad's grinning." Steph thought.

"Dad's here to kick some ass son. Besides these ugly bastards are trying to take my look, I'm supposed to be the Grim Reaper. What the hell are you doing here boy?" Vic said as a dark one lunged at him and he casually stabbed the bladed end of his staff through its forehead, before spinning the staff and removing the attacker's head. Before Steph could answer, Vic had spun the staff behind his back, slicing off the swinging arm of another attacking dark one, and without stopping the staff from spinning brought it around over his right shoulder to take the head off yet another one.

Steph was shocked, as it looked to him like his father was holding the top of a helicopter, the way he spun the bladed staff, slicing away at attacking dark ones.

Steph did not answer Vic, instead he resumed his dance with the blade, with a renewed energy. His father's bravado inspired him, it motivated him, and somehow, he felt the need to impress his dad. He had never known anyone who was more fearless than his father and he wanted more than anything to make him proud before he fell in battle to these evil creatures.

Grifter raised his head, seemingly aware of his surroundings for the first time since he had collapsed on the ground. He saw the human guardian, Steph, still fighting the never-ending swarm of dark ones with fearless determination. He glanced over his shoulder, still on his knees and saw a human, who had no aura of a guardian and no blessed weapon, fighting off just as many dark ones and smiling while he did it. Grifter, felt ashamed. His pack had resisted fighting, despite the blood oath that needed to be paid. His pack had betrayed him and retreated like cowards and now he found himself with a human guardian who fought against the entire dark one horde without flinching and still took the time to protect him…a Roken he didn't even know.

One could say it was because he had become a guardian, but what of this other seemingly ordinary human, who fought fearlessly with smile on his face, seeming to welcome death.

"NO!!!" Grifter roared. "I will not die lying on the ground! I will fight with this pack! I will defend this pack! I will honor my oaths!" he roared as he slowly started to rise.

"Your dog, gonna stop licking its wounds and fight with us now son?" Vic yelled, as he swept his staff low, cutting off the legs of two dark ones, before spinning it back around to take their heads.

"You dare call me a dog, human?!" Grifter roared as he finally got to his feet.

"You heard me, Rover. You're barking like a German Shepherd, can you bite like one?" Vic said without sparing Grifter a glance.

Grifter was shocked. He couldn't believe that a human would dare speak to him like this, he was tempted to kill the man, but at the same time he immediately respected this human even more. After all the human was right to mock him, he had fallen to die while the guardian had protected him and this new human had dove into certain death, to fight his last fight with them both.

Grifter pushed the pain from his wound that still bled profusely out of his mind, just like he pushed the rage at his pack's betrayal out of his mind and he decided he would show these humans what a Roken was capable of.

"I am a Roken, human, and it will be an honor to die with you both," Grifter growled.

Vic spun the staff with incredible speed and slit the throats of two dark ones that rushed him from either side. As their heads dipped down, where he had slashed, them, he spun past one, then the other, severing the heads from the bodies.

As his motion ended, he glanced at Grifter for the first time and said, "Who the hell said anything about dying?! I'm here to do the killing."

Just then G'noch burst through the wall of dark ones, to their right, swinging his mighty club as he did, splattering several dark ones to pieces. The large T'kche warrior was bleeding from wounds all over his body and had battle rage in his eyes.

"Little foot Vic, come to die with warriors?" G'noch said to Vic, giving him that same toothy grin that he was accustomed to giving.

"Theres my bigfoot buddy! What you get lost over there by yourself?" Vic asked with a smile and then said, "I'll tell you like I told the hound dog over there, I didn't come to die, I came to save your asses!" Vic directed his attention back towards a dark one that leaped through the air at him, caught the creature in the chest with the blade of his staff and used it to slam the creature to the ground. Then he kicked the dark one in the face and spun the staff, slicing its head off while it was still lying on the ground. As he did it he muttered, "All this talk of dying, we're suppose to be doing the killing."

Grifter took it all in and then leaped into the battle, sweeping across half the circle, taking the heads off the front line of dark ones, before skidding to a stop and letting out a howl in the middle of the circle.

"Now that's what I'm talking about Rover!" Vic yelled.

"G'noch like this Roken." G'noch said, as he swung his club through another patch of dark ones. Grifter glanced at G'noch and asked, "Where is Yokan, T'kche?"

"Roken friend help. Dark ones kill." G'noch said, still swinging his club.

Steph didn't really ignore them, but he didn't really pay them any attention either. He was overwhelmingly inspired at not only how his father dove into certain death to fight by his side, but how he somehow managed to rally a resistance in mere seconds. Steph fought with renewed determination, and for the first time since the battle began, he didn't worry about when Mila would do, whatever Brites do. It didn't matter anymore. He was proud to be fighting side by side with his father and would be happy to die this way if that's what it came to. In the process though, Steph was determined to make him proud.

CHAPTER 34
Saving the World

Samuel skidded the bike to a stop in front of Eva, who had been running towards the battle.

"You keep going that way, you'll end up dead before they even know you were on the way. You come with me and maybe we can help Halbred save our world. The choice is yours Eva." Samuel said coldly.

Eva stared at Samuel and then back at the countless numbers of dark ones ahead of her. She knew he was right. She just hadn't known what else to do, and had refused to just stand there while her husband and son died fighting.

"Okay Samuel. What do you have in mind? How do we stop so many of them?" Eva asked. "One at a time Eva. Get on." Samuel said.

Eva jumped onto the motorcycle behind Samuel and as soon as she was positioned he took off. Samuel circled wide past the massive gathering of dark ones that were focused on killing Steph, and now Vic too, and headed straight for the massive 'blur' that so many other dark ones were pouring through.

As he got closer to it, he used one hand to pull the shotgun off of his shoulder and handed it to Eva. "Try to clear us a path. I want to get past them and fight them back, not chase them through." Samuel yelled.

"Clear a path through that?? Ok, Samuel, but I'm starting to think you've been spending too much time with my husband, if you think that will work." Eva said as she used her legs to hold onto the bike and took aim with the shotgun.

Samuel laid on the throttle and did his best to navigate the speeding bike through the thick mass of dark ones fighting to get through the 'blur'. Eva began using the shotgun with what seemed like precision, taking the heads off of ones that stood in their way.

Samuel rode straight over bodies as they fell, continuing to push the bike as hard as he could to fight through the massing of creatures. Claws slashed open their legs and arms, but he kept pushing the bike onward. Two different dark ones had tried to leap at them through the air, but Eva had managed to greet them both with shotgun blasts, before they made it to them.

Eventually, the bike pushed its way through the 'blur', skidding and wobbling before crashing into a burning police car.

They jumped off the bike and Eva turned and kept firing at the dark ones that rushed after them. Samuel rushed past her without pulling any weapons and began to engage the charging mass of dark ones with his bare hands. They would attack and he would dodge, counter, or block, each touch of his hand freezing the enemy where they stood.

In seconds he had created almost a barrier of frozen dark ones between them and the rest of the masses that were still pouring through the 'blur'. The wall of frozen dark ones gave them a break from the attacks, as the rest of the horde seemed to spill in around it. Neither of them had been given a second to take in their surroundings until then and they were both shocked when they did.

They were in the middle of a small, town square of some sort. Several police cars were destroyed and burning and at least ten bodies of fallen officers were scattered around the square. There was a stone fountain in the center of the square and shopping strips all around them, with what appeared to be lofts above them. Samuel could see the broken windows and hear the screams of people whose homes were being invaded by the dark predators from another world.

He saw what looked to be two apartment or loft complexes several stories high, just past the strip malls around the square and could see dark ones scaling up the sides.

In the center of the square, not far from the fountain, was what appeared to be a giant dark one. It looked just like the other creatures swarming everywhere, but it was huge, a literal giant. A few feet from the giant, fighting with what looked like a brick in each hand was Halbred.

The old soldier was surrounded by four dark ones, who battered him with their claws, but despite their efforts the claws could not break through Halbred's impenetrable skin. No matter how much they hit and clawed at him, he just kept on bashing away at them with the bricks. He seemed to be trying to fight his way to the giant in the center of the square.

"Eva! To Halbred!" Samuel yelled, and the two of them began jogging across the town square that had become something straight out of a horror movie.

A dark one here or there noticed them and rushed in, but they were either frozen in seconds by Samuel or beheaded by the shotgun that Eva wielded before they were able to slow the two down.

As they approached Halbred, Samuel grabbed two of the dark ones from behind and froze them instantly. Eva shot a third in the head with the shotgun, while Halbred kept on smashing the fourth one's head in with his pair of battered bricks.

Samuel lightly touched Halbred's shoulder and the old soldier leaped up at him with the bricks, fury and rage in his incoherent eyes. Samuel did not freeze his old friend, he simply sidestepped the attack and said "Halbred! It's me! Snap out of it soldier!"

Halbred blinked and seemed to recognize Samuel and then Eva after a couple seconds. Then he turned his eyes towards the giant dark one, in the center of the square.

"He's got Roid's talisman. That damn path or 'blur' or whatever you want to call it, won't close until we can take it from him. We've got to get that damn thing closed or the entire world will end up turning into these things, Samuel." Halbred said.

"Roid's talisman? How did he get one and where is he? He attacked the cabin with flutter days ago and tried to kill me and Vic when we were in jail." Samuel said in surprise.

"Long story, don't know where he is now, those things threw him in a dungeon or something… wait, what the hell were you and Vic doing in jail, Samuel?" Halbred replied with what seemed to be an equal amount of surprise.

"Long story. We're going to need help here." Samuel said.

Halbred looked at him and patted one of the pouches on his belt, which seemed to be the only article of clothing on the old soldier that wasn't torn to pieces and said "I've radioed it in. Military will take time to get here though, time I don't think we have, but they're coming. They said they have some private contractors they might be able to get here quicker though. I didn't have time to talk to them more than that."

As Samuel listened to Halbred's report out, it triggered a thought. He quickly typed onto the watch he wore, thinking to himself "Any help we can get is better than none".

Then Samuel looked at Halbred, and said "Here", as he pulled the short broad sword out of the sheath on his back and handed it to Halbred. "This might work a little better than those bricks."

"That'll do Samuel. What are you going to use? Those pistols won't do much, you just plan on playing freeze tag with them?" Halbred asked.

Samuel nodded, but before he could respond Eva thrust the shotgun into his chest and said, "Might as well use this until you're out. The Roken gave me weapons that work better against these things than any of ours." As she said it, she engaged the gauntlets and a long blade emerged from each of them.

"The Roken huh? So, saving those hairy bastards turned out helpful." Halbred said. Eva nodded and replied "Yeah, turns out you were right Halbred."

"We've got to move, but when this is all over, I'd be curious to know what a Roken is." Samuel said.

With that the three of them began to work their way across the square towards the giant dark one, that seemed to be watching the chaos and hissing orders.

The sounds of breaking glass and screams of people being attacked seemed to fill the air around them. They saw a crowd of dark ones gathered around the giant, making it clear that they'd have to fight their way to him. As they neared, the crowd saw them too. Eyes locked and just before the dark ones rushed them, two police cars, with sirens blaring came driving through the square towards the giant.

They skidded sideways about ten feet from the giant and the mass of dark ones around him. The officers jumped out of their cars and used the open driver side door as cover and holding assault rifles over the doors. There was no shouting of 'freeze' over the loudspeaker or any words for that matter, the officers just started unleashing a hail of bullets into the gathering of dark ones surrounding the giant.

Instantly the dark ones turned their attention to the officers and rushed at them, paying the bullet wounds that they took on the way no attention at all.

They leapt onto the police cars and in seconds the sounds of gunfire had ceased, only to be replaced once more, by the sounds of screaming and destruction coming from all the buildings around them.

The distraction gave the companions the opening they needed and they took full advantage of it. By the time the gunfire had stopped, they were all but on top of the remaining dark ones gathered by the giant. Halbred, led the charge and dove in swinging the short broad sword like a medieval warrior, hacking, and slashing dark ones on every side of him as he worked to cut his way to the giant. Samuel began firing with the shotgun, walking at a steady pace, with Eva right beside him. Any dark one that managed to make it past the deadly shotgun blasts was met with Eva's bladed gauntlets and a flurry of stabs and slices, until a head rolled free from a dark one's body.

Samuel and Eva's tactical approach seemed effective and allowed them to cut the adversaries between them and the giant, although they both knew that some of their success was really due to Halbred's less refined approach serving as quite the distraction.

An opening presented itself and Samuel shifted his aim towards the giant. He unleashed the shotgun, less concerned about a head shot and more focused on slowing the giant down enough to get to him, he aimed for the legs, firing several rounds at the giant.

The gunfire exploded on the giant's left leg and blood burst from huge wounds that opened up. The giant dark one let out a mighty hiss that echoed across the square, and turned and rushed at Samuel, with speed that made the fastest dark ones look slow.

Before it connected with Samuel however, a battered Halbred cut it off. Rushing in swinging his short sword furiously at the giant dark one's right leg, hacking away at it.

The beast staggered and Samuel aimed for its head and pulled the trigger, only to hear a "clicking" noise instead of the roar of a gun blast. The shotgun was out of ammo.

The giant kicked Halbred back, just as Eva danced past its injured left leg and sliced the wounds open even more with her deadly gauntlets. Her attack seemed effective for but a second, before the giant swung hard with its left arm, hitting her in the chest and sending her entire body flying through the air and crashing into Samuel. Both of them hit the concrete fountain with incredible force. They looked up, as they tried to rise and saw the giant holding both its hands together and beating Halbred with the interlocked fists.

They staggered to their feet and saw six dark ones rushing them from each side. Samuel tossed the shotgun aside and faced off against the attackers to his left barehanded, while Eva rose to her feet shakily, facing the six rushing in from the right.

As she did, she said "There's too many of them Samuel. How are we ever going to stop them all?"

Samuel didn't answer. They both knew there was no answer to that question, just like they both knew that they would keep fighting until they were eventually overwhelmed by these deadly creatures.

Before the group to the right made it to Eva, a flurry of motion seemed to stop the creatures in their paths. There was a flash of something or someone, the dark one in the lead lost its head and the flash appeared behind the group, where another dark one was decapitated. In seconds, the six dark ones that had been rushing her were nothing more than headless bodies. Shocked, Eva looked over her shoulder past Samuel and saw the same thing happening to the group that had been rushing him.

As the last one fell, the blurry appearing and disappearing of what seemed to be a figure, stopped and they saw Dante standing before them in all black, wearing his crisscrossed straps across his chest that held countless daggers and holding something that resembled a samurai sword.

He looked at them both, then locked eyes with Samuel and said, "Gotta take their heads huh?" Then Dante shifted his eyes to the giant and exclaimed, "And I thought the one at the jail was big?! What did you guys get yourselves into?"

CHAPTER 35
The Call

The alert on his phone went off for the third time before Dante decided to see what it was. He was alone in his loft, thinking through the chaos of the previous days. When he finally picked up the phone, he saw that Riker had been reaching out, claiming it was urgent.

He hesitated for a moment before deciding with a dramatic sigh that he might as well see what job Riker was offering him and clicked on the icon that would contact Riker.

Riker immediately picked up and said, "Got something for you. It's from the government and they're willing to pay big, real big, but you gotta get there now Dante. They only reached out to me because they know what you can, you know 'do'. If you can get there and hold off the enemy forces until my men and the government reinforcements arrive, you'll have enough money to quit taking jobs all year if you want to. What do you say, Dante?"

It took Dante a moment to digest everything that Riker had said. The mercenary had spit it all out so quickly that it was hard to follow. After a few seconds it all sunk in and Dante responded by asking, "What is the job? Why do they need someone to teleport there now?"

Riker responded by saying, "Not just someone, Dante. They need you specifically, and that's because of the job." When Dante didn't reply, Riker kept going, "Remember the thing you fought in front of the jail? Well, it's them, smaller versions of them, but still those things, lots of those things Dante. They're coming out of some kind of gateway and terrorizing a small town. The government needs it contained and under wraps. They asked for you, since you can mobilize faster than the rest of us and because you already faced off with one of these things and came out on top."

Dante was shocked by what he was hearing. "How in the world do they know about me battling that thing in front of the jail, Riker? How do you even know about it?" He exclaimed.

"Come on, Dante. You know we comb through all the satellite feeds of our team's engagements. I know, I know, you're a subcontractor, not part of the team, but I watched it anyway. Nice moves by the way. You sliced that muscle bound monster up, man." Riker said.

"Riker?" Dante said impatiently.

"Ok, yeah, well you were in front of a jail and a ton of cops got killed. Did you not think they would comb through all the video footage? They didn't even need our satellite feeds, there were cameras everywhere. Did you know that thing disappeared after you diced it up?" Riker said

As Dante was listening, he noticed the watch that Samuel had given him, blinking from across the room where it sat on a counter. With Riker still on the phone, he walked over to the watch and saw the distress icon flashing its location.

"Riker, what are the coordinates?" Dante asked.

As Riker read off the coordinates, Dante stared at the watch and saw that they matched the exact location of the distress signal from Samuel. "Definitely not a coincidence," He thought.

"Send me pictures of the location. I'll be there as soon as I load up… and Riker, don't come, I work alone remember," Dante stated firmly.

"Dante, the feds are en route and there's a ton of them, you sure man?" Riker asked.

Dante didn't answer. He just hung up the phone and walked across the room. He was still wearing his boots and tactical pants, so he just threw on his black jacket, strapped the crisscrossed dagger holders across his chest, picked up the phone again opening the video clip that Riker had sent of the location.

Dante stared at it for a moment, locking the mental picture into his mind, and then paused just before he teleported. Something Samuel had said ran through his mind, "You have to take their heads".

Dante walked over to the closet, opened it up and stared at the variety of knives and blades hanging on the wall. He reached up and grabbed a samurai sword from a bracket on the top of the wall.

"This should work. I'm sure not going to try to cut their heads off with daggers," He thought. With one final look around, Dante closed his eyes and disappeared.

A split second later, he was standing in the midst of pure chaos. Creatures that looked eerily similar to the muscular beast he had faced ran through the streets. These creatures were not abnormally large and muscle bound, like the one he faced, though. They were leaner, and all wore tattered black cloaks that did little to hide their translucent skin and claw-like fingers and toes.

The creatures dove through the windows of stores and the lofts that sat above them. They scaled the exterior walls of what appeared to be apartment buildings or lofts right behind the stores in the main town square, where he stood. The air was filled with noises of destruction and screams of terror and death.

As Dante took it all in, three creatures spotted him and rushed towards him, flickering their long black tongues and reaching with their claws. Dante, immediately shifted his attention from surveying the destruction around him, to the first of the enemies he was sent to "contain". Right before they were upon him, he disappeared and reappeared directly behind them. With one strong sideways swipe of the samurai sword, he took two heads off. The third creature turned and dove at him. Right when the claws were sinking into his arm, he teleported behind it and took its head as he had the others.

"Ok. No standing still with these things, they're just too fast. Slice and move, slice and move. I got this." Dante thought to himself. Then he noticed the giant in the middle of the square. He didn't know what to think as he stared at the massive creature. He finally snapped out of it, when he realized the giant version of these vile creatures was actually being attacked and then attacking back.

It took only a second for Dante to recognize Halbred. Then he saw a woman get struck and she flew into another man, both of them crashing into the side of a stone fountain set in the middle of the town square. As the two got up, Dante realized it was Eva, Vic's wife and Samuel. He also realized that while the two of them were getting their bearings, they were about to be attacked by a half dozen creatures from each side.

"Ok, Dante. Slice and move, slice and move. No standing still to fight these things." He said out loud to himself and then he teleported directly behind the group rushing for Eva.

CHAPTER 36
An Honor and a Privilege

"I see you got my call," Samuel said to Dante.

"Yeah, I got a couple calls, Samuel. The government is sending more help, but I have no idea how long it will take," Dante replied somberly as he took in the rest of the scene around them.

More and more dark ones were gathering near the giant, seeming enthralled or excited to see the giant one of them furiously beating Halbred into the ground.

Others still scattered about the square and could be seen taking off past the buildings, spreading their terror to the homes on the outskirts of the town square.

"Where do we start, Samuel? Fighting one of these things is hard enough, but there are so many of them and they're everywhere," Dante said in defeated tones that showed his youth.

"They're going to keep coming too, Dante, if we don't stop the big one. He's holding a circular stone in his hand, like the one around my neck. If we can take it from him, or kill him, the path closes. That's priority number one. Once we cut off their way here, we'll worry about killing the ones that made it to our world," Samuel stated firmly, in such a determined tone that it made Eva and Dante wonder if he noticed how many of these creatures were all around them.

"He has definitely been spending way too much time with Vic," Eva thought.

"Ok, but what about the group of them gathering around him, that just started staring at us?" Dante asked.

Samuel and Eva quickly turned their heads towards the giant dark one, who was still beating Halbred with interlocked fists, and saw that Dante was right. The entire crowd of dark creatures that had gathered by the giant was now staring at the three of them. Then, as if they had been waiting to be noticed before attacking, they all began rushing towards them at once.

"Teleport past them, move fast, take his legs and his body, chop him down and take his head or take the hand that holds the talisman. That's all that matters Dante. We'll take care of them and then we'll join you," Samuel said, as he slowly began walking towards the approaching wave of creatures.

"We'll take all of them and then help him with the giant?!" Eva asked in clear disbelief. "Do you even have a plan or are you just planning to rush in and hope it all works out like my husband does?!"

"Stay behind me Eva, I'll freeze them, you take their heads. If any of them get past me, yell." Samuel said coldly, as he continued to walk towards the approaching mass of beasts with his guns still in their holsters, and his bare hands clenching and unclenching.

"Holy shit! Is he serious?!" Eva exclaimed.

"Come on, Eva, we both know that Samuel's always serious. Good to see you again, by the way.

Hope you don't die," Dante said in response, and then he was gone.

Eva looked up and saw Dante appear behind the giant dark one and immediately slash open the back of the dark one's left leg. She watched the beast shift its attention from the unmoving body of Halbred and turn towards Dante in a rage. As it spun around, she saw Dante disappear again and once again reappear behind the massive dark creature only to slash open the back of its right leg.

Figuring that Dante knew what he was doing, she shifted her attention to Samuel, just as the first of the dark ones reached him.

Four of the creatures dove at him at the same time, two went low towards his mid-section, while the other two leaped directly over them, obviously going for his head. Samuel ducked under the ones leaping at his head and as he did, he punched the two diving towards his midsection in their faces. Both of his fists, both their faces, freezing both of them on contact at the same time. Then without missing a step he reached up and touched a leg of each of the dark ones that were flying over his head. Their bodies were frozen still, as they crashed to the ground.

The next wave followed the first one, and Eva watched as Samuel ducked and dodged swinging claws, each blocking move or counterpunch left his adversaries frozen. In seconds the fight had completely changed. She saw Samuel dancing around the frozen bodies, using them as cover. He would duck behind a frozen dark one as another attacked, only to spin out from the other side of the frozen beast and punch the attacker in the head or body. Where he hit them varied, but every hit, added another frozen creature to the town square that had become this bloody battlefield.

Eva counted thirteen frozen dark creatures and watched as Samuel continued to fight into their ranks, filling the square with living statues as he did. She snapped herself out of the momentary amazement at what she was witnessing, thinking to herself, "He might really be able to take out an entire army".

Then Eva shook her head and got to work. She started with the closest ones and began using her gauntlets to cut the heads off of frozen dark ones, while Samuel continued to fight and freeze an army of the vicious creatures on his own. Eva quickly felt more like she was cutting firewood than battling enemies, but Samuel's plan seemed to be working and she knew she would not likely fare as well if she chose to dive into the melee with him, so she kept on. Head after head, she kept on. Each time she relieved a frozen creature of its head, the body slumped to the ground, frozen no more.

"Oh shit, he's fast!" Dante thought as he sped up his teleporting and slashing around the giant dark one. Each time he reappeared to slash at the dark one, the creature was just a little closer to catching Dante with its wild swings. Dante knew that if he slowed down, even slightly, this thing would surely catch him and was starting to think that if he didn't speed up, he'd be caught eventually too.

He moved faster, and saw the giant fall to its knees, the constant slashing finally paying off. Dante did not stop though; he continued to teleport around the beast slashing at its back and the sides of its arms with the samurai sword.

Halbred climbed out of the indentation that his body had made in the ground, shakily. He looked over at the giant dark one, mumbling to himself "That's twice today this damned oversized hell spawn has literally beaten me into the ground. I'm going to kill that damn thing if I have to chew its freaking head off with my teeth!" His mumbling got louder as he spoke and grew angrier.

As the rage built up, it finally registered to him that the giant was on its knees and being cut to pieces by someone teleporting all around it. Halbred instantly recognized Dante, thinking "I thought the kid was dead. Huh? Well, he doesn't get to show up and finish that damn thing off on his own."

Then he noticed that the giant was just swinging one arm wildly, but looking to the opposite side of its body from where it was swinging and held its free arm up, with claws pointed. "He looks like it's waiting to spear a fish… oh hell! Dante's the damn fish!" Halbred thought as he began running towards the giant. He wasn't far away. It took four strides and then he leaped for the giant's upraised arm.

Halbred hit the arm with his body, just when Dante appeared in the spot the giant was staring at and struck. The claws would've surely impaled the young man's entire body had Halbred not hit the large beast when he had. The result was that Halbred knocked the giant's arm off course and its claws pierced through Dante's right arm, instead of the center of his body. Dante dropped the sword and fell to the ground, holding his right arm.

Halbred hit the ground next to Dante, grabbed the fallen weapon, and spun around stabbing the samurai sword into the giant's left eye. The beast roared out in pain and rage, and grabbed Halbred by the throat with its free hand, screaming "Why won't you die?!!!"

Then it stopped screaming. It stopped moving altogether and Halbred easily slipped out of its grip, only to see Samuel standing next to the giant beast that he'd obviously frozen.

The chaos everywhere around them stopped. Every single dark creature that they could see stared at them, with hateful, deadly eyes.

As more poured through the open 'blur' they instantly stopped and stared too, like they could feel what had happened to their apparent leader.

"Nice for you to finally join the fight, Samuel," Halbred said with a grin.

"Take off its head quickly, to close the path Halbred. We have to stop more from crossing over before we're overrun by the ones staring at us." Samuel said coldly.

Halbred looked around the square that was now as crowded as could be. Tightly packed with these dark creatures that had crossed over. He glanced at Dante bleeding on the ground, then at Eva who now stood by Samuel looking bloody and exhausted, then to Samuel who was bleeding from countless claw wounds across his body, but stood unfazed, staring at the enemies around them.

"He just thinks about the next task. About what has to be done. About the mission." Halbred thought admirably. Then he thought, "He's right though. The rest of them can die, and he knows we'll never make it past this many of these creatures."

All Halbred said though was, "It's been an honor and a privilege to serve this world with you, Samuel." He gave Samuel a stern meaningful look when he said it and then the old soldier raised his arms back and swung the samurai sword for the giant's neck as hard as he could. Before the head was severed from the body, though, they were all blinded and time seemed to stop.

CHAPTER 37
The Fall of Heroes

By the time the flood of dark creatures stopped pouring out of the burning pyramid, or dark temple, there were almost three thousands of them crowded onto the plains. Many were pushing and shoving, fighting for their turn to try to squeeze through the giant 'blur' on the battlefield, while all the rest seemed to be trying to crowd into the giant mass circling the only remaining resistance.

In the center of that shrinking circle of resistance, four beings fought on. A human father and his son, a betrayed ruler of the Roken people, and a lone T'kche warrior whose family had been taken from him. All battered and bleeding, all facing certain death, yet all fighting with a sense of honor and determination that seemed to fuel the others around them.

They were literally keeping each other going. Each of them drawing inspiration from the courage and ferocity of the one fighting next to them, and that and Vic's taunting too…

"I'm starting to think that's the only move you got, Rover!" Vic yelled out, as he lunged low and forward with the spinning staff, cutting open the chests of four dark ones before him. As he did, they hissed at him, stretching their necks out, just enough for him to come back around with the spinning, bladed staff and remove their heads.

"You just keep running and scratching, no finesse. While me, on the other hand, I could win the Olympics of staff fighting! These ugly bastards aren't even getting close to me! Take some notes, you might learn a thing or two," Vic said, as he jumped into the air avoiding a dark one that dove low at his legs. He landed back a few feet from the creature, taking another of many nasty claw wounds to his legs from the dark one before beheading it with a downward spinning motion of his staff.

"Much of your blood soaks this land, for them not to be getting close to you human!" Grifter roared in response, as he slashed away at the dark creatures pressing in before him.

"Must be their blood. They ain't touching me, Rover!" Vic yelled back, as he sidestepped another clawed lunge and took the head off the creature before him.

Steph heard his father keep prodding at the three of them and heard it becoming more and more forced. They all could see they were getting forced back, as the circle shrank on them from the press of countless creatures relentlessly attacking them. He knew, that soon-very soon-they would have no room left to maneuver with their weapons. They all knew it. Just like they all knew that the battle would be over when that moment came.

G'noch swung steadily with his club, never seeming to tire. Clearing patches with every devastating swing, but the openings filled faster and faster with more and more enemies. Steph danced with the large two-handed blade, slicing away at foe after foe, but more and more kept coming.

As the circle shrank, more and more dark ones made their way into the clearing. None of them had lasted long, but almost every one of them had drawn blood from someone in the group. They were all wounded and bleeding-G'noch and Grifter, worst of all.

Steph worried that each of them would fall from sheer loss of blood soon. Yet somehow, he was still amazed at his father, whose clothes were now covered with blood they all knew wasn't from the dark ones, yet he hadn't slowed down at all. Vic just kept spinning the staff, with grace and precision, shredding and beheading one enemy after another. Steph realized in that moment that this man was more to him than just his father-he was his hero, pure and simple.

Steph's thoughts of admiration and his dance of the blade were all interrupted when the battle drastically changed all of a sudden.

One of the dark ones picked up a tire from the motorcycle Vic had hurled earlier. The creature jumped into the air with the tire and threw it at Vic with incredible force. Vic, still spinning his bladed staff into the attacking horde, never saw it coming.

The tire struck Vic in the midsection, sending him flying back into the center of the clearing and crashing hard to the ground, with the breath knocked out of him. Knocking him aside presented an opening in the defenses that the attacking creatures immediately took advantage of.

They rushed into the circle with force.

Steph felt his father's body hit his legs and looked down; he saw Vic lying on the ground, holding his stomach with one arm and reaching for the staff he had dropped with the other. Steph looked back and saw the dark creatures rushing in towards them. He leaped over his father's body and slashed at the attacking flood with his massive sword. Cutting the bodies of the first three rushing in, in half. As he turned his back to defend his father though, the creatures behind him slashed his back open down the middle.

Steph tried to swing back at them, but when he did, his arm was ripped open from the claws coming from the other side. He yelled out in pain and saw a large club strike down on the dark ones attacking him from one side. From the corner of his eye, he also saw that when G'noch turned to defend him, he had left himself open to attack. Rather than jumping on his back slashing away at the T'kche again, several dark ones rushed into his legs, knocking the large T'kche off his feet and sending him crashing to the ground. In an instant G'noch could barely be seen as countless dark ones dove onto him slashing and biting at him. Steph roared and slashed at the ones on top, but when he did, he noticed several more creatures lunging in at his fallen father, so he pivoted and slashed at them, cutting them off before Vic was covered up, like G'noch.

Steph felt his left calf get torn open. When he swung at the attacker, he felt his right side get torn open. He fought to remain on his feet and defend his fallen father and felt Grifter shoulder-to-shoulder with him trying to do the same.

He saw dark ones fly into the air, as G'noch emerged from the dog pile swinging his massive fists at dark ones, having lost his club somewhere in the battle. Steph saw that the large T'kche's stomach had been torn open and that massive amounts of blood were pouring out of those wounds, including one on the side of the T'kche's neck. Then Steph felt the burn of a claw ripping open the front of his chest, while another one ripped open the side of his neck. He staggered and dropped his sword, although he still stood over his fallen father. Black spots filled his vision, and he heard G'noch howl out in pain.

Then suddenly they were all blinded. Time itself instantly seemed to stop. Pain seemed to stop. Breathing and bleeding all seemed to stop. There was no noise, just the silence of nothingness and an overwhelming brightness that consumed them all.

The bright explosion of pure white light enveloped everything, not only across not just the world that they had come to know as the 'other side', but it also flooded through the open pathway, or 'blur', covering the home world of the companions. There was no way to tell how long the light lasted, as it truly seemed to stop time. They didn't know if everything stood still for a second or for a thousand lifetimes, but when the light finally cleared, everything was different.

CHAPTER 38

Changing of Seasons

The never-ending brightness finally faded, and Samuel blinked his eyes, trying to regain the sight that had been stolen from him. As his vision slowly returned, it was the silence that struck him first. There were no more screams or sounds of destruction or anything else for that matter, just silence.

He saw that the giant 'blur' that had served as a path to the 'other side' was gone. Turning his head, he saw that the giant was gone too. Where it had been was nothing but a small circular stone talisman lying on the ground. Samuel reached down and picked it up, placing it securely in the pocket of his badly disheveled coat as he continued to look around.

There were no more dark ones anywhere, as far as he could tell. The destruction and devastation left behind from their apparently short-lived invasion was everywhere, but the creatures themselves were gone. He heard moaning and looked over to see Dante on the ground, holding his injured arm. Halbred stood over him and was helping him up. Samuel looked to his left to see a bloody and beaten, Eva, standing there dazed, blinking her eyes, trying to regain her sight as he had just done.

Samuel turned his attention back to surveying the square and said out loud, to no one in particular, "They're all gone."

It was Halbred who responded, saying, "Yeah, but how? What took them out and how the hell are we still standing?" The old soldier said it with Dante's arm over his shoulder, helping the young man walk over towards Samuel.

Eva walked over to stand by the others and said quietly, "Mila."

They all looked at her with puzzled looks and then what she had said seemed to hit both Halbred and Samuel like a ton of bricks. Without another word, Samuel stepped forward and initiated the sequence on the stone talisman that he wore engaging it. Almost instantly the 'blur' appeared, and without a word Samuel stepped through, followed by Eva.

"What the hell are they talking about and why did they just cross back over when we barely stopped those things? They could all be right on the other side of that damn blur." Dante asked in surprise.

"You've got a lot to learn kid. We'll bring you up to speed, but not now. For now, just come on, I'll help you." Halbred said kindly, as he helped Dante through the 'blur' with him.

As Samuel emerged from the 'blur' onto the blood-soaked plains of the 'other side' he saw exactly what he had expected, not a dark one in sight. The temple or pyramid that they had been swarming out of was now nothing more than a pile of stone and rubble.

Then he looked across the plain and saw Steph standing up rubbing his eyes. Next to him G'noch was sitting on the ground rubbing his eyes as well. Then Samuel noticed Vic lying at Steph's feet, along with another man who lay naked on the ground not far from them. Other than that group, the destroyed temple and what was left of Vic's exploded motorcycle, there was nothing else at all on the plains as far as his eyes could see.

Eva rushed past him, running with a clear limp, but running nonetheless towards Steph and Vic. Samuel followed and, without meaning to, found himself running as well. Overwhelmed with concern for these people he had come to care for so much.

As he ran, he found it ironic that mere minutes before, he had known they would all die at the hands of the dark ones and now he found himself clinging to hope that his friend was somehow still alive.

Eva got to them first and embraced Steph. Eva squeezed him with the type of hug that only a mother hugging her child whom she thought she had lost could produce. After a moment, she released him, stepped back looking at him strangely and asked in bewilderment, "How do you not have a scratch on you, Steph?"

Steph seemed confused by the question, but when he looked down at himself, he realized that he no longer had any wounds. He wasn't bleeding. His body didn't hurt. He was in better shape than he had been when he had entered the battle.

Stunned and in shock, he looked over at G'noch who was picking himself up off the ground. He noticed that his large T'kche friend also looked perfectly fine. He didn't believe his own eyes, having just moments before watched the dark creatures tearing the flesh off of his friend. Yet now, here he was, just like Steph, standing there without a scratch.

Hope replaced shock as he looked down at his fallen father, but he did not see what he had hoped for. Vic was still covered in blood, lying still on the ground. He felt his voice get caught in his throat and was unable to move or speak. He just stared at his father lying there.

Eva followed Steph's eyes and when her own eyes landed on Vic, she gasped. She stood staring, just like Steph, not moving an inch.

Samuel however, knelt down next to Vic and put one hand under his head and the other under his friend's back, sitting up the tall man. To everyone's surprise, Vic started coughing up blood and choking. Samuel patted his back and held him up in a sitting position until the coughing fit had stopped. Then he took his hand from behind Vic's head, still holding him up with the other hand, and wiped the blood from his eyes.

Vic blinked and looked around, then he mumbled something faintly.

No one could make out what he said, so Samuel leaned closer and said, "What is it, Vic?"

Again, Vic mumbled the words. Obviously, it was a struggle to get them out, and the man was in much pain, But he managed to say them loud enough for everyone to hear this time, saying "I told you I was gonna kick their asses."

Samuel grinned and shook his head, while Halbred, who had finally made it over to them with Dante just said, "Yep, Vic's alright."

Eva leaned down and embraced her husband, albeit gently, so as not to hurt him any more than he was already.

Steph just stared at his father in shock.

G'noch on the other hand, walked over to where Grifter lay on the ground, bloody and in his human form. The large T'kche felt his chest and leaned down to listen, then picked him up in his arms and said, "Roken hurt bad. Need help."

"Looks like Vic does too, Buddy, " Halbred said. "Let's get these boys back to the cabin. We can see to their wounds there."

Halbred used the talisman he wore to open a pathway, or 'blur', next to them all and then looked at Dante and said, "You OK to stand on your own, kid?"

In response, Dante pulled his arm free of Halbred's support and stood there on his own, cradling his injured arm. In truth, he had forgotten about his injury. He was just staring at G'noch with his mouth wide open.

Halbred looked at him strangely, then patted him gently on his back and said, "Shake it, off kid, it's just our friendly neighborhood G'noch."

Samuel picked Vic up off the ground gently and said, "You fought well, friend, I got you." Vic looked up at Samuel and surprisingly didn't say a word.

Then Steph walked over to Vic and Samuel and while Samuel still held Vic, Steph put his forehead against his father's and began to cry.

"I love you Dad. Thank you," Steph said.

Vic said, "I love you too. You fought well. I'm damn proud of you, son."

Samuel didn't move, refusing to interrupt this priceless moment between father and son. No one there did.

The two stayed that way for several minutes, before Steph turned from them and wrapped his arms around his mother once again. While holding her close and still weeping, he said out loud through his tears, "She's gone. She said that she loves you both, but that this was her destiny. She gave herself to this world, to save it, or to change the seasons. I couldn't stop her, and I couldn't save her, so I helped her instead. I don't know if you'll understand, and I'll miss her forever, but I'm not sorry. It was her destiny and she fulfilled it well. I'm proud of my big sister."

When Steph finished talking, Eva yelled, "No!" and began to cry herself, squeezing Steph tighter as she did. "She can't be gone! She was just a child!" Eva yelled through a fit of tears.

"You know she was far more than that, Mom. She was something beyond us all. She was chosen and she saved all of us and this entire world, maybe both our worlds, by fulfilling her destiny." Steph said lovingly through his tears, still holding onto his mother tightly.

The only thing Vic said was, "Put me down Samuel."

Samuel gently eased his tall friend down onto his feet, holding him up and steady as he did. He saw that Vic was bleeding from wounds all over his legs, arms, neck and back, but that it was his mid- section that he leaned into, appearing to hurt there the most. Despite the injuries, Vic stood on his own and slowly walked over to his wife and son and wrapped his long, bloody arms around them both. Tears flowed from his eyes as he did, but no more words were said.

As the rest looked on, G'noch slowly made his way over to Halbred and handed the unconscious Grifter over to the old soldier. As he did, he said, "Help Roken, friend. He warrior like us."

"Sure thing, big guy, but we're all going to the same place. Why give him to me?" Halbred said in response.

G'noch gently put his hand on Halbred's thick shoulder and said, "G'noch stay. G'noch guardian to this world. Be safe, little foot Halbred. Keep friends safe."

Halbred looked up at the large T'kche to argue but saw clearly in the large warrior's eyes that there would be no talking him out of this, so he remained silent and simply nodded.

As the embrace finally ended, Steph wiped away his tears and stepped back from his parents.

Then he said, "I'm staying here too. I cannot go back with you." "What are you talking about, Steph?!" Eva exclaimed.

"G'noch is right. We were chosen. We are guardians of this world now. We have a duty here. I don't know how to explain it. I don't even understand it. I just know it's my destiny to stay here." Steph said firmly and stared at his parents, hoping they would understand.

"No!" Eva said. "This isn't even our world! It cannot have both of my children! It cannot have you too, Steph!" As she yelled, her tears returned.

"I know it isn't easy to understand mom. How do you think we got here? How do you think we got these weapons and knew to lure the beasts outside, so Mila could destroy them all? We are guardians and our place is here. Like I said, I don't understand it either, but I know it's where I belong. I'm sorry. I love you both and I'll miss you." Steph said, fighting to keep from crying again.

He didn't second guess his decision, though; if anything he felt more and more sure about it as he tried to explain it.

Vic nodded and stepped closer to his son. He took his watch off and put it on Steph's wrist himself, saying, "This time keep it on. We'll be coming to visit." Then he looked up into his son's eyes and said, "Do what you have to do. I'm proud of the man you are, Steph… and don't you dare get yourself killed."

Then Vic looked over at G'noch and said, "Don't you let anything happen to him, hairy!"

G'noch simply nodded.

"Take care of yourself, Steph. You turned out to be one hell of a soldier. I hope to see you again, son," Halbred said, then he looked at Dante and said, "Alright, let's go, kid." He stepped through the 'blur'.

Dante followed Halbred through the 'blur' without a word.

Samuel looked at G'noch and Steph and felt like he was losing a part of his family as well. As he looked from one to the other, he said, "I will sincerely miss you both. I have come to care for you like family. Take care of yourselves, and if you ever need help, step through to the 'top side' and hit the beacon on your watch. We'll come for you." With that, Samuel turned and walked through the 'blur'.

Vic embraced his son once more, and Eva joined in. After several more minutes of hugging and 'I love yous,' the couple turned and stepped through the 'blur' to the 'top side'. It disappeared behind them, leaving G'noch and Steph standing alone on the blood-soaked plain.

Steph looked at G'noch and asked, "How do you think we ended up without a scratch?" In response G'noch said, "Brite heal guardians."

"If Brite's heal guardians, then why aren't there ever any other surviving guardians, G'noch?" Steph asked in response.

G'noch simply said, "Wounds heal. Dead is dead. We not die." Then the large T'kche began walking off, in the opposite direction of the forest that they had entered the plains from.

Steph stood there and seemed to think about G'noch's response for a moment, and then jogged to catch up with the large T'kche, picking his sword up on the way, as G'noch had done with his massive club.

"So where do we go?" Steph said as they walked.

G'noch just shrugged and kept walking. Then, as if on cue, a leaf carried by a breeze from nowhere blew right in front of Steph and almost hovered for a second.

Out of instinct more than anything else, Steph snatched it out of the air. When he did, a shock ran through his body and for just a moment his eyes glowed. He stopped walking and G'noch stopped as well, staring at him with interest.

After a moment, Steph looked up at G'noch and said, "We must go to the coast to the south. There is a small village. The creatures there will need our help." As he said it, the leaf in his hand crumbled to dust and blew away.

G'noch stared at Steph but did not say a word. Steph stared back, in shock at the realization and clarity of what must be done that had just hit him when he touched the leaf. He was just as shocked at what he had said without even meaning to. After a few long moments of silence, the two began walking again, shifting their direction to the south.

CHAPTER 39

Homeward Bound

The group remained silent as they emerged from the 'blur' and let it close behind them. Despite the victory of sorts, they all felt the heavy weight of loss on their shoulders. The silence, along with their feelings of loss and sadness, were interrupted, however, by the roar of the helicopters that were landing at various spots around the destroyed town square. The helicopters were all black, with no markings or insignias on them anywhere.

Samuel counted six of the large helicopters, and watched as heavily armed soldiers in all-black uniforms poured out of each one, taking up positions around them and aiming their rifles at the group of companions.

"Stay calm. I'll handle this," Halbred said quietly to them all, as he stepped forward, still holding the bleeding, and unconscious Grifter in his arms.

"Put your guns down and help us, dammit! I'm Commander Halbred and these people need medical attention!" Halbred bellowed out at the soldiers surrounding them.

"We know who you are, Commander." said a large man, with a thick grey mustache. Everything about him seemed military, but if he wore a uniform, it could not be seen under the thick black overcoat that he wore. He had a black beret on his head and spoke gruffly, his voice seeming to carry over the sound of the helicopters and across the square without him yelling.

Everyone in the small group shifted their attention to the man, who was obviously in charge. "Ok, you know me. Now who the hell are you, and why are your men still aiming their weapons at us?!

Don't you realize we are the ones that just neutralized the enemy threat that could've potentially wiped out everything and everyone everywhere?!" Halbred roared.

"I do. I watched it all on the satellite feed, well, watched it all until everything blinked out," The man responded roughly. He shifted his gaze across the group for a moment before resting his eyes back on Halbred and continuing.

"I also realize that two of the men with you are wanted for the murder of several jailors and police officers in two different towns. Now, where we go from here depends entirely on you, Commander, well, you and young Dante there." The man said roughly.

Before Halbred could respond again, Samuel spoke up. "If your satellite feeds let you see this battle against a foe you've never dreamed of, then surely they showed you that we weren't the ones responsible for any of that!"

"Perhaps, Agent 17, and perhaps we make it all go away. Right now, though, people can't know what attacked this town, or the jail for that matter, and blaming you and Victor there is the easiest explanation for it all. That is, unless Halbred and Dante agree to come help us." The man seemed to pause for effect, before continuing.

"Really, we may expect help from all of you, but for now, we'll give you a lift back to your cabin, while Commander Halbred and young Dante come with us. Yes, we know about your 'secret cabin' too. So, what do you say, gentlemen?" The strange military man in charge said to them with a sinister grin.

"Well, shit. Not much of a choice here, fellas, unless we all want to try to slip back to the 'other side' before one of these boys can stick a bullet in us," Halbred muttered quietly to the group gathered around him.

"We could always kick their asses." Vic managed to mumble, while he coughed a little more blood up.

They all looked at him and shook their heads. Then Halbred looked at Samuel and said, "I'll get a signal to you, if you need to make a break for it. Until then, hang at the cabin and let the wounds heal up." As the old soldier spoke to Samuel, he handed him the still unconscious body of Grifter and then turned his attention to Dante.

"Look kid, I know you can disappear out of here in a flash, but I'm counting on you not ditching us. I figure if you were willing to come help save our asses, you might as well stick around long enough to see why these boys are asking for you and me by name. What do you say?" Halbred asked Dante.

"Yeah, let's go, but Halbred, the minute things look sketchy, I'm out of there. You and the rest of them will have to figure it out from there. I don't owe any of you anything." Dante said coldly, yet loud enough for the entire group to hear.

"Fair enough kid. Fair enough." Halbred said. Then he looked up at the man in the beret and the black over coat and asked, "So, where are we going?"

"Come with me. The rest of you go to that chopper, they'll take you back to the cabin." The man said pointing at a large chopper across the square. With that said, he turned his back and headed to the closest helicopter. He hopped in and sat in a seat without looking back.

Halbred and Dante, walked across the square, followed by six soldiers, and joined him the helicopter. When it took off, all of the remaining soldiers around the square loaded back up into their respective helicopters and took off, leaving just one helicopter with two soldiers and the pilot. They were obviously waiting to take the remaining companions back to the cabin, or so they said.

"We might as well go with them." Samuel said to Vic and Eva, as he began walking towards the helicopter. The couple slowly followed him, and in seconds they were airborne. All of them sat in seats except Grifter who was strapped down to a gurney in the middle of the large chopper.

They silently stared at the destruction of what was once a small-town square, as they lifted off and left it behind them. The chopper headed north, in the direction of the cabin, while the battered and beaten companions sat in a heavy silence.

The End

Epilogue 1

"Wow! You guys sure did a number on her." Riker said as he looked at Flutter's dissected body on the large table. Her head had been removed, cut in half, and placed on a separate table. Her body had been cut open and spread apart, and now lay dissected with many strange organs scattered all over the table.

"Yes, Captain Riker, we learned much in the process. The weaponizing of these creature's eggs could completely change the world as we know it," The man in the lab coat standing next to Riker said with a hint of pride.

After a moment of seeming to reflect on his accomplishment, the man in the lab coat continued, "We must verify its level of success before we can move on, though! So far, none of your men have returned from the reconnaissance efforts. Are you sure these two will fare any better?"

Riker stared at the smaller man in the lab coat for a long moment, letting his anger at being questioned be felt before answering. Finally, he responded,, "I told you this is the play. The kid's just a damn knife fighter with a disappearing act, but he'll get them in and out. The old man is tougher than a tank, and the things you're trying to create can't bite him. We'll get our answers as long as you play it like I said and don't slip up. Those two must think this is a sanctioned government operation. So don't screw it up!"

It was obvious that Riker was more than angry by the time he finished responding. He continued to stare at the man in the lab coat for another minute before adding, "And Doc, don't question my effectiveness again, or you'll end up on a table in pieces just like her. I don't need a damn lab coat to dissect your ass, little man!" Riker said viciously as he pointed at what was left of Flutter on the table.

The man in the lab coat didn't respond. Instead, he looked down, so as not to provoke the volatile mercenary any more than he already had.

Riker tapped the earpiece that he wore and then addressed the soldiers and the other men in lab coats in the room, saying, "That's the signal, the Colonel has them. Get in your positions and get everything ready."

As he finished, everyone in the room started scrambling, before the man in the lab coat could walk away, Riker grabbed him by the arm and leaned in close, saying, "Don't ever question me again, little man. Remember your place and you just might live long enough to see out the rest of your science project." As Riker finished talking, he shoved the man away and turned his attention to the preparations being made in the room.

Epilogue 2

He didn't know how long he'd been in the pit, or even how long it had been since the ceiling seemed to crash in on him, but he knew it was time. As the last streams of sunlight seemed to poke through the rubble like needles, slowly started to fade, Roid began to climb up the bricks and debris that had come crashing down into the pit, that had been his cell.

He had to use all of his incredible strength to move chunks of stone that were bigger than him, but outside of the barriers, the climb out of the pit was made relatively easy. The destruction of the pyramid poured down into his cell, but now that the dust had settled, it almost gave him a stairway out.

Roid didn't know how long he climbed and dug, but eventually he shoved the last large stone out of his way and emerged into the darkness of the open night. He stood in the center of the plains on a pile of stone and rubble that was once the pyramid of the dark ones. There was nothing around him as far as he could see.

Roid soaked in the nightand relished his newly acquired freedom, before his thoughts slowly turned to hatred and vengeance. He thought of the creatures that had imprisoned him, he thought of Halbred, who had been so close to him, yet still out of reach. Then he thought of the little knife fighter that had injured him and forced him to retreat, which led to his capture. His thoughts went to Samuel and Vic at the jail. As he thought through all of them, all of the reasons to kill all of his enemies, he strained to catch their scent on the breeze, strained to feel their presence, but none of them seemed anywhere. Then his thoughts went to where his pursuits had begun. He thought of the T'kche and the young man and the glowing little girl. He thought of his pursuit of them and their escape, then the scent hit him. He could not smell or sense the glowing girl, but the scent of the T'kche was unmistakable and he could smell the young man too. They felt close, they felt within his reach.

"That's where we start then, and as each is slaughtered, they'll lead me to the next. I'll make sure they do." Roid thought to himself, as his mind was flooded with sinister visions of the atrocities planned for all of those that had led him to this, that had betrayed him.

"First, it's the boy and the bigfoot though." As Roid settled himself down with the final thought, he took off across the plains, headed south as fast as he could. Desperately trying to cover as much ground as he could before he was forced to hide from the sunlight that would eventually come.

Reflections of Worlds: Volume 3,
"Worlds Collide" coming
soon!